Flawfully Wedded

Wives

Flawfully Wedded Wives

Shana Burton

www.urbanchristianonline.com

Urban Books, LLC
97 N18th Street
Wyandanch, NY 11798

ISBN 13: 978-1-60162-764-3
ISBN 10: 1-60162-764-5

First Printing August 2013
Printed in the United States of America

10 9 8 7 6 5 4 3 2 1

Distributed by Kensington Corp.
Submit Wholesale Orders to:
Kensington Publishing Corp.
C/O Penguin Group (USA) Inc.
Attention: Order Processing
405 Murray Hill Parkway
East Rutherford, NJ 07073-2316
Phone: 1-800-526-0275
Fax: 1-800-227-9604

This book is dedicated to my friend, publicist, writing sister, cupcake provider, and inspiration, Davidae "Dee" Stewart. I miss you so much, but I know you're looking down on all of us. I promise to make you proud!

It's also dedicated to my brave friend Aaliyah James. Not even a brain tumor could keep you down! Love ya, chick!

Acknowledgments

"The LORD is my strength and my shield; my heart trusted in him, and I am helped: therefore my heart greatly rejoiceth; and with my song will I praise Him." (Psalm 28:7). Lord, thank you for this gift and opportunity to write. Thank you for always taking care of me and for giving me such an awesome life! It's not perfect, but you are, and I can rest knowing that.

Myrtice C. Johnson, I know I thank you in every book, but I have to, because you're the best mother and grandmother ever! You've set a very high standard of excellence, but I'm trying to live up to it. Thank you, Shannon and Trey, for being the best kids ever! You give me purpose, you make me laugh, and you're a constant reminder of how blessed I am. I love you so much.

To the rest of my immediate family—James L. Johnson, Sr., Myrja Johnson Fuller, James "Jay" Johnson, Jr., and Matthew Watkins—I love you and thank you for being on Team Shana. You have given me the greatest support system in the world. Thank you, Jenny Scott, Rhonda Burton Bell, and Latoya Burton Ficklin for never treating me like an in-law. I'll always love you and consider you family.

Thank you to my dear friends and true soul mates, who hold me up and keep me going. Thank you, Deirdre Neeley, Therese Tarver, Lola Oyenuga, Tammy Dunlap, Stephanie Smith, Tralia Matthews, Tanisha

Fowler, Rashada Ross, and Shameka Powers for all the long talks, laughs, weekend trips, and endless glasses of wine, and for just being your fab selves.

Thank you to all of my guy friends who go hard for me on a daily basis. My life wouldn't be the same without you. Thank you, Demetrius Hollis, Douglass Smith, Scott Harris, Baron Samuel, Mychal Epps, Thomas Tomlin, Jude Ratleff, Damon Wilson, Daniel Dukes, Christopher Jackson, and especially my brother and bestie, Adrick Ingram. A special thanks also goes to Dwarka Jackson. Before I met you, I was one bad date away from becoming a bitter, angry black woman. You changed all that with one smile and made me believe in love again. I don't know how to thank you for that, but I'll love you forever. Maybe that's a start. . . .

I love my writing sisters sooo much! Thank you, Crystal Pennymon, Melissa Jones, Lisa Gibson, Traci Williams, Kim Timsley, and Nicole Ingram for not only encouraging my writing dreams but also for having the courage to pursue your own. You all are such talented writers, and I feel honored to be among such awesome women.

I would also like to thank Dwan Abrams, Rhonda McKnight, and Tiffany Warren for inspiring me as an author, and my editor, Joylynn Jossel-Ross, for your patience and for letting me push the boundaries a little more with each book.

Thank you, Omolola Oyenuga, Ryan Golphin, Marie Payne, and Phillip Lockett for gracing the cover of this book. It's my absolute favorite cover *ever* :-). Thank you to my cousin, Yaz Johnson, and to Yaz Photography for bringing my vision to life in such beautiful fashion.

I would be remiss if I didn't mention all the wonderful people I've met as part of Leadership Macon's 2013 class—best class *ever!* I feel so blessed to have met all of you. Thanks for your support!

Thank you to my spiritual family at Beulahland Bible Church and to Pastor Maurice Watson for your prayers and for keeping me covered by the Word.

Thank you to all my friends on Facebook. Thank you for being a part of my social networking life. Y'all know Facebook is my therapy! Thank you to all the bloggers, book clubs, radio personalities, and librarians who have helped me along the way. There are too many of you to name (especially since I'm already super late turning this manuscript in!), but please know that I thank you and appreciate everything you do for me. I thank every other author trying to have a voice in this industry. I thank God for you daily. I hope that I've enriched your lives as much as you've enriched mine.

Most of all, I want to thank all the Shana Burton readers! I'm *your* biggest fan! I love hearing from you, and there are no words to express how much you mean to me. Thank you for continuing to support me. Know that I'm praying for you all the time, and I'm so grateful that you've let me into your lives. Happy reading and be blessed!

Chapter 1

*"She'd be as eager for the world to know about
her past as you are for the world to know that you
jumped back in the sack with Vaughn and nine
months later out popped that little girl in there!"*
—*Angel King*

Lawson Kerry Banks's eyes passed over the elegant
spread of gourmet cookies, teas, and sandwiches on
display across her best friend, Sullivan Webb's posh
living room table during what Sullivan had coined the
Aunt Tea, a first birthday tea party for infant Charity
and Sullivan's closest sister friends. The four ladies and
Mount Zion Ministries members assembled that Sep-
tember afternoon, fought each other as hard as they
loved one another, laughed together as often as they
cried together, and usually gave as good as they got.

"Something's missing," observed Lawson, the mother figure of the bloc. She more than made up for her pe-
tite frame by being a verbal powerhouse and a spiritual
force to be reckoned with.

Lawson's younger sister, Reginell, and good friend
Angel King, nodded in agreement.

Sullivan, a stylish and high-maintenance diva, adjusted the big pink bow wrapped around one of Charity's Afro puffs. She inspected her work. At one year
old, Charity was every bit the fashion maven that her
mother was. "Yes, what's missing is your gratitude for

all the hard work I put into preparing all this food," retorted Mount Zion Ministries' first lady and magnet for drama and controversy.

Lawson eyed her with suspicion.

Sullivan relented. "Okay, all the hard work our maid put into it."

"It's all very lovely, Sully," acknowledged Lawson. "But there's still something missing."

Angel plucked one of the decorative tea lilies next to her and secured it to the natural ringlets dripping from her head. "You mean *someone*."

Sullivan huffed and rolled her eyes. "If you're talking about Kina Battle—"

"Of course we're talking about Kina," interjected Lawson, referring to the absence of her ousted cousin, who had once completed the circle of friends. "We started this journey together. The four of us were there when you found out you were pregnant with Charity. It doesn't seem right that Kina is not here to celebrate Charity's birthday with us. Charity has never even had a chance to meet Kina and get to know her like she knows all of us."

"And why should my daughter get to know the woman who almost destroyed our family?" argued Sullivan.

Angel raised an eyebrow. "Um . . . that woman would be *you*, Sullivan. You're the one who cheated on your husband."

"Yes, but Kina is the one who told him about it." Sullivan was never one to be caught without an excuse or someone to blame. "She also tried to convince him that I was carrying another man's child."

"It ain't like Kina was lying," uttered Reginell, a cocoa-skinned beauty, as she absently braided her kinky twists into one thick plait.

While it was true that Sullivan's brief affair with mechanic Vaughn Lovett could have very well resulted in Charity's conception, Sullivan had chosen to ignore that possibility and had set her mind—and both hers and Charity's futures—on Charity being the daughter of her husband and esteemed pastor, Charles Webb.

Sullivan continued. "Say what you want about me, but I've never tried to hurt anyone."

"That's only because you and Vaughn had a safe word," cracked Reginell.

Sullivan responded with an icy glare. Despite the fact that Sullivan and Lawson were more like sisters than friends, she and Reginell had been sworn frenemies since childhood.

"Kina knows what she did was wrong, and she apologized to you more than once," recalled Angel.

Sullivan fumed. "Are you all forgetting that Kina nearly killed my husband? He had the stroke right after she blabbed about me being pregnant with Vaughn's child."

Angel sighed, exasperated. "She didn't almost kill him. Charles had a stroke. I'm sure his years of unhealthy eating were a much bigger culprit than Kina."

"No bucket of fried chicken ever did as much damage to my husband's health as Kina and her vicious character assassination on me. What Kina did was cruel, and it was done for no other reason than to destroy my marriage so she could have my husband for herself. Thank God Charles either doesn't remember her telling him or has chosen to ignore it."

"And if Charles can forgive you for cheating and all your other sins, which far exceed Kina's, surely you can forgive her temporary lapse in judgment," Lawson pointed out.

"I don't know about y'all, but I miss her," admitted Reginell. "I've barely even talked to Kina since she jetted out of Savannah a year ago."

"I never told her that she had to leave town. I told her she had to leave my husband and me alone."

"At least we get to see her every week on TV," noted Angel. "How wild is it that she was chosen to be on a weight-loss reality show?"

"You actually look at that mess?" grumbled Sullivan. "I don't think I can make it through a whole episode without retching."

Lawson playfully nudged her. "Don't act like you've never tuned in to see our girl Kina."

"I won't say *never,* but devoting an hour of my Saturday every week to watch this charade of Kina's is not at the top of my to-do list."

Lawson chuckled, in awe of her cousin. "You've gotta hand it to her, though. Kina is not afraid of going after what she wants."

"Apparently, those wants include my husband. I'm tired of talking about Kina. New subject please." Charity began whining. Sullivan cradled the child in her arms to quiet her. "You see that? The mere mentioning of Kina's name brings my baby to tears."

Reginell shook her head as she rummaged through Sullivan's selection of herbal tea bags with her claw-like, iridescent fingernails. "What's up with all this bougie tea you got us drinking?" she asked, crumpling her nose at a Fruits d'Alsace tea bag before dunking it into her teacup filled with hot water. "You too good for regular ole Snapple?"

Sullivan grimaced. "It's a tea party, you twit! Forgive me for trying to introduce a little culture into your back-alley world."

Reginell fluttered her mink eyelashes in indignation. "*Back-alley?* You grew up in the same hood that me,

Lawson, and Kina did! You lived right across the street, remember?"

"I grew up in the hood, but the hood didn't grow in me," scoffed Sullivan and kissed her daughter. She gawked at Reginell's exposed midriff and tight snake-skin pants with disapproval. "Now that I think about it, I may need to start limiting your contact with Charity. I don't want your heathen ways and hood rat–inspired fashion sense rubbing off on her."

Reginell gave Sullivan the once-over. "Is taking after her gold-digging, bed-hoppin' mama any better?"

"Can you not act like this in front of the baby?" requested Angel, weary of her role as constant referee between Sullivan and Reginell. "I swear, at one year old, Charity is more mature than both of you! It's no secret that we've all been guilty of some things I'm ashamed to say out loud, but I do have to give Sullivan some credit. She's turned out to be an excellent mother."

Sullivan smiled, both smug and proud. "Thank you."

"Yeah, Sully, even I have to admit that I didn't think you could do it," confessed Lawson.

Sullivan hid her face with her hands, playing peeka-boo with Charity. "Do what?"

Lawson snickered. "Keep this child alive for a whole year!" Reginell and Angel joined in her laughter. "We didn't even have to call child services out here once."

"Yeah, I lost twenty dollars on *that* bet," grumbled health-conscious Angel as she waded through Sullivan's sea of scones in hopes of finding something to eat that met her low-fat, low-calorie, gluten-free dietary demands, needed to maintain her athletic physique.

Lawson stacked her plate with goodies. "Don't cash out on that bet just yet. Charity's birthday isn't until tomorrow. She still has twenty-four hours to go."

"Very funny." Sullivan tilted her arms so they could all see Charity. "As you can all see, Charity Faith Webb is alive, well, and thriving, not to mention absolutely stunning, like her mother."

"It's not like we can attribute any of her looks to her father, seeing as how you don't know who he is," ribbed Reginell.

Sullivan laughed bitterly in sarcasm.

"All right, don't be mean, Reggie," Angel scolded playfully. "Everybody knows that this is Charles's baby."

Reginell sucked her teeth. "I'll believe it when Maury and a DNA test confirm it."

"We don't need any tests," retorted Sullivan. "Charles knows in his heart that Charity belongs to him, and so do I."

"Just look at those cheeks and those big brown eyes," cooed Angel, looking down at Charity's cherub face. "It's like Pastor Webb popped them right out of his own sockets and put them into hers. Any fool looking at Charity would know she's Charles's daughter."

"What about last week, when you said Charity's nose and mouth couldn't be anybody's but Vaughn's?" Reginell reminded her.

Angel gulped, and her pecan complexion blushed from embarrassment. "Did I say that?" She quickly recovered. "At this age, babies change so fast that they don't really look like anyone for more than five minutes."

"Personally, I think she's the spitting image of her gorgeous mother," said Lawson, planting a kiss on Charity's cheek. "Of course, now the prayer is that she doesn't *act* like her!"

"I've been the model first lady, wife, and mother," insisted Sullivan, tossing a cluster of thick manufactured curls over her shoulder.

"You sure have," chimed in Reginell. "It's been at least a year since your last infidelity scandal!"

"A year and a half," Sullivan replied, correcting her, and laid Charity down in her playpen.

"I guess this means you really *can* turn a whore into a housewife," cracked Reginell.

"No doubt that's what your fiancé told himself before asking you to marry him," shot back Sullivan, alluding to Reginell's days as an exotic dancer. "At the very least, I'm sure that's the sound bite Mark uses whenever he runs into one of your old pole patrons in the street."

Reginell geared up for an acidic reply. Lawson stopped her. "Remember you started it, Reggie."

"Sully, you have to admit that Reggie has come a long way from the wild child we had to anoint with oil a few years ago," conceded Angel, pouring another cup of tea.

"We've all come a long way," affirmed Lawson. "No more stripping for Reggie, no more creepin' for Sully." She lifted her eyes toward Angel. "No more Internet porn for you."

"Must you keep bringing that up?" questioned Angel, a little testy. "Mind you, my brief foray into porn also occurred during the time I was competing with my fiancé's dead wife for his love and attention. It was my coping mechanism."

"*Coping mechanism?*" repeated Sullivan with skepticism.

"Yes, the same way downing bottles of tequila used to be *your* coping mechanism," blabbed Angel. "We all have our vices. Mine just happened to be naked and online. These days, I only use the Internet for what it was created for—shopping."

Reginell sifted through Sullivan's assortment of gourmet cookies. "We've all made changes in the right direction except you, Lawson."

"What have I done?" balked Lawson, grabbing a smoked salmon finger sandwich.

"It's what you *haven't* done," Angel informed her. "You still haven't forgiven your husband."

Lawson averted eye contact. "I forgave Garrett for his affair with Simone a long time ago."

Angel softened her tone. "Yeah, you've said the words, but what counts is what's in your heart. If you have truly forgiven him in your heart, you wouldn't be still punishing him and little Simon."

Despite the effort Lawson and her husband had made to move past his one-night stand with his construction company's interior designer, Simone, the evidence still lingered in the form of his four-month-old love child, Simon.

"Like Garrett, I'm guilty of screwing up every now and then," conceded Sullivan.

"More like 'screwing around,'" Reginell said, butting in.

Sullivan went on, ignoring Reginell's dig at her. "All I'm saying is that we've all come short of God's standards, and it's not as if you're blameless in all this, Lawson. Garrett never would've stepped out on you if you hadn't lied to him for months, secretly taking birth control pills while knowing that he wanted a baby."

Reginell added, "Not to mention how crazy you got after Mark and I started dating."

"Reggie, we all looked at you a little sideways about that one," divulged Angel. "After all, Mark *is* Namon's father and the man your sister lost her virginity to."

"That's not the point!" Reginell swept her braids off of her shoulders. "Lawson, the point is that you made Garrett feel disrespected and unloved. You shut him out."

For once, Sullivan sided with Reginell. "Between your lies and your neglect, you did everything except gift wrap Simone's panties for him, Lawson."

"Whatever." Lawson put down her plate, having now lost her appetite. "I've owned up to my mistakes, but no one, not even Garrett, can expect me to warm up to the one thing that's a living, breathing constant reminder of my husband cheating on me."

"Simon is not a *thing,* Lawson!" blurted out Reginell. "He's Garrett's son and your stepson—"

Lawson held up her hands to cut her sister off. "Simon belongs to Garrett and that tramp Simone. He has nothing to do with me."

Sullivan sat down next to Angel on the sofa. "And it's *that* attitude and your refusal to accept his son that are going to drive your husband away and right back into Simone's waiting arms. Is that what you want?"

"None of this has been what I wanted. My marriage would be fine—*perfect*—if it weren't for that woman and her child," griped Lawson, balling her fists in frustration.

Sullivan shook her head and glanced over at Charity. "No marriage is perfect, honey, believe me!"

Reginell wrapped her arm around her sister. "Garrett and Simon are a packaged deal, like you and Namon were when you met him, and you need to find a way to make peace and deal with it."

"The difference is that Garrett went into it knowing I had a child."

"But you agreed to stay married and work things out, knowing that Garrett had a child on the way." Angel sipped her tea. "Lawson, that kid isn't going anywhere, and your husband loves him. Don't force Garrett to choose between the two of you. You'll lose every time."

Reginell spoke up. "Plus, it's not fair. He's never made you choose between him and Namon, not even when Mark got in the picture."

"Again, the circumstances are different." Lawson sat down across from Sullivan and Angel. "I had Namon when I was sixteen. I didn't even know Garrett existed. My husband got this chick pregnant less than a year after we were married! There's no comparing the two situations."

"Maybe not, but you're going to lose your husband if you can't find it in your heart to love and accept his son," warned Reginell.

Angel checked the time. "Ohhh, it's almost seven o'clock!"

Sullivan rolled her eyes. "And?"

Lawson stood up to turn on the television. "Sully, don't act like that. *Lose Big* is about to start. It's down to the final two episodes, and Kina is one of the top three finalists."

"Personally, I can't wait to watch every episode," disclosed Angel, sliding in next to Lawson. "I've been very proud of Kina and how she's represented herself."

Sullivan frowned. "Why? I can't stand the way she tries to market herself as this devout Christian whenever she spies a camera nearby."

"Kina *is* a Christian, Sully, and she's not ashamed to let the world know it. I say amen to that." Lawson raised her teacup.

The television screen flashed a montage of the contestants during their weekly workout routines as a voice-over narrated.

Angel pointed at the television. "Look at Kina kickin' butt and taking names on all those obstacle courses. She's been puttin' those young chubsters to shame!"

Reginell agreed. "I know, right? Who knew she was so athletic?"

"She's always had it in her," replied Lawson. "In high school Kina was a cheerleader and on the track team. She didn't start to lose herself until she got mixed up with E'Bell."

Angel beamed. "Well, she's definitely finding Kina now!"

As Kina completed the course, she lifted her hands and head toward heaven, silently praising God.

Sullivan smirked. "I wonder how eager she'd be to let the world know about her non-Christian activities, like trying to seduce my husband, or her lesbian lover, Joan."

"She'd be as eager for the world to know about her past as you are for the world to know that you jumped back in the sack with Vaughn and nine months later out popped that little girl over there!" Angel remarked.

Sullivan sulked in silence.

"Do you see how great she looks?" added Reginell, noting that Kina's once round body had been sculpted into a new, svelte figure. Silky weave now flowed down her back replacing the short, stubby hair that refused to grow.

Angel turned up the volume on the television. "Look, Kina's talking!"

"Yesterday was very grueling for me," recalled Kina during the video-diary session of the show. "The rain was pouring down, and we were all so tired and still had half a mile to run in all that rain and mud. Just when I was at my wit's end and about to give up, I looked up at the sky. I remembered that God promises that rain doesn't come down and go back up until it's done everything it's supposed to, just like His Word. It was all I needed to get my second wind and go on to victory!" Kina lifted her hands, and the camera cut to her crossing the finish line, soaked and covered in mud, surpassing her competitors. "God gets all the glory! It's none of me and all of Him!"

Sullivan booed and threw a pillow at the television.

"Real mature, Sully," admonished Angel.

"Do you honestly think she meant a word of that? It's totally scripted!" insisted Sullivan.

Lawson turned to Sullivan. "Scripted or not, if it helps someone else or leads someone closer to God, it's all good."

"You mean it's all *fake*," Sullivan muttered.

Angel pinched her. "Stop hatin', Sully. You're just mad you're no longer the center of attention."

"Call up Vaughn and make another sex tape and leak it on the Internet, Sully," suggested Reginell. "You'll be trending again in no time."

After a few more minutes of watching Kina trample her competition, Angel stretched and stood up. "Well, ladies, as fun as this has all been, duty calls."

Lawson looked up from the television screen. "You headed to the hospital?"

Angel nodded. "From eight to eight, like every weekend for the past three months."

"Angel, between your personal care business and the hospital, you're working sixty hours a week. How long do you think you'll be able to keep this up?" asked Sullivan.

"Until I can build up enough cash flow not to. Guardian Angel is practically bleeding me dry. I've got to work at the hospital to stay afloat."

Sullivan squeezed Angel's hand. "I told you I'd loan you the money to tide you over for a while."

Angel was confused. "What money, Sully? You don't work. You spend your husband's money, remember? Besides, I can do this, with the Lord's help and your prayers."

"You know I'll be praying for you, girl, as always."
Lawson stood up. "In fact, there's no better time than
the present to put in a little prayer for all of us."

Sullivan and Reginell peeled themselves away from
their seats and joined hands with Lawson and Angel.

"In the name of Jesus, Lord, we come praising your
name. Thank you for grace. Thank you for your Word,
and we thank you for bringing us together today for
such a joyous occasion. Thank you so much for our precious angel, Charity Faith. She has brought nothing but
love and happiness to everyone in this room and our
entire church family. Continue to strengthen her. Make
her virtuous and kind. Give her a desire to follow your
ways and to know you, Lord. Watch over her parents.
Give them the wisdom, resources, and compassion
needed to bring up this child in the way she should go.
We ask for your protection over her entire family for all
the days of their lives.

"God, we know that you provide and bless according
to your riches and glory. We know that through faith
and patience, we inherit your promises. You've promised to take care of our every need, so I ask that you
bless Angel abundantly in her finances, knowing that
she works for you and will be a faithful steward over
that which you bless her with. Help her to remember
that you are her source and that jobs are only resources. Give her the strength and energy she needs to make
it through this week and beyond.

"Lord, I thank you for my friends, whom I call my
sisters. The soul of each one of us is knit to the other
like your servants David and Jonathan. Let this friendship be the impetus to strengthen, not tear down one
another. Thank you for the love between every woman
in this room. And while we treasure these friendships,
we know that friendship with the world is enmity to

you, so let us be in this world but not of the world. Keep our eyes stayed on you. Let everything we do exalt you, Lord. We thank you and praise you in advance for all you're doing in our lives."

"Amen," said Angel, Reginell, and Sullivan in unison.

"And, Lord, please watch over Kina," Lawson added. "Give her the courage and knowledge to carry out your plans. Keep her safe and bring her back home to us very soon."

Kina Battle stared out of her high-rise hotel window into the starry California night. A few short months ago she had barely had money to put food on the table and had maxed out her credit cards to buy plane tickets, leaving Georgia with nothing but a hope and a prayer. Now she was ordering room service and lounging in designer robes. Both life and God were indeed good.

She looked over at her thirteen-year-old son, Kenny, who was brooding, as was usually the case these days. "Did you finish your homework?"

Kenny didn't look up from his electronic tablet to answer her. "Nope."

"Why not?" demanded Kina.

"'Cause I didn't feel like it. I hate that school, and I hate this place! Why can't we just go back home?"

"This is our home, Kenny. It is for now, anyway." She looked out the window again. "Besides, there's nothing left for us in Savannah."

"Maybe not for you, but my friends are there, and so is my family. I miss Reggie and Lawson and Namon. I miss everybody."

"So do I, but sometimes you have to make a fresh start," she told him. *Because you've screwed up too much to go back home,* thought Kina.

"Can't we at least go home for the holidays?" pleaded Kenny.

"I've already booked us a trip to Cabo for Thanksgiving. You're gonna love it!" she promised, forcing herself to sound excited. "We're going to have so much fun boogie-boarding and snorkeling, you won't even remember to think about going to Georgia."

Kina's enthusiasm fell on Kenny's deaf ears. "I'm going to always miss being in Georgia."

Kina sighed. She missed home, but there was no turning back for her. Between her abusive husband's death at the hands of their son, falling for a woman, then her best friend's husband, and being barred from the only women she'd ever been able to call friends, Savannah was the last place Kina ever wanted to set foot in again.

Chapter 2

"The only person in this equation who has an opening to leave is me."
—*Lawson Kerry Banks*

"Is the food okay?" asked Lawson.

Her husband of two years, Garrett, nodded and swallowed. "It's great, babe. You've always been a whiz in the kitchen."

Lawson smiled a little. It wasn't just the compliment. She was also grateful for the break in the dead air between them. Dinner that night, as with most nights since the birth of Garrett's son four months prior, involved little to no discourse. The clanking of forks on plates was the only sound drowning out the silence between them. That sound used to irritate Lawson, but she'd gotten used to it, as it had become the new normal of their dinner routine.

"How was the tea party?"

"It was what you'd expect from Sullivan—sweet and over the top, like Sullivan."

"Is Namon still at Mark's?" asked Garrett, finishing the last of his stewed chicken.

She nodded. "I feel like he's practically living over there these days."

"I can't say I'm surprised. Namon is almost seventeen. He's a young man now and wants his space and his freedom. We both know that Mark doesn't hold the reins nearly as tight as we do."

"I know. Reggie is there, too, and I know he's crazy about his aunt, who seems way cooler to him than his mom does."

"That shouldn't surprise you. Reggie's only twenty-five. She's practically a kid herself. Plus, Mariah came down this weekend. You know how much he enjoys spending time with his little sister."

"Sometimes I wonder if I've driven Namon away," admitted Lawson.

"You haven't done anything wrong. You're a wonderful mother. He's growing up, but I wouldn't worry too much. You've done an excellent job raising him." Garrett warily broached the next topic. "Speaking of children, Simon had his four-month doctor's visit earlier today."

Lawson clenched her teeth before clamming up, knowing what she had to ask but not wanting to hear the answer. "So what did the pediatrician say? How's . . . how's Simon?"

Garrett let out a deep breath. "Do you really care, or are you just making conversation?"

She replied with a terse, "If I didn't care, I wouldn't have asked."

Garrett wiped his mouth. "According to Dr. Ratleff, Simon is great. The doctor said his weight is okay. His sleeping and appetite seem normal." Garrett smiled. "Of course, he went ballistic when they tried to give him his shots. I think Simone was crying worse than the baby—"

Lawson butted in, cutting him off. "Uh-huh. Glad it went well." She bolted from the table. "I guess I better start on these dishes."

The irritation registered on Garrett's face. "Dang, you couldn't even give my son five minutes of your attention?"

Lawson continued gathering their plates. "I was listening, Garrett. I can do two things at once, you know?"

"Whatever," murmured Garrett, and he rose from the table. "I'll be back."

She stopped moving. "Where are you going?"

"Simone has plans tonight. She needs me to watch the baby for a while."

Lawson slammed the plates down hard on the table. The loud crackle startled her husband.

"What's with you?" asked Garrett, alarmed.

"Sorry . . . They slipped."

"Lawson, don't put up a front with me. I know you better than that."

"It's nothing. I'm fine." Lawson took a deep breath and leaned forward. She gripped the table and shook her head, forcing back tears. "No, I'm not."

Garrett sidled up behind her. "What's wrong, babe? Talk to me."

Lawson dropped her head and lowered her voice to practically a whisper. "Do you know what it does to me every time I hear that woman's name?"

He wrapped his broad arms around her waist and kissed her on the cheek. "I'm sorry, sweetheart. I didn't mean to upset you. I know you're trying."

She yielded to Garrett's loving embrace and caressed his hand. "I know you didn't do it on purpose. You don't mean to hurt me, and I don't mean to hurt you, but lately it seems like that's all we're doing."

"Yeah, I know. It's going to take some time for us all to adjust. We both need to try a little harder, that's all."

Lawson broke away from him. "Try a little harder to do what? Pretend like your affair never happened? Pretend that I'm not constantly reminded of it whenever you mention Simon? Pretend that it doesn't kill me inside every time you leave me and our family to go be with another woman and her child?"

Garrett was at a loss for words. "How do you expect me to answer that, Lawson?"

"I don't." Lawson shook off indignation and scooped up their glasses. "Are you bringing Simon back here?"

"I'd like to if that's all right."

The prospect annoyed Lawson, but she tried her best to conceal and suppress it. "Sweetie, I don't know if that's such a good idea. I've had a long day, and I've still got a ton of grad work to finish."

Garrett tensed. "So what you're saying is that you don't want my son here."

"I never said that. I just think Simon will be more comfortable in his own home, don't you?"

"Lawson, this is his home too."

Lawson was flustered. "You know what I mean—the home he's most comfortable in."

"I want him to feel at ease whether he's here with us or across town with his mother. If you were a little more welcoming, he would be."

Lawson stood with her arms akimbo. "I've been welcoming, Garrett. I've opened my life and my home to both your mistress and her child."

"Simone's not my mistress, and Simon is your stepchild. He's a part of both of our lives."

"I've accepted that." Lawson's temper flared. "I know he's your son, and I know you love him. I'm trying to get there too, but I'm not there yet."

"Lawson, this has been hard on all of us. I've been asking you for months what I can do to make this right."

She exhaled. "There's nothing you can do. It is what it is. Simon's here, and he's not going anywhere. Simone is his mother, and she's not going anywhere. You've made a commitment to the two of them, and you're not going anywhere, either. The only person in this equation who has an opening to leave is me."

Garrett pulled her to him. "No, you don't. We've been through all this before. You're my wife, and it's going to stay that way," declared Garrett. "My commitment to you and Namon is as important as the one I made to Simone to help her raise our son."

"I know you want to believe that, but Namon is not your biological child. I'm a mother. I know firsthand that the bond between parent and child is unbreakable. If you ever had to choose between Namon and me and Simon and Simone, you couldn't turn your back on the child who has your blood running through his veins any more than I could."

"Thankfully, no one is asking me to make that choice."

"No," replied Lawson. "Not yet."

Garrett stood back. "That almost sounded like a threat, Lawson."

"It's not." Lawson took a softer line. "Garrett, I don't want to fight with you, not tonight."

He yielded. "I don't want to fight, either." He leaned down and pecked her on the lips. "I just want to love you."

She smiled. "That's much better than fighting."

"I've been thinking . . . maybe we should consider going back to counseling. Look how much we got out of those premarital counseling sessions."

"Sweetheart, how many times do we need someone to tell us what we already know. Communicate more, spend time together, be each other's best friend, blah, blah, blah . . ."

"As many times as it takes to get this marriage back on track," proclaimed Garrett. "Lawson, I've been with you for almost twelve years now. In the ten years before we got married, our relationship was wonderful. Somewhere along the road to matrimony, we lost it. We need to go back to what made this relationship work, and it was those fundamental things they told us about in counseling."

"All of that was before Mark came into our lives and staked his claim on Namon, and before teaching and going back to school consumed so much of my time. It was also before I lied about taking my birth control pills, and before you broke our vows and slept with Simone, and before Simon even existed." Lawson shook her head. "Too much has happened for things to go back to the way they were before."

"A lot has changed over the last couple of years, I'll give you that. But what hasn't changed is the way I feel about you, Lawson. I love you today as much as I did two years ago, when we exchanged those vows."

"I love you too. I don't even think you truly comprehend how much. I want to be the kind of wife you thank God for sending to you. I just don't know how to right now."

"You're too hard on yourself, baby. Everything is going to be fine. I'm not going anywhere. You got that? I'm willing to do whatever it takes to work this out."

Lawson lowered her head. "Except the one thing that it would actually take to make this marriage work again."

"Lawson—"

"You better go," she insisted, turning her back to him. "You don't want to keep your child and his mother waiting."

Lawson held it together long enough for Garrett to get out of the house. Then she kneeled down to pray.

"Lord . . . Father, give me strength. I want to be able to walk before you in faithfulness, righteousness, and uprightness of heart, but I haven't been able to do that. I admit over the past few months I've separated myself from Garrett both spiritually and emotionally, and I know that's not your will for our lives or our marriage. Please tear down these walls I've built up. Break down that hardness in my heart that's directed toward my husband and his son. I know he's trying to be a good father to Simon and still be a good husband to me. Forgive me for making it harder on him than it already is. God, I don't want to be like this, but I need your help and your strength. I know that you are strongest when I'm at my weakest, and I don't think I can get much weaker than I am right now! Grant me the peace that surpasses all understanding. Empty this rage and pain and hurt inside of me. Fill me with your love so I can be the wife and woman you've called me to be."

And as she'd done nearly every day since finding out Simone was pregnant eight months ago, Lawson broke down and cried.

Chapter 3

"I learned long ago not to put anything past any-body, not even your so-called friends."
—Sullivan Webb

Pastor Charles Webb entered Charity's butterfly-themed bedroom as Sullivan was fastening a clean diaper on Charity's bottom. He kissed his wife on the cheek. "Do you know how sexy you look doing that?"

Sullivan rolled her eyes in jest. "I see Charity's diaper isn't the only thing in here that's full of it! How was the ministry leaders' conference?"

Charles loosened his tie. "It was good. I'm glad to be back home with my girls, though. Three days is too long to be away from the two most beautiful ladies in the world."

Sullivan lifted the baby from her changing table and lowered her into the crib. "When this one goes to sleep, you can show me how much you've missed me."

"Count on it." Charles winked his eye at her. "Did our little princess enjoy the tea party?"

"Of course she did. You know Charity loves being the center of attention. Like mother, like daughter, I guess."

"She certainly has her mother's gorgeous looks," remarked Charles, looking down at Charity in her crib.

"But she's smart and strong like her daddy." Sullivan's words were met with silence. Both she and

Charles felt an uncomfortable vibe blanket the room
as the proverbial elephant in the room reared its head
again. As an unspoken rule, they never openly dis-
cussed the likelihood that Charity could be Vaughn's
biological child. Sullivan hastily cut through the tension. "I think she's the perfect balance of both of her
parents."

Charles laid his hand on her shoulder, as if to reas-
sure her. "I think most children are."

"Not me," Sullivan averred. "Not that I know of,
anyway. Now that I think about it, my mother was a
whore, and my father was an adulterer. I may be more
like them than I want to admit."

"Sullivan, don't even joke around like that. Whatever
your parents are or are not doesn't have any bearing on
you. You're a wonderful mother and wife." He saw that
she was still troubled. "Not knowing your father has
really left a void in your heart, hasn't it?"

She nodded. "A lot of fathers underestimate how
much their daughters need them. People are always
saying how much little boys need their dad, but I
needed my father too. I needed his protection when
my mother's boyfriends were molesting me. I needed
his guidance when Vera was pimpin' me out for vaca-
tions and clothes. No matter what I have or accomplish
or get recognized for, deep down inside I'm still that
little girl who longs for her father's love and approval."
She playfully tousled her fifty-year-old husband's gray-
streaked hair. "Maybe that's why I've always been attracted to older men."

"You have that love and approval, Sullivan, in your
heavenly father. Deuteronomy reminds us that we
have a father who'll never leave us or forsake us, and
He's never left you. Earthly parents leave or die, some
go to jail or have any number of calamities befall them,
but God is always right there with you."

"I know, but it doesn't make me wonder about my biological father any less."

"When was the last time you heard from him?"

"I don't even remember," Sullivan stated sadly. "I couldn't have been more than six or seven years old."

Charles took a deep breath. "Sullivan, what do you know about your father? What does he do? Where is he from?"

She frowned and shrugged. "I don't know. Aside from telling me that my dad was a lying bastard and a cheating bastard and a no-good bastard, my mother rarely talked about him when I was growing up. I remember once, when I asked her where my father was, she told me he was with his *real* family and not to ask her about him again. It was one of the few times I actually obeyed her."

"So Vera never told you anything personal about him?"

"Not really. I don't think he and my mother had anything serious. I've never known Vera to be serious about any man, only his bank account. Samuel was probably just one of many pit stops on her road to financial security."

"Is that why you haven't tried harder to find him?"

"I guess I always assumed if I mattered to him, he'd try to find me."

"Do you think you would know him if you saw him?"

"Honey, Vera had so many men in and out of the house, I don't think I'd recognize him if he was standing right in front of me." She stopped for a moment and set one of Charity's stuffed animals down in the crib with her. "I do remember his smile, though. He wasn't around enough for me to remember much else."

"Oh."

Sullivan turned to face Charles. "Why the sudden interest in my father?"

"There was a pastor at the conference by the name of Samuel Sullivan, from Milwaukee. He recently moved to Georgia to pastor a church in Duluth, outside Atlanta."

Sullivan's curiosity was piqued. "Really?"

"The name is probably a coincidence, but I figured it was at least worth mentioning to you."

She was hopeful for a moment, before reality set in. "I doubt it's him. Samuel is a pretty common name, and so is Sullivan. I mean, what are the odds, right?" Sullivan said, not allowing herself to consider the possibility.

"Stranger things have happened. Look at your friend Lawson and how she ended up working alongside the long-lost father of her child."

"Yeah, but Savannah is a pretty small place. Lawson was bound to run into Mark sooner or later. My surprise is that it didn't happen sooner." Sullivan veered the conservation back to Samuel Sullivan. "Did you talk to him?"

"Who? Pastor Sullivan? Yes, but it was just small talk. I met his lovely wife, Martina. They both seem like good, salt-of-the-earth people. They have big plans for taking Friendship Temple to the next level."

Sullivan turned up the corners of her mouth. "Humph."

"He said they have two grown children. Two sons, I believe."

"No mention of a thirty-three-year-old illegitimate daughter with a drunken, chain-smoking hussy?" joked Sullivan.

Charles chuckled. "Not that I can readily recall."

"Figures."

"To be honest with you, I don't think that a man who professes to love the Lord and to be called by Him could abandon a child that way."

"Not every pastor has the same morals that you do, Charles. More than one professed preacher has darkened Vera's doorway, including ones with wives and children at home."

Charles shook his head. "I don't see it, not coming from him."

"I learned long ago not to put anything past anybody, not even your so-called friends. Any man can play the role of a devoted husband and father long enough to get through a ministry leaders' conference."

"On the off chance that he is your father, would you even want to see him?"

Sullivan rolled the scenario over in her mind. "I can't say. A part of me would like to see my father again and get some questions answered, but why bother? If he hasn't thought enough of me to pick up a phone or try to find me in all these years, is he really the kind of man I'd even want in my life? I went through hell growing up. I don't think it would've been that way if he'd stuck around."

"I can't imagine what that must've been like for you."

"The sad part is that that's the way it's been in my family for generations. I've carried the scars from my childhood for a long time, but I guess you know that better than anyone. It means the world to me that life will be different for my daughter." She looked down at Charity. "But it makes me kind of sad that she'll never know her grandfather, and even sadder that the only grandparent she'll ever know is Vera."

"I hate that my folks passed away before they could meet her." Charles grinned. "They would've spoiled her rotten."

"I think we're doing a pretty good job of that without any help," mused Sullivan.

"Every little girl deserves to be her daddy's princess, even you, Sullivan. It breaks my heart that you didn't have that."

"Vera would be a strong contestant for the Worst Mother Ever title, but I can't blame her or my dad for the mistakes I've made as an adult. It makes me sick to my stomach when I think about how much I've hurt you."

"I'm strong, Sullivan. I'm okay. I went into this marriage with you with my eyes wide open."

"Yeah, but I know I made you want to close them and pretend this was all some horrible nightmare! You couldn't have predicted my drinking problems, the affair with Vaughn, or my psychotic mother."

"We've all made our mistakes, Sullivan, myself included."

"You're no saint, Charles, but compared to me, you're seated on the throne next to Jesus!"

He laughed. "You're not so bad, my beauty. The drinking, Vaughn, and that whole mess are all in the past."

Sullivan nodded, looking down at her baby, who smiled at the sight of her mother. Sullivan desperately wanted to believe her husband and embrace the idea that all her past sins were behind her. After all, didn't the Bible say she was a new creature in Christ and had been forgiven? She allowed Charity to squeeze her finger. Though Sullivan returned Charity's smile, she couldn't shake the nagging feeling that, instead of being behind her, the living evidence of her sins was staring her in face.

Chapter 4

*"You're only young once, so I say live it up
while you can."*
—*Reginell Kerry*

Reginell broke into a smile the second she saw her fiancé sitting alone at the Green Truck Neighborhood Pub. Even in a polo shirt and jeans, his toned body, chiseled from his days as a football player, was something to be admired.

Reginell still had to pinch herself sometimes to believe that it was real. Even now that they were engaged, it was still hard for her to grapple with the fact that a man as handsome, smart, and kind as Mark Vinson would want her, that he'd chosen her over Lawson, who was much more his equal and the mother of his oldest child. Mark was aware of everything she'd done in the past, and loved her in spite of it. For Reginell, there was no clearer metaphor for understanding God's love for His wayward children than to see Mark's love for her.

"Did you order for me?" asked Reginell, joining her fiancé in the booth.

Mark passed her the drink. "Vodka and cranberry with light ice, exactly how you like it."

"Finally, a drink I can recognize! You wouldn't believe the crap Sullivan was serving." Reginell took a sip. "A couple more of these and I'll be straight!"

"You mean headed straight to bed, right?"

"No, I mean ready to get my party on," she sang, gyrating in her seat. "I'm in the mood to shake something."

Mark rose. "Good. You can shake something for me when we get to my house."

She pouted. "I thought we were going out."

"I thought you just wanted to meet up here for a drink, then go back to my place."

Reginell sulked. "Baby, it's the weekend. I don't want to be trapped in the house like some old fogys!"

"You won't be trapped. You'll be chillin' at home with your future husband."

She blew him off. "We have the next fifty years to sit home in front of the TV. YOYO!"

Mark returned to his seat. "I thought the saying was YOLO. You only live once."

"No, this is *YOYO*. You're only *young* once, so I say live it up while you can. Plus, there's a new reggae club opening. I want to check it out."

"I'm not feelin' the club scene tonight, babe."

"Mi no wan no wutless bwoy," protested Reginell in a pseudo-patois accent. "Mi wan dance!"

Mark chuckled. "Wa mek you so speaky spokey?" he asked, mocking her.

She pulled on his sleeve. "Come on, Mark, please! I'm way too crunk to spend the night at home."

"Babe, I'm tired. Why don't you go call up some of your girls and go clubbing with them?"

The offer was tempting, but Reginell knew that Mark would be disappointed if she actually took him up on it.

She sighed. "No, it's cool. We'll go to your place and watch some dumb romantic comedy and fall asleep on the couch . . . like we did last weekend and the weekend before that and the weekend before that."

"Oh, so you're getting bored with me already? I thought you promised me the next fifty years, woman?"

She kissed him and winked her eye. "You think I'm letting you off the hook with fifty? I've got you forever, playboy!"

"Don't worry. You'll have plenty of time to show off those dance moves in a couple of weeks," Mark announced.

Reginell perked up. "Is there another club opening?"

"Not exactly. My college football coach is retiring after forty years. The school is throwing a huge banquet in his honor, black tie and everything. So I need you to grab your baddest dress, your flyest heels, wrap those braids up in a nice li'l bun, and come on."

"Ohhh, how about that leopard-print dress I wore to your cousin's birthday party?" she suggested. "You know, the one that's kind of low cut and makes the girls sit up and pop!"

Mark laughed. "I know *exactly* which dress you're talking about, but the banquet is going to be formal. It's your chance to get red carpet ready, not cookout fresh. I'm sure you have a nice after-five gown in your closet somewhere. Lord knows, you've got everything else in there."

"I might." She withdrew a little, abashed. "I don't really get invited to fancy places like that."

"Get used to it, little lady! I get invited to this kind of thing all the time."

Reginell was less than thrilled by that notion. "Is the banquet going to be at the Civic Center?"

"No, it's going to be at one of the banquet halls on campus in Virginia."

The prospect of going to unchartered territory was even less appealing. "Are we driving?"

Mark reeled back. "Do you think I'm going to make my bride sit in a car that long? We're flying first class, baby."

Reginell hung her head. "I've never been on plane before, never been out of Georgia, really, except that time I went to New York, trying to get a record deal. Even then, I took the bus there and back."

"My lady doesn't have to travel by bus or car," he told her. "We do everything first class. That's what you deserve, Reggie."

Her excitement withered completely and was traded for self-consciousness. "Mark, are you sure you want me to come?"

"You're my fiancée. Why wouldn't I want you to come with me?"

Reginell shrugged. "All of your old professors and college friends are going to be there. Everybody will be there with all their degrees and high-profile jobs, and I didn't even finish college. Shoot, I barely *started* college!"

"Reggie, you have more charm and personality than anybody I know. When you open up your mouth to sing, there ain't a soul on this planet who can touch you! Anyway, having a degree doesn't necessarily mean you're smarter than the person who doesn't. It only means you had the drive to see something through."

"Baby, I don't want to embarrass you around all those educated and important people. What are they going to think when you show up with an ex-stripper on your arm?"

Mark reached for her hands. "Will you stop doing that? I don't care what other people think. I love you, and I'm proud to be your man. I'm proud that you're going to be my wife. I can't wait to show everybody that I bagged the finest woman this side of the Mississippi!"

"Just this side?" teased Reginell.

Mark kissed her on the cheek. "That's more like it. It'll be a blast. You'll see."

Reginell slowly started becoming used to the idea. "You might be right. It'll be fun to get all dolled up. Plus, you know I'm always looking for an excuse to go shopping."

"Yeah, I know," he murmured. Mark stood up and grabbed Reginell's hand. "So you ready to watch that movie? I'll even let you pick it this time."

Reginell slid out of the booth. "Yes, let's go."

As they were walking out, a group of loud, chatty females barged in. They appeared to be happy and having the time of their lives. Reginell glanced back at them in longing, remembering when that used to be her.

Mark held the door open for Reginell as they filed out. She gave him a quick peck before walking ahead of him. Reginell felt secure in her life with Mark and had never thought she could feel so much love for one person, but she hadn't expected to miss her old life so much, either.

Chapter 5

"I prefer to think of myself as a queen."
—Angel King

"The patient in room four has been evaluated, and he's resting," Angel reported to the patient representative at the front desk, removing her stethoscope. "And I'm going on break. I'll be back in fifteen minutes."

"You look exhausted, honey," the woman replied. "If you're not careful, you're going to end up in one of these hospital rooms yourself."

Angel yawned. "It's three o'clock now. Only five more hours to go. Hopefully, I can get in at least two hours of sleep before church."

The woman at the front desk shared an encouraging smile. "Hang in there. It gets easier."

Angel sighed, struggling to keep her eyes open. Working twelve-hour shifts at the urgent care center was not how Angel envisioned spending her weekends, but it was the only way to make payroll for her small staff and pay bills for the time being.

Walking toward the snack machine, she bumped into a man coming from the opposite direction. "I'm so sorry. I wasn't looking where I was going."

Her victim grinned. "It's okay. We're in a hospital, so I'm in the best place for a head-on collision."

Angel smiled. The man got a closer look at her face and identification badge. He squinted his eyes, searching for recognition. "Angel? Angelique Preston?"

Angel was stunned. Very rarely did anyone address her by her real name, and even more rarely by her maiden name. "Yes . . . Do I know you?"

"Yeah, you used to, anyway. Jordan McKay. I was your lab partner for two years in high school."

Angel thought back to her days of high school chemistry. Then she remembered the cute, bowlegged basketball player with the dimpled grin. The awkward lankiness of youth had been replaced by lean, hard muscles. Neatly trimmed dreadlocks sprang from his scalp, where a high-top fade had once been.

"Jordan McKay!" she exclaimed.

He flashed that dimpled smirk. "Do you remember now?"

"Of course!" She reached out to hug him. "It's so good to see you! Heck, it's good to see anybody from back home. That hardly ever happens. What are you doing in Savannah?"

"Making a fresh start. I moved down about six months ago."

"Wow! I think the last time I saw you, you were shooting hoops in the gym, wiping the floor with some gullible freshmen. We all thought you were going to be the next Michael Jordan."

He laughed. "I did too, but I'm an old man now. My jump shot is not as sweet as it used to be, but I can still give the young'uns a run for their money on a good day."

"Thirty-three is not old, at least not on me," she bragged, posing playfully for him.

He ogled her. "No, it actually looks rather good on you."

"So is showing off on the court what brought you here today?"

"Oh, no. There was a shortage in one of the breakers. They called me in to fix it. By the looks of it, I'd say a paycheck is what brought you here today too."

She smiled again. "Yeah, I have a personal care business, but I come in on the weekends to earn my shoe money."

"So you're a nurse?"

She nodded.

"That's cool. I can see you taking that route with your career. I remember you always helping people when we were in school. You didn't even mind the sight of blood. All the other girls would be somewhere squealing in biology when it was time to dissect something, but you were right there in the trenches with the fellas."

She was impressed that he remembered. "Nursing is my calling, my gift. So what do you do when you're not perfecting that jump shot of yours? You said something about fixing the breakers."

He reached into his back pocket and handed her a card. Angel read it. "You're an electrician, I see."

"Yeah."

"That's great."

He spotted Angel's last name on her badge. "You're a King now, huh?"

"Yes, but I prefer to think of myself as a queen," she joked.

Jordan laughed a little. "So you're married. I guess when I didn't see a ring, I assumed . . ."

"You assumed correctly," she informed him. "We're divorced."

"I'm sorry to hear that . . . kinda."

Angel blushed. "What about you? Any wives? Ex-wives? Baby mamas?"

"No . . . no kids, never been married."

"With that face? How's that possible?" she asked, catching herself flirting with him. "I thought Deidra would've made you wife her right after graduation."

"We still dated for a year after we graduated from high school, but you know how it is in college. It's easy to get distracted when there are a few states in between you."

"Yeah, but when you're eighteen and naive, you think you're going to be together forever, or at least I did. I met my ex the first day of class at Howard. We were married by my junior year and divorced a few months after graduation."

"There's nothing like young love."

"Then what accounts for the fact that I got engaged to him again at thirty-one?" Angel shook her head. "We broke up a year ago. This time it's for good. What about you? No love-and-war stories?"

"No, I mean, I've had a few girlfriends here and there, and times where things were serious for a while. I was engaged myself a couple of years back."

"What happened?"

"Just didn't work out." He sighed. "That's life for you, though."

"And love," she added.

He stared at her for a few seconds before speaking. "I guess I better let you get on back to work. It was good seeing you again, Angel."

"You too, Jordan." She smiled and turned to walk away.

Jordan reached for her hand. "You wouldn't mind if I called you sometime, would you?"

She hesitated. "I guess that would be okay."

"Well, you wouldn't mind if I asked you to join me for lunch one day, either, would you?"

She blushed. "No, I wouldn't mind that, either."

"Great." He pulled out his cell phone and handed it to her. "Why don't you lock your number in, and I'll give you a call one day next week?"

"Sure." Angel typed in her phone number and handed the phone back to him.

"Don't work too hard," he warned her. "I don't want you trying to use exhaustion or sleeplessness to back out of our lunch date."

"I won't," she promised him.

Angel smiled as she watched Jordan walk away. It was the first time since breaking up with her ex-husband–turned fiancé–turned ex-fiancé, Duke, that a man had made her smile. It was a ray of hope that she wasn't destined to spend the rest of her life as a single, overworked nurse. Hope was a fine thing. So was Mr. Jordan McKay.

Chapter 6

"It's about time you grew up and stopped running around, doing whatever and whoever your hormones tell you!"
—Lawson Kerry Banks

"Smile, Charity," Sullivan sang into the video camera the following afternoon, as Charles recorded the two of them. "Happy first birthday!"

Charles lowered the camera and turned it off. "All right, I think we can officially call it a wrap."

Sullivan exhaled and dropped the smile and sing-song voice. "Thank God. I thought all those children and their parents would never leave!"

Lawson and Angel laughed.

"At least you have another three hundred sixty-four days before you have to worry about it again," said Lawson.

Charity stretched out her pudgy arms to her father. "Oh, you want your daddy now?" Sullivan handed her off to Charles. "Can you get her ready for bed, sweetheart?"

"My pleasure. Come on, big girl!" As Charles hoisted Charity up over his shoulder, the doorbell rang.

"And can you get that too, honey?" Sullivan requested sweetly.

Charles kissed the top of Sullivan's head. "Anything for my beautiful wife." Charity squealed with delight as Charles carted her off with him.

"The two of them are so cute together," gushed Angel. "At this point, I don't think it even matters to Charles who her biological father is."

Sullivan craned her neck to make sure Charles was out of earshot. "It doesn't matter right now. I'm praying it'll stay that way."

"Do you ever hear from Vaughn?" asked Angel.

"No, I'm praying it'll stay that way too. The last thing I need is for Vaughn to start doing the math and asking questions about Charity. He needs to keep his tail in New York, where he belongs."

"Fingers crossed," swore Lawson.

"Well, look who's only two hours late," spewed Sullivan as Reginell barged into Sullivan's living room minutes after Charity's birthday party was over. "You were in charge of balloons, Reggie. I should have known that was too much responsibility for you."

"Where were you?" Lawson asked, fishing, as she took down some of the birthday streamers. "I tried calling you a couple of times."

"Planning this doggone wedding. The guest list is already up to two hundred fifty with all of Mark's country-bama kinfolks coming in from Texas," ballyhooed Reginell. "Do you have any idea how much wedding dresses and cakes and caterers cost? I sure didn't!"

"No one said you had to have some big, fancy wedding. Do what the two of you can afford," Angel advised.

"But I want the fairy-tale wedding. I'm planning on doing this only one time."

"I wonder how many men she's told that lie to," mumbled Sullivan.

"Of course, I did manage to save room for Vaughn to come, Sully, if you want to invite him," offered Reginell. "That'll be the perfect opportunity for him to meet Charity. You, him, Charles, and the baby could all pose for a nice family picture. We can even have the photographer insert little question marks over Charles's and Vaughn's heads and let people guess who the daddy is."

"Isn't it confusing enough that you're marrying your sister's baby's daddy and that you're being given away by your nephew stepson?" Sullivan retorted. "Do you really need to add more drama to the mix?"

Reginell expressed herself with a finger gesture toward Sullivan.

"Sully, stop being messy!" argued Lawson. "You know I'm perfectly fine with Reggie marrying Mark. It's enough to worry about my own husband. I don't have time to worry about hers too."

Reginell helped herself to a leftover cupcake. "On top of trying to pay for this wedding, I still have all my other bills to deal with."

Lawson clasped Reginell's shoulder. "Welcome to the real world, li'l sister!"

"Man, if I was still dancing at the club, I could pay for this wedding and everything else in two or three good weekends."

"If you were still stripping at that club, you wouldn't be marrying Mark, so there would be no need for a wedding," Lawson mentioned.

"He fell in love with me when I was stripping."

"Yeah, and he dumped you because of it too." Sullivan glanced over at Angel, who was humming, lost in her own world. "What's up with all that?"

Angel stopped. "All what?"

"All the smiling and humming."

Angel smiled. "Oh, was I doing that?"

Sullivan bumped her. "Um . . . yes, you were, ma'am, so what gives?"

"Nothing." Angel shook her head. "I mean, it probably won't amount to anything, anyway."

Lawson joined Angel. "What probably won't amount to anything?"

Angel tried to act blasé about it. "This thing with Jordan."

Sullivan was intrigued. "What *thing,* and who's *Jordan?*"

"He's a guy from back home in D.C."

Lawson winced. "Oh, Lord, don't tell me you're doing the online thing again."

"No, I ran into him at the hospital—literally."

Sullivan stacked the empty paper cups. "What's he doing in Savannah? Is he a patient?"

"No, apparently, he's living here now."

Sullivan raised an eye. "Is he living single?"

"He was when he asked me out," Angel replied with a smirk.

"Aw, sookie, sookie now!" exclaimed Lawson, wrapping up what was left of Charity's birthday cake. "That's wonderful, Angel. It'll be good to see you getting out and dating again."

Angel shrugged dismissively. "We'll see if anything comes of it. He was probably just being polite."

"*Polite* stops where the exchange of goods and services begins!" retorted Sullivan. "If he offered to take you out, he's more than just *polite*. He's interested."

"It's been so long since a guy has been interested that I can't tell the difference between the two," admitted Angel.

"You're a catch, Angel. Why wouldn't he be interested?" asked Reginell.

"Be sure to take it slow, though," recommended Lawson. "Take your time to get to know him. No need to rush anything."

Reginell edged closer to Angel. "How does he look?"

Angel fanned herself. "He's got skin like Hershey's, a body like 'Hurt me,' and swag like 'Have mercy!'"

The ladies all roared with laughter and smacked hands.

Once the hilarity died down, Sullivan started to speak, then stopped and sighed.

"What?" Lawson asked, pumping her as she watched her. "What is it you're *not* telling us now?"

"Yeah, Sully, it's much better when we hear these scandals from the horse's mouth, as opposed to reading about it online. Spit it out," Angel said, egging her on.

"This isn't a scandal, not *my* scandal, anyway," replied Sullivan.

Lawson eyed her with caution. "So whose scandal is it?"

Sullivan exhaled. "Okay, well, it is my scandal . . . sort of. There's this minister in Atlanta."

"Oh, God, not again," wailed Angel, assuming that Sullivan had bedded yet another man who was not her husband. "Sullivan, I know Charles is a patient man who loves the Lord, but he's still a man! How many times do you expect him to take you back after you step out on him?"

"And how many times do you expect *us* to keep quiet when you self-destruct like this?" Lawson wanted to know. "You have a child now. It's about time you grew up and stopped running around, doing whatever and whoever your hormones tell you!"

"Wait a minute," interjected Sullivan. "It's not what you think."

Lawson shot her an exasperated look.

"Ladies, I know I don't have the greatest fidelity track record, but this is different. I'm not sleeping with the minister."

"Then what are you doing with him?" inquired Lawson.

"Nothing! Charles said something about him the other day that I can't get off my mind."

Angel was curious. "What?"

Sullivan said aloud what had been on her mind all night. "He thinks this minister may be my father."

Angel was taken aback. "Really? Who is he?"

"And where did Charles find him?" Lawson added.

"In Atlanta, a few days ago."

"I thought he was at some kind of ministry leaders' conference," said Lawson.

"He was. That's where he met him. Apparently, there's a Samuel Sullivan who's the pastor of a church in Duluth."

Lawson was skeptical. "No offense, Sully, but do you honestly think a pastor could be your father? I mean, look at Vera."

"Whores attract good and bad guys alike," Sullivan disclosed.

"Yeah, but wouldn't a man like that, who feared and loved the Lord, have made some effort to find his daughter?" Angel wondered aloud.

"Not necessarily," countered Sullivan. "Especially if he has a wife and kids at home. Besides, who knows what Vera did to the poor guy? She probably threatened him and ran him off."

Reginell invited herself into the conversation. "So are you going to go up to Duluth and see him for yourself?"

"I don't know. I haven't even gotten the nerve to look him up on the Internet to see if it's really him," Sullivan confessed.

"What's stopping you?" asked Lawson.

"Who knows? I guess fear, scared to get my hopes up."

"So you want to see him?" questioned Angel.

"That's something else I don't know. I haven't seen this man in over twenty-five years. I have no idea what I'd say to him or how I'd feel seeing him after all this time. Maybe this is one of those times where it's better to leave Pandora's box unopened."

"Sully, you don't even know that this guy at the church is your father," said Reginell. "The least you should do is check him out. If he is your dad, decide what you want to do from there."

"To tell you the truth, I've had my fantasy father for so long that I'm afraid of what the truth might be."

Angel blinked. "Fantasy father?"

"Yeah. When I was forced to do Vera's bidding for her when she needed a bill paid or wanted a new purse, I'd always imagine that my father would come swoop down and rescue me." Sullivan looked off, as if in a daze. "In my mind, my dad was always this handsome man who smelled like wood and Old Spice, who had the kind of smile that could melt a girl's heart. We would have inside jokes together, and he'd call me his star baby. And he wouldn't hesitate to lay the smack down on anyone who even *thought* about bringing harm to his baby girl." She turned back to her friends. "Maybe that's the image I want to hold on to."

"Sullivan, you have to check it out if there's even the slightest chance this man could be your father," insisted Lawson.

"Do it to find out his medical history, if nothing else," directed Angel.

"My father skipped out on Reggie and me when we were kids. I didn't see him again until the day of his funeral. As much as I resent him for leaving us, I would give anything to see him again."

"It should be noted that's probably how Simon is going to feel about Garrett, so you shouldn't be so gung ho on keeping them apart," Sullivan noted.

"That's precisely why I don't keep them apart. As much as it tears me up inside to know that my husband is at that house with his jump-off and her son, I know Garrett needs to be there for his child. I'd never do anything to interfere with that."

"Sully, you have something that a lot of people don't get—a second chance to make things right. Don't waste it," Angel implored her. "It's been twenty years, but

I still haven't gotten over losing my father in Desert
Storm. If I could see him or hug him one more time, I'd
do it in a heartbeat."

Lawson playfully elbowed Sullivan. "Hey, what could
go wrong, right?"

"Everything." Sullivan pulled out her smartphone
and logged on to the Internet. "I believe Charles said
the church is called Friendship Temple. I know it's in
Duluth." The ladies crowded around her.

Lawson pointed to the screen. "Is that it?"

"We're about to find out." Sullivan clicked on the
link to the church's Web site. "It looks like a nice-size
church."

"Click on the 'Meet Our Pastor' link," instructed
Lawson.

Sullivan obeyed. A picture of Pastor Samuel Sullivan
and his family lit up the screen.

Lawson pointed at the church's pastor. "Is that him?"

"That's him." Sullivan leaned back in the chair and
exhaled deeply. "That's my father."

"Are you sure?" Angel squinted her eyes to get a better look at the picture. "I mean, you said yourself you
haven't seen the man in about twenty-five years."

"*That's him!*" insisted Sullivan. "I'm positive that's
my father. He's got the same smile and everything."

"So now what?" asked Lawson. "Are you going to call
him?"

Sullivan sucked her teeth. "And say what? 'Hey, I'm
the daughter you abandoned years ago'?"

"It's a start," said Angel.

Sullivan shrugged. "What the heck?" She got the
church's contact number and dialed.

"Are you calling him?" Angel asked, shocked.

"Yeah . . . shush. It's ringing."

Lawson tried to take the phone. "Sully, maybe we
need to ask the Lord about this first."

"It's a blessed day here at Friendship Temple!" greeted the voice on the other end of the line. "May I help you?"

"Yes," answered Sullivan. "I'm looking for Pastor Sullivan, please."

"May I ask who's calling?"

Sullivan hesitated. "Um . . . Lawson Banks." Lawson angrily nudged her. Sullivan signaled to her to be quiet. "Hold please."

"Why did you give them my name?" spewed Lawson.

Sullivan flung her hand to silence her. "Calm down. Nobody knows you."

A deep baritone voice piped through the phone. "Hello. Pastor Sullivan speaking. How can I help you?"

Sullivan was suddenly lost for words. She didn't recognize the voice on the other end of the line and realized she had no idea what she was going to say.

"Hello?" repeated the voice.

"Yes . . . hello, Pastor Sullivan. I think you can help me with something, at least I hope you can."

"I'll try."

"Did you ever live in Savannah, Georgia?"

Samuel Sullivan hesitated but then answered her question. "I grew up there."

Sullivan muted the phone. "He's from Savannah!" she whispered. "I think this is really him!"

Sullivan cleared her throat and unmuted the line. "Um, do you know a woman by the name of Vera Jackson?"

"Is she a member here?"

Sullivan began pacing the floor, her heart pounding a mile a minute. "No, she's lives on St. Simons Island, but she used to live in Savannah."

"Sister, I haven't lived in Savannah for nearly a hundred years! If I did know anyone by that name, the memory is long gone. Is there anything else I can help you with? If not, I need to get back to the church's business."

"Are you positive you don't know a Vera Jackson?" Sullivan asked, nearly convinced that the man on the other end of the line was her father. "She has a daughter. She was named Sullivan after her father . . . you."

Pastor Sullivan had no response.

Sullivan didn't know what to think. "Hello? Are you still there?"

"All right, who is this, and what do you want?" demanded the pastor, his voice now somber.

"I just need to know if I'm talking to the right man," explained Sullivan. "Did you father a child with Vera Jackson thirty-three years ago in Savannah, Georgia?"

"I told you, I don't know anybody named Vera Jackson or her child. I suggest you tell me what you want right now, or hang up and don't call back!"

Sullivan was offended. "I don't want anything from you, not the way you mean."

"Either tell me who this is or I'm hanging up."

"It's Sullivan, the daughter of Vera Jackson and Samuel Sullivan."

At that, the phone went silent.

"Hello? Did you hear me?" asked Sullivan.

"I'm afraid you have me confused with someone else. I don't have a daughter. I don't know who this is, but don't call here, trying to stir up trouble. Better yet, don't call here again."

Samuel Sullivan hung up the phone without saying another word.

Chapter 7

"Our sex life is like our marriage—could be better, could be worse."
—*Lawson Kerry Banks*

Armed with an extra hundred dollars in tips from her waitressing job and a nearly maxed-out credit card, Reginell scoured the mall for evening gowns, dragging her sister along in the process.

"OMG, how cute is this?" Reginell said, gushing, as she held up a designer cocktail dress. "It would be perfect for the retirement banquet. This dress was made for me!"

Lawson checked out the price tag. "No, this dress was made for someone who can afford to drop seven hundred dollars in one pop. You're not one of those people."

Reginell sulked and hung the dress back up. "I used to be. I could've made the money for this dress, plus a pair of shoes to match, in one night at Paramours."

"Yeah, but in the end, it would've cost you a lot more than the price of a dress and a pair of shoes."

"I know," Reginell replied wistfully. "I do miss it sometimes, though."

"What part do you miss, honey?" Lawson sifted through the evening gowns, looking for something her sister could realistically afford. "Having a bunch of strange men groping all over you, making you do things that would shame the devil, for a few lousy bucks? Do you miss having to get high or drunk to make it through your shift? Do you miss not having any self-respect?"

Reginell sucked her teeth. "It wasn't like that every night, Lawson. Sometimes it was a lot of fun."

"You didn't appear to be having much fun when you had to get that restraining order on your strip club stalker or when that crazy chick jumped on you for going into the champagne room with her boyfriend," recalled Lawson.

"It's not like waiting tables is that much better."

"At least it's honest work that you can be proud of. It's better to work for a living than to have to twerk for a living, Reggie."

"All right, all right . . . point taken." Reginell sighed. "I'm just saying money was the last thing I had to worry about then. It's the only thing I worry about now. This minimal wage BS ain't cuttin' it!"

"If you want to make some more money, do what the rest of us do—go back to school and finish earning your degree. Then you can stop waiting tables and make the kind of money you want—with your clothes on, I might add."

"Yeah, in the meantime I've got to keep bumming rides with you, because I can't afford to get my car fixed."

"I don't mind. Besides, why don't you ask Mark? I'm sure he wouldn't mind helping you out. He is your fiancé."

Reginell lifted a strapless gown. "He offered, but I turned him down."

"Why?"

"I don't want him to feel like he's marrying a freeloader. He already had to bail me out with the rent last month." She returned the gown, knowing without looking at the price that she probably couldn't afford it.

"Honey, Mark loves you. He wants to be there for you."

Reginell shook her head. "I'm going to figure out a way to handle it without asking Mark." She hesitated before speaking again. "I may ask Ray, though."

Lawson frowned. "Ray? Why would you ask that manager-slash-pimp for anything?"

"I made Ray a lot of money down at the club. The least he can do is let me hold a few hundred dollars."

"That's not the only thing Ray is going to have you holding, Reggie," warned Lawson.

"It's strictly business between Ray and me. He owes me."

"And you owe Mark more than to go sneaking behind his back to ask Ray for money!"

"Ugh!" groaned Reginell. "Why can't you stay out my business sometimes?"

"You're my baby sister. That automatically makes you my business. Mark is Namon's father, which makes *him* my business too. Reggie, you're just starting to get your life back on track. You're better than all that now. Don't go backward. You have a strong relationship with the Lord, you have a fiancé, and you're about to be stepmother to a young, impressionable girl, in addition to being a stepmother to my son. Think about everything you stand to lose by getting mixed up in that life again."

"Dang, Lawson, I didn't say I was definitely going to do it. I said I was thinking about it, so stop trippin'."

"Well, think about something else, like finding a dress over there on the clearance rack, where you belong. Better yet, borrow a dress from Sullivan, like I told you to do a week ago, when you found out about the event."

"That troll has nothing I want, and you know she'll make me beg to borrow one of her big-name dresses. I refuse to give her the satisfaction."

"Then I'll ask her. She knows better than to act crazy with me. I know too many of her secrets."

Reginell and Lawson wandered to the undergarment section of the department store.

"How are things with you and Garrett?" asked Reginell.

"We're great," Lawson lied. Reginell gave her a hard look. "We're surviving. Things are no better but no worse."

"Do you think your marriage can survive this situation with Simon and Simone?"

"I hope so, but I don't know. Despite everything that's happened, I still love my husband, Reggie," Lawson confessed. "It nearly killed me during those weeks we were separated. I can't go through that again, and I can't see myself without him."

"Then you've got to embrace Simon as your own child, like Garrett did with Namon, and you've got to let this thing with Simone go. Yeah, he slept with her and screwed up big-time, but he's not sleeping with her now. Forget about it and move on."

Lawson puffed up with rage. "It burns me up, you know, to look at her and her child and to know that she's given my husband something that I can't."

"Simone has given him something you won't. That's a whole lot different from *can't*."

"Reggie, I refuse to get pregnant in order to compete with Simone."

"Chick, you've got to be doing more than *sleeping* with your husband for that to even occur. How are things in the bedroom?"

Lawson recoiled. *"Reggie!"*

"What?"

"I know you're an adult, but you're still my baby sister. It feels weird talking to you about what goes on between Garrett and me between the sheets."

"It's not like I'm clueless as to what goes on behind closed doors. Maybe it's what's *not* going on that's causing a problem."

"Our sex life is fine, Reggie."

"What do you call *fine?*"

Lawson sighed. "Our sex life is like our marriage—could be better, could be worse."

"Humph. If I were you, I'd stop looking at those granny panties and get myself a couple of these." Reginell passed her a sheer, crotch-less negligee.

Lawson beheld it with disdain. "Reggie, nothing about this thing looks sexy or comfortable."

"You ain't wearing it for your comfort," said Reginell, hanging it back on the rack. "You're wearing it so Garrett can take it off! Sis, you may be the expert in teaching, but I'm the expert in *doing*. Trust me, I know what I'm talking about."

"I bet you do," murmured Lawson.

"I'm serious, Lawson. I can show you how to do a sexy lap dance for him that'll have Garrett eating out of your hands and anywhere else you want him to!"

Lawson couldn't help laughing. "Reggie, as you will find out whenever you and Mark jump the broom, sex is not a cure-all for everything that's wrong in a marriage. Sex is what got us into this predicament in the first place!"

"That's because he wasn't having it with you. I'm not saying it'll fix everything, but if you have ninety-nine problems, sex shouldn't be one of them. You and Garrett used to be hot and heavy all the time. You need to get back to that. Shoot, you never should've left it!"

"It's hard to be attracted to him when I'm worried about whether or not he's started back sleeping with Simone. When we're together, I find myself thinking, 'I wonder if he did this to her. Did she show him that move?' It takes all the romance out of it."

Reginell shook her head. "Lawson, what are you always telling me? If you're going to pray, don't worry. If you're going to worry, don't pray. Everybody knows if Lawson Banks does nothing else, she prays, so stop worrying about all that." Reginell whipped out her cell phone. "Besides, if you want to show Garrett some moves he ain't never seen before, I have this one hundred different sexual positions app on my phone. See? Check this out."

Lawson pushed the phone out of her line of vision. "That won't be necessary, Reggie. Thank you."

Reginell tucked her phone away. "Okay, do it your way, but don't say I didn't try to help out. This is a battle, but you've got home-court advantage. There's nothing wrong with using what you've got to get what you want, and what you want is all of Garrett's attention on you."

Lawson mulled it over and reluctantly chose a pink Chantilly lace garter belt and matching bustier from the rack. "Do you think they have this in black?"

Reginell's lips creased into a devilish smile. "That's what I'm talking about. I knew you had you some inner freak up under all that . . . anti-freak."

Lawson opted for the black version in her size and headed to the sales counter with Reginell. "This better work, because I have a lot more to lose than a few dollars spent on lingerie if it doesn't. I could also lose my husband."

Chapter 8

"There's half a million dollars on the line. Surely, you and your money-hungry tendencies can appreciate the magnitude of that."

—Angel King

Sullivan arrived at Reginell's apartment with both a designer evening gown and an attitude. Lawson had convinced her to let Reginell borrow one of the many dresses she had collecting dust in her closet, but that didn't mean Sullivan intended to do it with a smile on her face.

"I don't know why I had to loan her a dress and drive way over here to give it to her," whined Sullivan.

"Because that's the only way we could get you over here," revealed Lawson, leading her into Reginell's great room.

Sullivan was surprised to find Angel there, and a spread of vegetables, salsa, chips, cheese, popcorn, and wine as well. "What's going on?"

"We're having a viewing party," explained Lawson. "Tonight is the *Lose Big* finale. We'll find out if Kina wins the competition."

Sullivan whirled around. "I'm leaving."

Angel ushered her back into the fold. "No, you're going to sit your derriere right down here and watch to see if Kina will prevail. There's half a million dollars on the line. Surely, you and your money-hungry tendencies can appreciate the magnitude of that."

Fuming, Sullivan handed the dress to Reginell and sat down. "Do not return this dress with any grease stains, wine stains, or freak stains!" Sullivan warned her.

Reginell rolled her eyes and pulled the black gown out of the garment bag. "Oh, my, this is beautiful! Thanks, Sully."

Lawson and Angel moved closer to get a good look at it.

"I love this jeweled neckline," said Angel. "It's so elegant yet modern."

Lawson examined the gown's sheer cap sleeves. "Reggie, this dress is perfect for you. You can look sophisticated but still have a little sex appeal."

Reginell pressed the gown up against her body to gauge if it would fit. "Where did you get this from? Kohl's?"

Sullivan narrowed her eyes. "Kohl's? Did you say *Kohl's?*" Reginell nodded her head. "Reggie, that is a Badgley Mischka gown! They do not sell Badgley Mischka gowns at Kohl's."

"How was I supposed to know that?" asked Reginell. "I've never even heard of Bradley Mischka, or whatever the name is."

Sullivan shook her head. "Your hoodness never ceases to amaze me, Reggie. I hope you're able to stifle it long enough not to embarrass Mark at that dinner."

"Mark told me to be myself and everything will be fine," boasted Reginell.

"Reggie, please be anybody *but* yourself!" pleaded Sullivan. "Otherwise, Mark will be the laughingstock from here to Virginia."

"Don't listen to Sullivan," ordered Angel. "If Mark loves you the way you are, that's all that matters."

Reginell placed the gown back in the bag. "Thank you."

"Reginell knows what she's doing," bragged Lawson. "Trust me when I tell you she knows a thing or two about men. Heck, I've even started taking advice from her."

Sullivan was baffled. "Why?"

"Because I want to save my marriage," Lawson disclosed. "If turning up the heat in the bedroom is what it takes, I'm going full throttle! Namon is at home as we speak, setting up for a romantic evening."

"Namon?" questioned Sullivan. "Honey, don't you think that's taking the family involvement thing a little too far? He's going to need years of therapy after that!"

Lawson laughed. "He's just setting up lights in the backyard. I'm trying to re-create the night Garrett proposed."

"You mean the night you told him no?" wondered Angel.

"That's the whole point!" said Lawson. "I want to do it over and say yes to him this time—yes to our life together, yes to the vows we made, and yes to a fresh start."

"What about Simon? Is that a yes to him too?" Reginell wanted to know.

Lawson's joyful mood changed. "We need to fix the problems internally before we start reaching out to outsiders."

"Simon is not an outsider," said Reginell.

"We'll deal with Simon another time. Tonight is about Garrett and me reconnecting and getting back some of that spark we've lost, so you ladies will understand if I cut and run as soon as the winner is announced."

"Of course. Do your thang," Reginell said, encouraging her. "Or should I say, 'Do your husband'?"

Sullivan snatched the bowl of popcorn. "So, Miss King, are you and Jordan doing anything you're ashamed to tell us about?"

Angel walked by Sullivan and bopped the top of her head with one of Reginell's decorative sofa pillows. "No, we're keeping it very G-rated. Jordan is a sweetheart. We had coffee this morning, when I got off work. We sat there and talked for three hours. I can't tell you how nice it is to be with a man who doesn't have sex on the brain. It frees us up to talk and get to know one another."

Sullivan kicked off her stilettos. "So that's it? Coffee? That's the special date he promised you?"

"No, that comes next weekend."

"I may be in for a surprise of my own this week," Sullivan revealed.

Reginell poured a glass of wine. "Are you going to try to call that pastor again?"

"He's not just a pastor, Reggie. He's my father," Sullivan asserted. "I know he is."

"Unfortunately, he doesn't seem to know it, Sully," Lawson noted. "Let's not forget that you have no real proof that this is the same man. It could all be circumstantial."

"You didn't hear his voice change when I mentioned Vera and Savannah, but you're right. I have no proof, but I will. Watch me," Sullivan vowed.

"Have you talked to Charles about this?" Lawson asked.

"Girl, you know Charles. He wants me to be patient and be led by the Lord."

"That's good advice," Angel concurred.

Sullivan shook her head. "I've waited almost thirty years, and that's long enough. Somebody is going to give me some answers one way or another."

"All right, be quiet!" Lawson directed and turned up the television. "It's starting."

"We're down to our last two contestants, folks, our biggest losers for this season!" announced the neatly coiffed, tailored suit wearing host. The camera spotlighted Kina and her fellow competitor. "Ladies, tell us how you're feeling going into tonight's finale."

"I feel great," answered Kina. "This morning I got up around seven and had breakfast with my son. We prayed together. We went over the scriptures we've been focusing on and the promises that we're believing God for. We've had a lovely day. I'm not worried about the outcome of this competition, because I know God's will shall be done. I'm simply thankful He has allowed me to get this far, meet so many awesome people, and has given me the body I thought was gone forever! I haven't been a size ten since I was seventeen years old. It doesn't matter who takes home the trophy and the money tonight. I've already won."

"And is there anybody out there in TV land or back home you want to say hello to?" he asked her.

"Shhh. Let's see if she's going to give us a shout-out," said Lawson.

Kina paused to think. "I would like to say thank you to everyone who's been praying for me and following me on Twitter. Your words kept me encouraged every time I wanted to give up. Thank you all for taking this journey with me."

Sullivan smirked. "I'm sure she was thinking of all of you when she thanked her thousands of random Twitter followers."

"I think she's going to win," Reginell said, making a prediction, as the other contestant droned on with responses to the host's questions. "At least I hope so. I may need her to let me borrow a few bucks."

"We told you to stop planning the kind of wedding you can't afford," reproved Lawson.

"It's not even that. I've gotten behind on all my bills. Matter of fact, y'all need to enjoy looking at this fifty-inch television while you can. I may have to pawn it if I don't get some money soon."

"Reggie, you can't maintain the same kind of lifestyle as a waitress that you had as a stripper," said Angel. "Look at this expensive apartment and that convertible you drive and all these other amenities you have around here. It's time to face the fact that you may have to downgrade."

"Not necessarily," Reginell hinted. "I have options."

Lawson looked up at her. "Like what?"

"Stay out of my business, Lawson."

After nearly an hour of filler programming and clips from earlier in the season, the host of *Lose Big* was finally ready to announce the champion.

"The winner of this season's *Lose Big* competition and the winner of five hundred thousand dollars is . . ." He suspended his words to draw out the anticipation and suspense. "Kina Justine Battle!"

The live audience erupted into thunderous applause, and Kina fell to her knees as confetti rained down on her. "God is so good!" she declared. "He made this happen! He answered my prayers! I praise Him! I praise Him! To God be the honor and the glory!"

"She did it! She did it!" screamed Lawson, pumping her fists in the air.

"Oh, my God, I can't believe she won!" exclaimed Angel. "We love you, Kina! Whoo-hoo!"

Reginell hopped up on the couch and pointed at the television. "That's my cousin right there, y'all! Yes! She did the doggone thang!"

Sullivan yawned, unaffected by all the fanfare. "She won. Good for her."

"You're such a hater, Sullivan," accused Reginell, stepping down.

"I'm not hating," insisted Sullivan. "I'm glad she won. She can finally give Kenny the kind of life she always wanted for him, but don't expect the same Kina to return that left here, assuming she bothers to come back at all."

Lawson rolled her eyes. "Sully, we've been watching Kina on that show for weeks. She's still the same humble, sweet Kina she's always been."

"That's because she was still broke. Money changes things, and it changes people. Kina just got five hundred thousand dollars richer. It's only now that you're about to see the real Kina come out and play."

Chapter 9

"Yeah . . . some other night."
— *Lawson Kerry Banks*

Lawson's heart couldn't help but swell with pride as she watched her son, Namon, string up Christmas lights on the trees in her backyard. When she was a naive sixteen-year-old parent, she couldn't imagine the day that her son would be applying to colleges and prepping for his high school graduation. The traces of his baby face were starting to fade as he morphed into a young man who resembled Mark more with each passing year.

"Looks good," said Lawson, giving Namon an approving nod.

Namon looped the remaining string of lights around his hand. "I set everything up exactly like we did last time Dad wanted to pop the question."

Lawson smiled. "I'm glad you still think of Garrett as your dad, especially after everything that's happened."

"He's the man who raised me. Nothing can ever change that."

"What about Simon?"

Namon grimaced. "What Dad did to you sucked bigtime, but we've talked about it a lot. I forgave him. We all make mistakes. Anyway, Simon seems like a cool li'l dude. I kind of like having a little brother."

"That's very sweet of you to say."

Namon broke into a smile. "Did you see Kina on TV tonight? She won."

"Yeah, we saw it. I'm so proud of her."

"Yeah, me too. It's about time we got some ballers in the family! Do you think this means her and Kenny will be coming back soon?"

"I don't know, sweetie, but I'm praying that she does."

"If you talk to her, tell her I said, 'Congrats.'"

"Will do." Lawson clasped her hands together. "Okay, Garrett will be home in about an hour, so I better finish up out here."

"Do you need me to do anything else?"

Lawson looked around the yard. "Nope, everything looks perfect." She dropped her car keys into Namon's open palm. "Now, go make yourself scarce! I'll see you tomorrow. I love you."

"Thanks." He kissed her on the cheek. "Love you too."

"Go straight to your father's house," Lawson called after him as he jogged toward the house. "No speeding and stay off the cell phone!"

Lawson painstakingly re-created every detail from the night of Garrett's proposal, from the position of the candles to the strawberries he fed her, covered in whipped cream. She showered and doused herself with his favorite perfume. Her newly purchased lingerie was covertly hidden underneath her dress. This night would signal a new beginning for them, and Lawson couldn't wait another minute.

As she lit the last candle on the table in their back-yard, she heard Garrett calling for her inside the house.

"Hey, Lawson, where you at?"

"I'm out here in the backyard, honey. Why don't you come join me?"

Garrett approached the opened back door. "I would but . . ." He stopped, astonished by the alluring scene before him. "What's all this?"

Lawson strutted over to him and flashed a seductive smile. "Doesn't it look familiar?"

Garrett inched toward her. "Yes, it does. You look incredible, by the way. What's the occasion?"

"No special occasion." She threw her arms around his neck. "I thought it was time we—" She was interrupted by a loud, shrill cry from inside the house. "Is the TV on?"

"No." Garrett removed her arms. "That's what I was coming out here to tell you. Simon's here. He is asleep in his carrier. Make that *was* asleep in his carrier."

"Sounds like he's wide awake now." Lawson exhaled and tried to mask her disappointment. "Go check on him."

"He probably dropped his pacifier." He gave Lawson a quick kiss. "I'll be right back."

Lawson busied herself by grazing over the food. Garrett returned a few minutes later.

"Is he okay?" she asked.

"He needed to be changed. He'll drift off to sleep in a minute. I put him back there in Reggie's old room."

"I didn't know you were getting him today," replied Lawson, slightly miffed.

"I didn't either. Simone's best friend was in an accident today. She asked me to look after him while she tended to her friend. She's going to stop by and pick him up when she leaves the hospital."

"Okay." Lawson smiled up at her husband, determined not to waste another second discussing Simone. "Where were we?"

Garrett drew her to him. "I believe we were right here, Mrs. Banks."

"You remembered." She leaned in for a kiss.

Garrett stopped her when their lips were just shy of touching. "You know what? I think I need to get the baby monitor. If Simon starts crying, we won't be able to hear him out here."

"Garrett, he's fine. Let the boy sleep. That's what babies do best."

"I know. I want to be on the safe side, though." Garrett didn't wait for her approval before dashing inside to retrieve the baby monitor.

Lawson poured herself a glass of champagne to calm her nerves. She couldn't fault the baby for being a baby. She couldn't even be upset with Simone, because she would drop everything to be there for her friends too. She just wished that it could've happened any other night. Lawson had downed two glasses of champagne by the time Garrett returned.

He set the monitor down on the table. "I'm sorry about that, babe. I had to look for it."

She gritted her teeth. "It's fine. You're being a concerned dad. Nothing wrong with that."

"All right, no more interruptions," he announced and swept her into his arms.

Lawson yielded. "You promise?"

"Lawson, this is all very sweet. I love you for doing this."

"You're going to love me even more when we get inside." She lifted her dress enough to reveal the garter belt.

Garrett was aroused. "I can love you right out here if you want me to."

She giggled. "It's been a minute since we've done that . . . out here, at least." It felt good to flirt with him again.

The covered trays on the table caught Garrett's attention. "What's over there?"

Lawson walked over to the table and lifted one of the lids to reveal the plump ripened strawberries underneath. "See? Just like last time."

Garrett plastered a fake scowl on his face. He sat down at the table and pulled Lawson into his lap. "Wasn't it around this time that you were turning down my proposal?"

"Technically, I didn't say no. I said, 'Not yet.'"

"My ego took it as a no, ma'am."

"But we got through it, like I know we'll get through this." She poured him a glass of champagne and retrieved her glass. "What shall we toast to?"

"More nights like this."

As they clinked their glasses together, Simon's wails screeched through the baby monitor.

"*Seriously?*" Lawson thought aloud.

Garrett took a deep breath. "You know what? I'm going to check on Simon, and then I'm going to shoot Namon about fifty dollars to babysit for a couple of hours. How about that?"

"I sent him to Mark's house for the night so we could be alone." She exhaled and rose from Garrett's lap. "You might as well get up and check on him."

When Garrett returned, Lawson had blown out the candles and closed the strawberries and was drinking champagne straight from the bottle.

"Is it over?"

Lawson brought the bottle down from her lips. "You tell me."

"I, um, got a call from Simone while I was in with Simon. Her friend is going into surgery and doesn't have any family around here, so Simone wants to stay at the hospital. She asked if Simon could spend the night."

"Fine," said Lawson and finished off the bottle. "I'm not really up for all this anymore, anyway."

Garrett licked his lips. "What about . . ."

"I'm not up for *that* anymore, either." Lawson stood up. "I'm sleepy and a little drunk. I'm going to bed."

Garrett was as dejected as Lawson was. "Okay. I'll come join you in a minute."

"Why don't you sleep in the room with your son? That way you'll be close by if he wakes up."

"Is that what you want?"

"Garrett, I rarely get what I want these days. Good night."

"Hey, Lawson," Garrett called as she neared the door. "We'll make this up some other night."

She turned around and looked at him, feeling more distance between them than ever before. "Yeah . . . some other night," she repeated and went to bed alone.

Chapter 10

"We both know I don't belong here."
—*Reginell Kerry*

Dressed to the nines in her Badgley Mischka gown and with her braids neatly swept to the side of her left shoulder, Reginell stood before Mark in the lobby of their hotel. "How do I look?"

Mark gazed at her, drinking in her beauty and essence. "You're gorgeous, Reggie. I don't know when I've seen you look more beautiful—or any woman, for that matter."

"Are you sure?" She tugged on the gown. "I feel like it's a little tight. I guess I'm curvier than that stick-figure Sullivan."

"I love your curves." Mark curled his arms around her waist. "You look amazing."

Reginell bowed her head, staring down at the gown. "It's the dress, not me."

"You make the dress, baby. Trust me, Reggie, it's *you!*"

After a ten-minute cab ride, Reginell and Mark arrived at the banquet hall. Mark escorted Reginell inside. Tables and chairs were covered with pressed white linen, and glass drop chandeliers shined to an antique silver finish dripped overhead. It was all somewhat daunting to Reginell, who was more accustomed to a nightclub than a ballroom.

Mark spotted his former coach chatting with the college president. "There's Coach Parker. Come on so I can introduce you."

Reginell saw them, but she didn't see two men talking. She saw one man who was so revered that the school wanted to acknowledge his accomplishments in the most honorable way possible, and another man who had so much power that he met with dignitaries from all over the country on a regular basis. What kind of intelligent conversation could she possibly have with them? The last thing she wanted to do was make a fool of herself or humiliate Mark by saying the wrong thing. Reginell didn't know much about the Bible, but she knew Ecclesiastes stated that "there's a time to keep silence, and a time to speak." This was a time for her to keep silence.

Reginell tapped the side of her head. "Baby, you know what? I forgot to call Lawson and let her know we made it up here okay. You go on and speak to your coach. I'm going to step away for a second to call her."

"That's okay. I'll wait," offered Mark.

"No, you go do what you need to do. I'll catch up with you in a second." Reginell eased away from him to make her imaginary phone call. She returned when she saw Mark waiting for her by the entrance.

"There you are," said Mark. "I got us a table with a few of my old teammates."

Mark led Reginell to a table with three other dapper couples. "Everyone, this is the goddess I was telling you about, my fiancée Reginell."

"She's lovely, Mark," replied one of the women at the table.

"That she is." Mark faced Reginell. "Reggie, the charming young lady who just complimented you is my friend Gloria. She's married to that knucklehead sitting next to her, Greg."

"I bet this knucklehead can still kick your butt all over the football field," joked Greg.

Mark laughed. "You retired from the NFL a long time ago. Don't let your mouth get you in trouble, old man! Next to them is Tanya and her husband, Scott." Mark pulled out a chair for Reginell. "And here we have my college roommate Jason and his wife, Darla."

Reginell sat down. "It's nice to meet all of you." Reginell looked down at all the silverware arranged in neat rows, like soldiers, next to her Caesar salad. "What happened to a regular old fork and spoon?"

Gloria laughed. "Honey, work your way from the outside in."

Reginell smiled and nodded. She spread her cloth napkin over her lap, imitating what the other women had done.

Jason looked across the room. "Hey, is that Darwin Jackson over there?"

"Yep, good ole number twelve!" Mark removed his arm from around Reginell's shoulders. "Hey, babe, I'm going to go over there and holler at my boy. Are you going to be okay over here by yourself for a minute?"

"Yeah, I guess." Reginell's heart sank. The last thing she wanted was to be left at a table with a bunch of snooty-looking women she didn't know and probably had zero in common with, but she didn't want to deprive Mark of a good time.

"Go on, Mark. We'll take good care of her," said Darla.

Mark kissed Reginell on the forehead and scurried off with his teammates. She prayed that none of the women would try to strike up a conversation with her. All she wanted was to be treated like she was invisible. To her chagrin, the moment the men left, the ladies started talking.

"That gown is exquisite, Reginell," praised Darla. "Who's the designer?"

"Um . . ." For the life of her, Reginell couldn't remember the designer's name. "I don't know. Magda something, I think. The dress isn't mine. I borrowed it from a friend. This kind of thing isn't really my style."

"I'm sure it's not," muttered Gloria. The other ladies cut their eyes at Gloria, causing Reginell to feel even more out of place.

Tanya cleared her throat. "So, Reginell, how are the wedding plans coming? Have you chosen a theme and your colors?"

"Not really. I didn't know so much went into planning a wedding. I probably should've helped my sister out more when she was planning hers."

"Focus on the bright side," said Darla. "You're marrying the man you love, you're going to get a ton of fabulous gifts, and after all the wedding madness, you can relax and enjoy your honeymoon."

"Have you all chosen a honeymoon destination?" Gloria asked, piping up. "I highly recommend the Maldives. There's no place like it."

"Maldives? I've never even heard of it," admitted Reginell. "That sounds like something you sprinkle over chicken."

Tanya and Darla giggled.

"Oh, you've got to get Mark to take you!" continued Gloria. "It's magnificent."

"Is it down there by Jamaica and all those places?"

Gloria gave Reginell a sour look. "Um, not exactly. It's southwest of India."

Reginell nodded, not having the first clue as to where Gloria was talking about.

"Wherever you go, be careful," warned Tanya. "Scott and I went to the Turks and Caicos for our fifth anniversary and came back with a bun in the oven."

"Maybe we'll just go to the Turks, then," replied Reginell, still clueless.

"Most people don't do one without the other," Tanya explained.

"The Turks and Caicos are a part of a group of islands in the Lucayan Archipelago. Do you know where that is?" Gloria asked before taking a sip from her goblet.

Reginell shook her head. "I can't even pronounce it."

Tanya laughed. "She's so cute. Isn't she funny?"

Darla cut into her salad. "Did I tell you that my firm is downsizing again?"

"Oh, no," moaned Gloria. "How many are they looking to lay off?"

"At least fifty people. You'd think that an MBA and all those years of school would guarantee some form of job security. It's getting to where a master's carries about as much weight as a GED!"

"It's such a shame!" Gloria shook her head. "Where did you go to school, Reginell?"

"Beach High."

"No, I mean for undergrad," Gloria said, clarifying matters.

"Oh . . . well, I went to Savannah Tech for two quarters." They looked at Reginell, as if waiting for her to finish the rundown of her educational background. To save face, Reginell tossed out, "I've been thinking about applying at Savannah State too."

"You should definitely do that," Darla said, encouraging her. "Do you know what you want to major in?"

"Computers or business, but what I really want to do is sing."

Gloria nodded. "There's a lot of money to be made in the music industry. Do you write or produce as well?"

"No, but I guess I could if I really tried."

"I used to be an exec over at Zephyr Records, and I can tell you firsthand that there's not a lot of money in album sales these days or in just getting performing credits for a song. Most artists I know write not only for themselves, but for people in other music genres too. It's hard to make it solely by performing, unless you're headlining a major tour."

"And it's hard to do that if you're first name ain't Beyoncé or Madonna!" tossed out Tanya.

"So what are you doing in the meantime?" Gloria asked, pressing.

Reginell gulped down her tea, yearning for something stronger. "What do you mean?"

"Are you doing vocal coaching, entering competitions, posting some of your music online?"

"I sing at work sometimes, on amateur night."

"Where exactly do you work?" inquired Gloria. "Is it a jazz club? Do they feature live music?"

"No, it's pretty much a dive where people come to shoot pool and have a few beers with bad wings. They started doing open mic night to draw people in, but it's usually just me and some old dude who plays the flute who perform."

A collective round of piteous "Ohhs" went around the table.

"Speaking of flutes," interjected Darla, "did I tell you that Kara is going to be playing for the Queen?"

Tanya was bowled over. "Of England?"

"Yes, her school's band was invited to attend some big ceremony they're having over there. A few of her classmates aren't going, though, because they don't have passports, and the passports won't be back in time for them to go."

Gloria shook her head. "Can you believe that people in this day and age don't have passports?"

Reginell could believe it. She was one of those who didn't have one.

Gloria went on. "My Adrick has had his since he was six. He goes to China every summer, and he's gotten as fluent in Mandarin as he is in English. Too bad his parents can't say the same."

Everyone at the table laughed except Reginell. The joke was lost on her, unless the joke was that most of their children had done more by age six than she had done by age twenty-five. She continued sipping her tea in silence, wishing that the floor would open up and suck her in. She was going to kill Mark for leaving her alone with these debutantes for so long. She tuned back in to the conversation in time to hear Darla ask a question.

"Have you been keeping up with these drone strikes?"

"Who's on strike?" asked Reginell, attempting to contribute something other than pity to the conversation.

"No, I'm talking about the military drone strikes in Yemen."

"Thank God my brother Jarvis has been promoted to captain," Darla remarked. "We don't have to worry about him being on the front line as much."

"Captain at only twenty-six years old," Gloria observed, enthused. "You must be proud."

Reginell's self-worth plummeted. She and Darla's brother were virtually the same age, and he was already light years ahead of her in accomplishments.

Reginell sat quietly as the women talked over her head about foreign policy and the kind of financial problems she'd loved to have, like being forced to be put on a waiting list for a five-thousand-dollar purse and missing Fashion Week in Paris this year. She felt as if the women were speaking a foreign language to her, possibly Mandarin, which, apparently, she should have been able to understand by the time she entered first grade.

Reginell was damp from nervous sweat. "If you ladies will excuse me, I need to go to the bathroom. Do you know where it is?"

"Out those double doors and to your right," instructed Tanya.

Reginell couldn't get out of there fast enough. She went out on the terrace and bummed a cigarette from one of the cooks who was outside taking a smoking break. She felt way more at ease chatting with them than she did with the women at her table.

Mark found Reginell leaning over the ornate railing, alone, puffing on the cigarette. "When did you start back smoking?"

"I didn't." She ground the cigarette into the cement. "I mean, I don't unless I'm stressed out or nervous."

He draped his jacket around her bare arms. "And what is my bride-to-be stressed out about?"

"Mark, be honest. We both know I don't belong here." Reginell lowered her head. "I never should've come."

Mark lifted her chin. "Hey, wait a minute. Did those women say something to upset you?"

"No, they didn't mean to say anything, not intentionally."

"What happened?"

She sighed. "They were talking about their degrees and places they've been and a bunch of things I've never even heard of. I felt so out of place."

Mark held her. "Reggie, you have no reason to feel threatened by the women in that room or anywhere else. You're beautiful, smart, and talented, and there's no one in the world I'd rather be here with tonight than you."

"That's sweet of you to say, but look at those women and look at me. They're all so accomplished and professional."

"So are their husbands. Half of the guys in there went on to play for the NFL or for some other league overseas. Then there's me, a hometown football coach and math teacher. It would be real easy for me to be intimidated by all their accolades and success, but one thing my daddy always said is that a real man—or woman, in your case—isn't intimidated by anyone except God, and I don't believe anyone in there holds that title. Even with all their money and achievements, I wouldn't trade my life for theirs if I could. All we see is the outside. We don't know what kind of hell they're catching at home."

Reginell smiled up at him. "You always know what to say to make me feel better."

"Keeping a smile on that beautiful face of yours is one of my most important jobs, and I take that very seriously." Mark tilted his head down to kiss her. "So are you ready to go back in? They're about to serve the main course. It's steak."

Reginell thought steak was very apropos, considering that she felt like she was going back into the lion's den. For Mark's sake, she would grin and get along long enough to get through the evening, but she knew she didn't fit in with that crowd any better than she fit into Sullivan's gown. As soon as they got back to Georgia, she was going back to the people and place where she knew she belonged.

Chapter 11

"Let me guess. Garrett was mad at me, and you just happened to be right there to comfort him with your vagina."
—*Lawson Kerry Banks*

Lawson stood in front of the door with her arms crossed and a glower splashed across her face. Simone Atwood's presence brought a chill over Lawson that had nothing to do with the nip in the night air. It was her Christian duty to be cordial, but it was her obligation as a scorned wife to make Simone feel as unwelcomed as possible.

"If you're looking for Garrett, he's not here," she barked to Simone, who was standing on the other side of the door.

"Actually, I just wanted to drop Simon's jacket off. It's not too bad right now, but the temperature is supposed to drop later on tonight, and all Simon has on is his sweater. I don't want him out in the cold with no protection."

She extended the jacket to Lawson, who practically snatched it from Simone's hands. "Fine . . . Thanks. They went to Garrett's parents' house, but I'll be sure to give it to him when they get back. Is there anything else?"

"As a matter of fact, there is. Do you have a minute?"

"I'm in the middle of typing a paper for class so, no, I really don't have any minutes to spare."

"I think we need to talk . . . woman to woman. It won't take long."

"It's more like mistress to wife." Lawson sighed and stepped aside, allowing Simone to come in. "Make it quick. I have a lot to do."

Simone spun around and faced Lawson in a defiant stance. "I want to know what your problem is."

Lawson narrowed her eyes. "Excuse me?"

"I want to know what your problem is," repeated Simone. "What is your issue with me and my son?"

"I don't have an issue with Simon. He's a baby. He's innocent in all this."

"Then what's your problem with me?"

Lawson laughed, astounded by Simone's gall. "You've got to be kidding me!"

Simone exhaled. "Look, I know what Garrett and I did was wrong, but it was only one night. You all were separated at the time, and it didn't look like you were going to get back together—"

Lawson interrupted her. "A separation is not the same thing as a divorce, and it doesn't change the fact that you slept with a married man, and had unprotected sex at that."

"Lawson, it wasn't like we planned for that to happen. It was one of those nights. Garrett was upset and—"

Lawson flashed her hand. "Please spare me the details. I think I can pretty much figure it out. Let me guess. Garrett was mad with me and you just happened to be right there to comfort him with your vagina. Does that pretty much sum it up?"

Simone rolled her eyes. "It was never my intent to break up your marriage. I even changed jobs because

I felt so guilty about what happened and couldn't face working with Garrett again."

"Wasn't that noble of you?" Lawson offered a mordant simper. "Then again, why settle for merely working with Garrett when you can have his baby?"

"It wasn't like that. At first, I wasn't even going to keep the baby."

"Then why did you?" Lawson shot back. "You knew he was married and had a family. Why didn't you just put the baby up for adoption or something?"

"Because I loved my child too much not to have him and not to keep him. I didn't care whether Garrett stepped up as a father or not. I was going to keep my baby. But I did think he had a right to know and be a part of his son's life."

"You make it sound so magnanimous and selfless, but I wasn't born yesterday, sweetheart. I know exactly what this is about."

"It's about Simon. That's it."

"No, it's about the fact that you still want him, don't you?" asked Lawson.

Simone looked up. "What are you talking about?"

"My husband," answered Lawson. "Admit it. . . . You still want him."

Simone exhaled. "What I want is a father for my son. I also want the peace and security of knowing that he'll be treated like a part of the family when he's here, not like some discarded outcast. I want to know that I can leave him alone with you without having to worry."

Lawson was taken aback. "I can't believe you said that to me! I'm a mother, Simone. I could never hurt another child, not even yours!"

"That's all I needed to hear. You don't have to like me, and I darn sure ain't got to like you, but we do need to be able to peacefully coexist for the sake of my son and your stepson. That's the only thing I want from you."

"Surely, that's not the *only* thing you want from me, Simone." Lawson circled her. "Yeah, you'll take that, but if you can have my husband too? Well, that's icing on the cake, isn't it?"

"Garrett is a good man. He's kind, hardworking—"

"I don't need you, of all people, to tell me about my husband!" bellowed Lawson.

"Like I said, he's a good man, but he's *your* man. I'm not trying to take him." She paused for a moment. "However, he is the father of my child, and nothing would please me more than for us to raise Simon together as a family. Now, if you don't want Garrett or, better yet, don't know how to keep him, I'll be more than happy to fill that position and show you how it's done."

"You make it very hard not to hate you." Heat rose to Lawson's face. "If I wasn't a saved, 'sanctified by the Holy Ghost' woman, the police would be outlining your body with chalk right now," she spewed.

Simone laughed a little. "If you weren't a lot of things, like frigid, judgmental, and self-righteous, we wouldn't be having this conversation right now, would we?"

Lawson had to do some fast praying not to haul off and slap her.

"But don't get your church hat in a bunch," said Simone, needling her. "I told you, I'm not going after your husband. But if he comes after me, I'm not turning him away." Simone pranced to the door. "You have a good night, Mrs. Banks. Be sure to give Garrett that jacket. I want my baby to stay warm." Before leaving, Simone turned around and said, "Be sure to tell your husband I said hello, and I'll see him tomorrow . . . to drop the baby off, of course."

Lawson slammed the door behind her. Under different circumstances, she might have been impressed with Simone's ability to play both the martyr and the predator simultaneously, but Lawson knew she couldn't rest on her laurels, considering that the role Simone secretly wanted to play more than any other was that of Mrs. Garrett Banks.

Chapter 12

"Are you even capable of saying anything that isn't wrapped in a lie, Vera?"
—Sullivan Webb

Vera Jackson opened her front door, surprised to see both her daughter and granddaughter standing on the other side of it. Sullivan frowned. Her mother's wig was way too blond and wiry for Sullivan's liking, but Vera was never one who had an appreciation for tact or subtlety.

Vera gulped down her cocktail and reached out for Charity. "It's about time you brought this child over here to see me."

Smelling the familiar stench of cigarette smoke on her mother, Sullivan stepped back and held Charity close to her chest and out of Vera's grasp. "Don't you come anywhere near this child until you wash your hands and change out of that smoke-infested robe."

Vera sucked her teeth. Wanting to see Charity out-weighed Vera's desire to stand there arguing with Sullivan. She let the two of them into her seaside St. Simons Island cottage and pointed to the sofa. "Y'all can sit over there while I change, but don't go looking through my stuff. Keep that baby out of those ashtrays," Vera ordered and disappeared into her bedroom.

Sullivan had endured a tumultuous and often violent relationship with her mother for as long as she could remember. While Vera had schooled Sullivan on sex and how to use it as a weapon, she had never taught her daughter about love. Even though they'd made modest strides in their ability to communicate with one another, Sullivan and Vera's relationship was still shrouded in dysfunction. None of that mattered today. Sullivan needed answers, and Vera was the only one who had them.

Vera returned, wearing a fitted Christian Dior T-shirt and tight jeans molded around her slim frame. For a woman nearing sixty, she still maintained a figure that rivaled her thirty-three-year-old daughter's.

"Hmm . . . Dior. The porn business must be booming," noted Sullivan, referencing Vera's live-in boyfriend's job as an adult film director.

Vera sat down next to Sullivan. "You tell me. You're the one with the sex tape."

"I'm sure I'm not the only one. Is Cliff home?" asked Sullivan.

"No."

Sullivan removed Charity's jacket. "Is Cliff *ever* home?"

"What's it to you, Sullivan? Cliff is my man, not yours. If I'm not worried about where he is, why are you? Now, hand me that grandbaby of mine."

Sullivan grudgingly handed her daughter over to Vera.

Vera stood Charity up on her knees. "Did you ever figure which man was the daddy of this child?"

"How many times do I have to tell you that this is Charles's baby?"

"Uh-huh. I guess time will tell, won't it?" She kissed Charity on the nose. "She doesn't look like either one of 'em if you ask me. Knowing you, there's probably no telling who her daddy is."

Sullivan adjusted her sitting position. "Speaking of telling . . . why don't you ever talk about my father?"

Vera rolled her eyes and sat Charity down in her lap. "What is there to talk about?"

"Who is he? Why did he leave? How did the two of you meet?"

Vera twisted her face into a scowl. "Why do you care? That man ain't bothered to even show his face around here in almost thirty years!"

"I know that. What I want to know is, why not? What went down between you two?"

"Nothing. He was married, I was his side chick, and you were something that was never supposed to happen. End of story."

Sullivan glared at her mother. "You can be so cruel sometimes, you know that?"

"Well, Sullivan, you asked for the truth, and I gave it to you. Don't start whining because you don't like it."

"The truth?" echoed Sullivan. "Are you even capable of saying anything that isn't wrapped in a lie, Vera? It's no wonder Samuel got as far away from you as fast as he could."

Vera immediately took offense. "Oh, so you assume I was the problem, huh? I did something to run him off, right?"

"Are you going to tell me that *I* did?" shot back Sullivan.

Vera set Charity down to let her explore the living room. "I don't know what kind of fantasies you got going on in your head about Samuel Sullivan, but he wasn't no saint. Far from it."

"Well, that's obvious by the mere fact that he slept with you!" Sullivan watched Charity fling magazines off of Vera's coffee table. "I can only assume you weren't half the shrew back then that you are now."

"Believe whatever you want to believe, Sullivan."

"Why won't you just tell me about your relationship with my father?"

Vera was annoyed. "What for?"

"For me. For your granddaughter. She has a right to know where she comes from."

Vera howled with laughter. "That's funny coming from you, considering you don't even know where she comes from!"

"You're not going to distract me or stop me from digging by insulting me," warned Sullivan. "I'm not leaving until you give me something to go on."

"Just let it go, Sullivan. You're going to start digging around, and I promise you, you ain't gon' like what you come up with. People who go looking for something usually find it."

"All I want is to know the man who gave me life. Why is that so bad?"

"If he wanted you to know him or if he wanted to claim you, don't you think he would've done something about it by now?"

"Not if you made it clear that he wasn't welcome."

"When a man loves his baby, there ain't nothing you can do to keep a man from that child." Vera frowned. "Why are you worried about him all of sudden, anyway?"

"I called him."

"Called who?"

"Samuel Sullivan." Sullivan's eyes met her mother's. "I think I may have found him."

Vera ceased to budge for a moment before regaining her composure. "Girl, you're talking crazy. You ain't found your daddy."

"Actually, I wasn't the one who found him. Charles ran into him at a ministers' conference."

Vera laughed to herself. "I see Samuel Sullivan is still frontin' like he's a preacher."

"So you knew he was a minister?"

"I knew he was a man who *claimed* to be one. I can't rightly say that he is a minister, not a real one, anyway."

"He hung up the phone as soon as I told him who I was, so I'm thinking about going to see him," revealed Sullivan. "He can't avoid me if I'm right in his face."

Vera scooped up Charity as she hobbled toward the fireplace. "Sullivan, that man doesn't want to see you."

"How in the world could you possibly know that, Vera?"

"Did he ask you to come? Has he made any effort in all this time to see you?"

"I can't say for sure that he hasn't tried to get in contact with me. I don't put it past you to have purposely kept the two of us apart."

Vera shook her head. "If believing that helps you to sleep better at night, Sullivan, have at it!"

"Well, then, what's the reason? Why did he stop coming around?"

"I told you he already had a family. You, me—we were outsiders. You were never going to be a part of the family no matter what I did or didn't do."

Sullivan crossed her arms. "How do I know you're not lying?"

"You don't." Vera blew raspberries at Charity. "But you'll see. If I were you, I'd pretend Samuel Sullivan didn't exist and focus on my beautiful grandbaby. You've got enough to worry about trying to figure out who her daddy is instead of trying to dig up yours."

"I don't care what you say, Vera. I'm going to see my father."

Vera shooed Sullivan away. "Fine. Go see him. Just don't believe anything that man says. I doubt that he's changed much, and once a liar, always a liar."

"Thanks for the warning, but I want to see for myself. Besides, he can't be as bad a parent as you were."

"For all you know, he could be worse. You mark my words," Vera warned her. "You're going to regret the day you let that man into your life."

Chapter 13

"I think it's a new season for me. . . ."
—*Angel King*

Almost two weeks following their initial encounter, Angel and Jordan finally squeezed enough time out of their hectic schedules for an afternoon lunch. After gorging on fried green tomatoes, roasted tilapia, and shrimp panini at the Cotton Exchange Tavern and Restaurant, Angel and Jordan attempted to burn off the excess calories with a romantic stroll along Savannah's famed River Street, taking in the sights, smells, and sounds of the tourist district.

"I can't believe I ate like that," said Angel as she and Jordan walked along the cobblestoned path following their lunch. "I'm usually very particular about what I allow inside my body. You're a bad influence on me, Mr. McKay."

He winked at her. "You loved every bite of it. Admit it."

Angel sneered, unable to deny it.

"Why are you so worried about what you eat, anyway? You're not even close to being overweight. Everything—and I mean *everything*—on that body of yours looks great. Even better than back in the day."

"I certainly hope so! I wasn't much to look at back then," lamented Angel.

Jordan smirked. "You were cute, but you have a different kind of beauty now. It's still soft, but there's a strength to it as well. It's very attractive."

"Thank you."

"So do I look the way you remember?" asked Jordan.

"No." She stared into his deep-set russet eyes. "You look better."

A smile escaped from his lips. "Now, you know I'm too dark for you to have me over here blushing."

Angel winked at him. "You look cute doing that too." Angel looked at the sun reflecting off the river as they strolled by. "I love this time of year, with all the festive colors and the crisp air."

"Yeah, it's beautiful here." He looked over at Angel. "It's beautiful everywhere."

"You can literally see the seasons change. The Bible talks a lot about there being an appointed time and season for things to happen in our lives. I think it's a new season for me."

"I feel the same way."

"You said you came to Savannah to make a fresh start, but you could've gone anywhere in the world for that. Why Savannah, Georgia?"

Jordan kicked a pebble down the street. "I'd been here a few times before. We have family in Augusta and South Carolina, so we'd drive down here to go to the beach sometimes. I don't know what it is about this place, but I've always felt at peace and at home here. What about you?"

"My college roommate lived here. She and I are best friends. When my marriage fell apart, she invited me to stay with her for a while. I came and never left."

"Are you and your ex still cool?"

Angel nodded slowly. "Yeah, we're friends. We talk, and I still spend time with his two daughters. We just weren't meant to be a couple, that's all. It took me a long time to accept that, but after three failed attempts at a relationship, I finally got the message."

Jordan appeared to be deep in thought.

Angel nudged him. "Hey, what are you thinking about over there, McKay?"

"To be honest, I'm over here trying to figure out why you're still single."

Angel laughed. "Oh, I could give you about a thousand reasons!"

"I mean it," affirmed Jordan. "You're gorgeous. I'm in love with all this natural hair." He ran his fingers through a cluster of curls. "You're smart . . . sexy." She blushed. "You've got good conversation, and you're successful. You're the total package."

"Well, I do have two things working against me," she divulged. "One is that I work too much and hardly have time for a social life. The second is that I'm celibate. Those two words aren't usually a turn-on for most guys."

His eyes bulged. "Celibate, huh? As in no sex, period?"

"Yes, I'm saving myself for my husband. I want him to know that I loved him enough to wait for him and to do things God's way." Angel waited for Jordan to react. "Uh-oh, there it is. . . ."

"What?"

"The look that means 'Lose my number.' I've seen it more times than I care to count."

Jordan laughed. "Not at all, Angel. I respected you anyway, but I respect you even more now than I did before. I think waiting is very admirable."

"So if we were to date, you honestly wouldn't have a problem with my being celibate?"

"No. In fact, I've been kind of on a break myself. I haven't been with a woman since I moved down here."

"Wow, I guess there are at least two of us taking cold showers in Savannah," she joked.

"Just look at it as us doing our part to conserve energy and protect the environment." They both laughed again. Jordan reached for Angel's hand as they neared her parked car. "I really want to see you again, Angel."

"I'd like that too."

"I think I'd like to see you as much as possible," confessed Jordan.

Angel nodded and smiled. "I think that can be arranged."

Jordan checked his watch. "I know we both have to get back to work, but I'm not ready to be dismissed from your presence."

"It's just temporary, right?"

"Better be. I already have a place in mind for our next date."

"Where's that?"

Jordan shook his head. "It's a surprise. I think you'll approve, though."

"I can't wait," she gushed. "I love surprises."

Jordan opened Angel's car door for her. "I guess now comes the awkward part. Do we kiss? Do we hug? Should I pound you up like you're one of my homies?"

She giggled. "What would you like to do?"

He swept a strand of hair out of her face. "I would very much like to kiss you."

Angel wrapped her arms around his neck. "So kiss me."

Jordan placed his hand on the small of her back and leaned down into her. He set his lips on top of Angel's for a lingering kiss that left her a little breathless.

"Was that okay?" he asked, releasing her.

"That was perfect."

"Good." Jordan smiled and helped Angel into the car. "Get back safely. I'll call you later, all right?"

"I'm looking forward to it."

Angel watched Jordan walk away. She let out a deep breath and placed her hand over her heart, but she didn't need to feel it to know how fast it was beating. There was no denying that Jordan McKay was responsible for making her feel things in places where she hadn't felt anything in a long time.

Chapter 14

"I let them know who the queen is and make those wenches bow down!"
—*Sullivan Webb*

Sullivan arrived at Angel's house and dumped a bag full of newly purchased shawls and scarves into Angel's lap as Lawson looked on. "Here."

Angel picked one up and frowned. "What's this?"

Sullivan flopped down on the sofa next to Lawson. "I gave up. The whole knit-one-purl-two thing is *so* not my scene. It was way less hassle to just buy the dog-gone things and be through with it."

Angel shuffled through the items. "Some of these aren't even shawls! You've got scarves and do-rags in here too." Angel thrust them back into Sullivan's arms.

"Three years ago we all agreed to knit these shawls to donate to Shelia's Shawls in honor of Kina, and every October we find an excuse not to do it, but we promised that this year would be different," said Lawson. She shook her head. "Are you philosophically opposed to committing to anything, Sullivan?"

Sullivan set the bag down. "Maybe doing anything for Kina is the part I'm philosophically opposed to."

"Then do it for all the other domestic violence survivors the Silent Witness National Initiative helps," urged Angel. "Handmade, not store-bought."

"Ugh," grunted Sullivan. "Pass the dang yarn and needles!"

Lawson snickered and obliged Sullivan. "Try to not poke anybody's eye out with those things!"

Sullivan began wielding the needles. "It's a good thing I didn't have these when I went to see my mother the other day."

"How did that go?" asked Angel.

"As expected. Vera is still a psychologist's wet dream. I swear the older she gets, the more intolerable she is."

"Just keep praying for her, Sully. You know she has a lot of demons."

"Lawson, Vera doesn't have demons. She *is* a demon! But I will say that she seems to love Charity. It's the only proof I have that she's actually human."

"I'm sure Vera loves you too, in her own twisted way," Angel told her. "Did she tell you anything about your father?"

"Nothing useful. I think I'm going to go to Atlanta and see this Samuel Sullivan for myself and let the chips fall where they may."

"Are you sure that's a good idea?" Lawson asked, pondering aloud.

"What other option do I have? He's certainly not going to come to me. I can't even get him to come to the phone."

"Just don't set your expectations too high. He may be less than thrilled to see you," Angel advised, speculating.

"While we're on the subject of people showing up unexpectedly, I had a visitor." Lawson turned her needles and knit the purl stitches.

"Who?" asked Sullivan, looking up from her own halfhearted knitting.

"My husband's baby mama, Simone."

Angel groaned. "What did she want?"

"She wanted to know what my issue is with her."

Angel stopped and frowned. *"Seriously?"*

"Oh, it gets better! She officially put me on notice that she expects me to treat Simon like my own child and that, while she isn't going to chase after my husband, she has no qualms about letting him chase after her."

"How considerate of her," Angel remarked, ruminating. "And I'm sure it's all in the name of 'just wanting a daddy for my son.'"

"Of course it is," agreed Sullivan. "Some women have no problem stooping to use a baby to get exactly what they want. I know. I've done it before!"

Lawson shook her head. "Obviously, she's waiting with open arms, as well as various other parts, for Garrett to come trotting back to her."

"Lawson, the only power she has is the power you give her," insisted Angel. "That child is the only thing she has on you and her only connection to Garrett. You take that away, she has nothing."

"But we *can't* take him away—that's the problem! As long as Simon is in our lives, Simone will be too, always lurking in the shadows somewhere, waiting for the opportune time to pounce."

"You're the one Garrett loves. She's the baby mama. That's it. Don't be scared off by that slut puppy!" advised Sullivan.

"Sometimes it's hard not to be," Lawson revealed, no longer hiding her insecurities. "Ladies, my marriage is a mess right now. We argue all the time, and things are incredibly tense at home. I wouldn't be all that surprised if he did go running back to her."

"You're playing right into her hands, Lawson. Honey, do you have any idea how many desperate, hat-wielding, Bible-thumping heifers try to push up on Charles? I don't run away with my tail between my legs when they show up. I let them know who the queen is and make those wenches bow down!"

"See? That's what I'm talking about!" exclaimed Lawson. "I don't want this to turn into some big competition between Simone and me. That's not what I want my marriage to be about."

Angel was baffled. "So you're just going to roll over and sign away your husband to her?"

"No, but I'm not going to fight dirty, either. I think the Christian thing to do is to take the high road."

"I'm all for that," said Sullivan. "You can take the high road. When you do, though, make sure Simone's in the middle of it so you can run her over and toss her off the side of it."

"You've always been such a fighter, Lawson," noted Angel. "You seem to have lost some of that edge. What happened?"

"I guess I feel like I'm at a disadvantage."

"Why?" asked Angel.

"Because I can't bring myself to love Garrett's child. I'm sorry, but I look at him, and I'm reminded of everything that has gone wrong in my marriage, from Garrett pressuring me to have children to his affair with Simone. I know I'm hurting my husband, because he loves us both." She paused. "Sometimes I think setting him free is the kind thing to do."

"Yes, *kind of stupid!*" Sullivan scoffed. "Lawson, your marriage can be whatever you make it. You and Garrett write the rules, not Simone and not Simon. I'm not excusing Garrett's behavior or his affair, but it happened. Forgive, forget, and get over it. Simon can be a blessing to you if you let him be."

"This is all about your pride, Lawson, pure and simple. You already know that the Bible says pride comes before destruction and a haughty spirit before a fall. Don't let your pride and the pain you want to hold on to destroy your marriage. That's a much bigger threat to your relationship than ole Simone is," Angel said.

Lawson hushed them. "Enough about my depressing love life. I want some happy couples news. Angel, what's going on with you and Jordan?"

Angel broke into a smile. "We had our first date . . . and our first kiss!"

The women oohed like schoolgirls.

"I can't wait to see him again," Angel added.

Lawson started knitting again. "So you think this might actually amount to something?"

"I hope so. I really like him, and you know I haven't felt this way about anybody since Duke and I called off the wedding."

"I think you reuniting with Jordan is proof that calling the wedding off was the right thing," concluded Sullivan. "You know . . . that and the fact that you were practically cheating on him with his cousin and developed that nasty little porn addiction in the process."

Angel set her needles and yarn down in her lap. "You really know how to suck all the fun out of a room, don't you, Sully?"

"I know that this is all exciting for you Angel, but don't move too fast," Lawson advised, lecturing her.

"Lawson, I've known the guy almost twenty years, and we're just now getting around to our first date! I think it's safe to say we've taken things pretty slow."

"No, you knew him in high school," Lawson replied, drawing the distinction for her. "It's not the same thing as interacting with someone for twenty years."

"Well, I say go for it!" Sullivan said, pushing Angel. "Angel, you deserve to have some fun and enjoy yourself. You haven't had a date, not to mention what else, in nearly two years. Seize the day and the man!"

There was a knock at the door before Angel could respond.

"I bet that's Reggie," said Angel, rising from the sofa to answer the door.

"Another unwanted visitor," Sullivan muttered.

Lawson faced Sullivan. "So you're really just going to show up at the church, demanding to see Samuel Sullivan, without so much as a phone call or warning?"

Sullivan shrugged. "Yes. What's the worst he can do?"

"Have you thrown in jail for trespassing and stalking."

Angel yelped. Sullivan and Lawson whirled around in the direction of her cry.

"Is everything all right?" called Lawson.

Angel returned with a woman barely recognizable to Lawson and Sullivan at her side. "As you can see, everything on this body is great!"

"Oh, my God!" Lawson gasped. "It's you!"

Chapter 15

*"I've found strength in the Lord and in myself that I
never even knew existed."*
—Kina Battle

They all stared at her in disbelief. Gone was the
pudgy, self-conscious woman who was almost afraid of
her own shadow. The woman who stood before them
now was stylish, confident, and fifty pounds lighter.

Kina offered a shy wave. "Hey, cuz."

"Oh, Kina!" Lawson leapt from the sofa and hugged
her. "You look . . ."

"Fabulous?" Kina replied, filling in the gap made by
Lawson's silence.

"Different." Lawson offered a loving smile. "But fab,
no less. What are you doing here?"

Kina squeezed Lawson's hand. "I wanted to see you
guys. I missed you."

"Aww . . . ," Lawson cooed and hugged her cousin
again. "Where's Kenny? Is he with you?"

"No. I went by your house first, Lawson. Namon is
the one who told me you were here. Kenny stayed at
your house with him. He's missed his favorite cousin
like crazy."

"We've missed him too," said Angel. "We've missed
both of you." Angel glanced over at Sullivan. "*All* of us
have."

Kina cut her eyes to Sullivan. "I don't think all of you have missed me, but thank you."

Angel looked Kina up and down, still amazed. "I can't believe you're here!"

"Believe it." Kina nodded toward Sullivan. "Hello, Sullivan."

Sullivan continued knitting without looking up. "Kina."

"Last time I saw you, you were out to here." Kina extended her hand to the size of Sullivan's pregnant belly back then. "Now you don't even look like you've had a baby."

"I assure you that I did." Sullivan refused to make eye contact with her. "Don't tell me you've forgotten, Kina. After all, you were the one who announced my pregnancy to Charles, nearly killing him with your lies about my baby's paternity."

"Sullivan, don't start," groaned Angel.

"It's okay," Kina reassured her. "Sullivan is . . ."

"*Right?*" Sullivan proposed.

"I was going to say, 'Still in that same dark, angry place you were in before I left.'" Kina brightened her tone. "So how's the baby?"

"Her name is Charity, and she's great. So is Charles. So is my marriage."

"Charity just celebrated her first birthday," Lawson announced, cutting in, sensing the argument Sullivan was about to instigate. "She's gotten so big, and she's so beautiful and smart, isn't she, Sullivan?"

"Congratulations, Sullivan," Kina said, extending a compliment. "I'm sure you're an excellent mother."

Sullivan knit and didn't respond.

Angel diverted Kina's attention. "Congratulations to you too on everything. We never missed an episode of *Lose Big*. You should've seen me running around here and shouting like a fool when you won."

Kina untied the silk scarf from around her neck and sat down on Angel's love seat. "Thank you."

Lawson scooted in next to her. "So are you back for good?"

"I don't know. Right now I'm down here shooting some scenes for my reality show. You know, sort of giving a tour of my hometown and where I come from."

"Are you going to be on another reality show?" asked Angel.

"Well, it's not official, because I haven't signed on the dotted line yet, but my agent has been pitching a show about my life to some TV execs. She thinks there will be a bidding war for it. Apparently, the viewing audience can't get enough of me," she bragged.

Lawson swelled with pride for her cousin. "You certainly were the breakout star of *Lose Big*. You had the whole world rooting for you."

"You should've seen my Web site and Twitter feed the night of the finale. I think my site crashed at one point from so many people logging on."

"All hail Queen Kina!" mocked Sullivan. "The new queen of trash TV!"

"Sullivan, please . . . ," hissed Angel.

Kina wasn't shaken. "It's okay. I've heard it all, from I lost weight because I had lipo to I beat my child because he brought a bag of potato chips into the house. I'm used to the negativity. I'm just thankful that television has given me a platform to talk about the Lord and lead people to Christ. I get letters and e-mails all the time from people saying how I've inspired them to reconnect with Jesus or turn their life over to the Lord. That's what really matters."

"You developed a tough skin out in L.A.," observed Lawson. "I'd like to see E'Bell try to push you around now!"

"I've found strength in the Lord and in myself that I never even knew existed," said Kina. "Moving out there and getting on that show was the best thing that could've happened to me. It turned me into a new woman."

"We're so proud of you, Kina," said Angel. "A lot of women in your situation would've caved in, given up, and quit, but you took everything the devil tried to use for bad and made it work for your good. That's a testimony."

Kina nodded. "Do you mind if I let my camera guys in?" Kina jumped up without waiting for Angel to reply. "I think they should be capturing this."

"*Camera guys?*" echoed Sullivan as Kina raced out of the door. "Is she serious?"

"Sully, give the girl a break, all right? We all know what Kina has been through over the past few years. She was beaten by her husband. She went through that horrible time of trying to cope with the fact that Kenny shot and killed his own father. Then all that stuff with questioning her sexuality and getting involved with Joan to the guilt of falling in love with Charles. Not to mention that you tried to beat her up when you found out about it and totally exiled her from our circle, knowing that her friends were the only support team she had. She's been to hell and back. She deserves some happiness right now," asserted Angel.

"Okay, you can set up over there," directed Kina, coming back into the house with her camera crew. "Ladies, don't mind them. They need to get some footage for the show."

"I thought you haven't signed on for a show yet," noted Angel.

"I haven't, but I will. I've been shooting for weeks. I need to have material already in place when my agent reaches a production deal. I've been uploading snippets on my Web site to let the fans know what I'm up to." She fluffed her hair a little. "Okay, let's act natural and talk like we've been doing."

Angel blinked and used her hands to block out the glaring light. "What's natural about having this camera in my face like this?"

"Don't worry. You'll forget it's there after a while. Maybe we should re-create that scene again where I was talking about God and using my platform to lead people to Christ," Kina said, pondering aloud.

Lawson was a little irritated. "It wasn't a scene, Kina. We were having a conversation. That was a natural moment."

"Sometimes natural moments need to be tweaked, Lawson, but we won't worry about that now." Kina pointed at the shawls spread around the room. "What's all this?"

"Oh . . ." Angel picked up the shawl she had been knitting. "You remember how we said we were going to knit and donate shawls in October since it's domestic violence month? We're finally getting around to doing it."

"I think it's wonderful you all are doing this. Let me help." Kina looked directly into the camera. "As a domestic violence survivor myself, I would do anything to help the women currently suffering at the hands of their abusers. I've walked in their shoes. I've been where they are," she stated with affectation.

Sullivan rolled her eyes. "Did you get all of that, cameraman?"

Kina suddenly turned dramatic, tearing up as she spoke. "Sullivan, don't you dare trivialize what I've been through! I barely escaped from E'Bell with my life. I suffered years and years of threats, terrorization, and abuse at his hands. My son and I lived in constant fear. You see this?" She lifted her bangs off her forehead to reveal a scar. "Every time I look in the mirror, I'm reminded of the day my husband beat me so badly that I thought I was going to lose my very life. I probably would have if Kenny hadn't been there to protect me, so don't you dare ridicule what happened to me or what happens to millions of women all around the world every day. It's only by the grace of God that we are able to go on." Kina took a deep breath.

"Take a bow, Kina!" Sullivan clapped. "That was beautiful. Did you get all of *that?*" Sullivan asked the film crew, unfazed by Kina's speech. "Maybe they should shoot it again. Only this time, Kina, when you cry, try to do the Denzel Washington one tear thing. You know that earned him the Oscar for *Glory.*"

Lawson and Angel groaned.

Kina mouthed, "Edit that out please," to the cameraman.

"I have a nice biblical scripture for you, Kina," Sullivan continued. "'Woe unto you, scribes and Pharisees, hypocrites! For ye make clean the outside of the cup and of the platter, but within they are full of extortion and excess.' Matthew twenty-three, twenty-five."

"You know, I think we could all use some fresh air and a bite to eat," suggested Angel, trying to sound cheerful.

"I know I certainly could use a drink right now," retorted Lawson.

"No, you go on," said Kina. "I can't drink. I need my head to be clear in case I get called on to minister to someone."

"Good grief!" exclaimed Sullivan. "I'll be outside. I need some fresh air. All the hot air in this room is making me gag."

They watched Sullivan storm out the front door.

"Some things never change," mumbled Kina. "Or should I say some people?"

Lawson flipped her hand. "Girl, you know Sullivan likes to put on a good show. You've gotta love her, though. She keeps things interesting."

"If you say so. I just wish she'd let go of all that anger toward me. I know I hurt her, but I'm not going to keep apologizing for something that happened two years ago. Jesus did not die on that cross for us to walk around in condemnation. That's the beauty of being under God's grace. 'In whom we have redemption through his blood, the forgiveness of sins, according to the riches of his grace,'" Kina said, ending with a quotation.

"Now, Kina, you know Sully is a drama queen, but she'll come around," promised Lawson. "She misses you, even if she won't admit it. She even tuned in to watch your show once or twice."

"So what's up with you?" squealed Angel. "You've got lights and cameras following your every move. You pulled up in a big customized Range Rover. It looks like you bought the good, expensive hair weave. You're officially a Hollywood starlet!"

"God has been good to me," declared Kina. "This is the life He's always wanted me to live. It's the kind of life He wants all of His children to live. Do you have any idea how good it felt to be able to go to that car dealership and pay for my car in cash? I remember how I used to drive around in that ole raggedy ten-year-old Civic, praying that it wouldn't cut off in the middle of the road. Now look at me!"

"I guess that smile is what being half a million dollars richer will do for you," stated Lawson. "Now, don't go blowing all that money, Kina. I'm sure all these cameras and equipment must be costing you a pretty penny."

"They do," Kina conceded. "But I'll make all of it back and then some once the show gets picked up. The way I see it, it's an investment."

Lawson eyed Kina's feet, recognizing the pricey Casadei sandal strapped around them. "I guess the same holds true for these designer shoes and fancy clothing labels."

Kina brushed it off. "It's only money, Lawson."

"*Only money?*" repeated Angel. "You really *are* Hollywood!"

Kina patted Angel on the knee. "Don't you ladies start worrying. I've given the Lord His ten percent. I've put some money away for Kenny's college fund. I'm setting aside some cash to buy a little condo once I decide where I want to settle down, and I'm investing the rest into Ki-Ki's Tees."

Lawson was thrown. "Ki-Ki's Tees? What's that?"

"It's a T-shirt line I'm starting," announced Kina. "The viewers really took to all those inspirational sayings and Bible verses they heard me use on the show, so I decided to capitalize on that with the shirts. We go into production in a few weeks."

"How much is all that going to cost?" asked Lawson, now concerned.

"Cuz, you have to spend money to make money. I told you I have this under control. Stop worrying!" Kina pulled out her compact to make sure her makeup was still intact. "Now, there is one other thing I've done with the money, and it involves all of you. Well . . . maybe not Sullivan, but definitely you, Angel, and Reggie."

"Kina, we don't want you wasting money on us. That money is to secure your and Kenny's futures," Lawson maintained.

Kina playfully elbowed her. "Will you stop acting so noble? What's the good of me having all this money if I can't share any of it with the people I love most? Now, tell me, how do you feel about spending the weekend spread out on some marvelous powder-sand beach in the middle of the Bahamas? I've rented a four-bedroom villa for all us to get away, relax, and reconnect. What do you say?"

"It sounds wonderful," said Angel. "But money is kind of tight for me right now. I don't even know if I could afford the plane ticket."

"Then let me buy the ticket for you," proposed Kina. "It's the least I could do for the woman who gave me my first real job."

Angel shook her head. "Kina, you're already paying for the villa. Now you're going to buy my plane ticket too? I can't let you spend that kind of money on me."

"You can and you will," asserted Kina. "So both of you go ahead and mark your calendars for the last weekend in October."

"Are you inviting Sullivan?" asked Lawson.

Kina stood up. "She's free to come, but she'll have to abide by my terms. My dime, my rules, which means no bringing up the past."

Angel grabbed her purse. "Are you joining us for a bite to eat?"

Kina checked her Tank Française watch, which sported a pink mother-of-pearl dial and a stainless-steel bracelet.

"Fancy watch you've got on there," observed Angel.

"It's Cartier," bragged Kina. "I've always wanted to be able to say that."

"It's nice," said Lawson. "So are you and your Cartier watch having lunch with us or what?"

"Actually, I need to run. I've got to pick up Kenny, and I need to post a new blog to the site. I'm working on a piece called *Let Her Return Home*. It's all about my spiritual and emotional journey to get back here. You all should check it out."

"Definitely," said Angel.

Lawson walked Kina to the door. "Where are you staying?"

"I have an executive suite at the Westin. It's not quite up to the standards I'm used to in L.A., but it's the best Savannah has to offer. It'll do for now." Kina summoned the camera crew to follow her. "It was really awesome to see you guys today. You have no idea how many times I thought about you while I was away and how much I missed you."

Lawson hugged her again. "We missed you too. Welcome home."

Kina hugged Angel and left.

"So what do you think?" Angel asked once they heard the door close shut.

"*Think?* I'm still trying to figure out what just happened."

"What do you think about this trip to the Bahamas? Do you think we should go? It doesn't feel right to help Kina blow all her money."

"She said she can swing it, so I believe her. Truth be told, I could use the time away," Lawson replied.

"What about Sully? Do you think we'll be able to convince her to go?"

"Angel, Sullivan is many things, but stupid isn't one of them. There's no way she's going to turn down a free weekend in the Caribbean, even if Kina's name is attached to it."

Angel nodded slowly. "Kina is really starting to come into her own. Are you concerned?"

Lawson thought for a second. "Not really."

Angel narrowed her eyes. "Did she come off as a little . . . I don't know . . . *smug* to you?"

"She's been in Hollywood, Angel. That's not exactly a haven for reality."

"I don't want to see her get caught up in that life and forget who brought her out and blessed her with this opportunity."

"Angel, if Kina is nothing else, she's grounded in her relationship with Christ. Yeah, I admit, she's feeling herself a little right now, but she'll float back to earth soon enough."

"Okay, but you better hope she comes *floating* back, not crashing hard and hitting rock bottom!"

Chapter 16

"To be honest, it's pretty safe to say that I've been a mess for most of my life."

—Sullivan Webb

"I just wanted you to know that I made it up here safely," Sullivan reported to Charles from Friendship Temple's church parking lot after a nearly four-hour drive to Atlanta the following Wednesday afternoon. "How's my princess?"

"She's fine. You're the one I'm concerned about. You know I wanted to come up there with you."

"And *you* know I didn't want to leave Charity with a sitter, especially with her coming down with a cold. Don't worry. I'm a big girl. I can handle this alone."

"I would've felt better if you weren't facing all of this by yourself."

"Babe, we've talked about this. We've prayed about it. I honestly feel like I'm doing the right thing. Thanks again for getting me on his secretary's calendar."

"Well, you know I'm not too proud of that," Charles moaned.

"You didn't lie, Charles. I fully intend to tour their children's building and talk to the youth minister for ideas to revamp our children's ministry at Mount Zion . . . right after I talk to my father."

"Just don't go in there with unrealistic expectations."

"I'm not going in with any expectations at all. I want to see him and let him know who I am and where he can find me if he wants to stay in touch. The rest is up to him."

"Be careful, Sullivan. Samuel is a man of God, but you never know how a person might react to something like this, especially if he feels threatened. I'm praying that God keeps you covered."

"He will. Relax, Charles. I'll be fine. Anyway, I've got to go. I'll call you the minute I leave here."

Sullivan hung up the phone and made her way to the pastor's office suite. She approached the pastor's administrative assistant.

"Hi. I'm Mrs. Webb from Mount Zion Ministries in Savannah. My husband scheduled a one o'clock appointment to see Pastor Sullivan," Sullivan reported, careful not to reveal her first name. "He couldn't make it, so I came in his place."

The assistant verified the appointment on her computer. "Ah, yes, he is expecting you. He's in with the first lady right now, but I'll let him know you're here."

The assistant slipped into the pastor's adjacent office and returned a few seconds later.

"He's ready to see you," she announced, holding the door open for Sullivan to pass through.

"Thank you."

"Sister Webb, we're honored to have you here," greeted Samuel Sullivan, with his arms outstretched. "It's great to finally meet you. How was the drive up?"

Sullivan's feet felt cemented to the floor, but she mustered the strength to lift them to embrace her father. "I thought I'd never get here."

"That's Atlanta traffic for you, honey!" exclaimed the woman Sullivan presumed to be his wife.

"Sister Webb, this is my wife, Martina." Samuel turned to the woman. "Dear, this is Pastor Webb's wife, from Mount Zion Ministries in Savannah. We met her husband, Pastor Charles Webb, remember?"

"Oh, yes. He's such a gentle spirit. Mount Zion is blessed to have such a godly man at the helm and a lovely young lady as their first lady."

Sullivan managed a smile. "Thank you, Mrs. Sullivan."

"Please call me Marti, sweetheart."

Sullivan nodded. "Will do."

Sullivan marveled at the stunning woman, who, while appearing to be around Vera's age, was the complete antithesis of her. Sullivan wondered how a man could be attracted to two women so seemingly different.

"She's here to look around at the children's building today," explained Samuel and faced Sullivan again. "Forgive me. I don't think I caught your first name."

"It's Sullivan."

Samuel froze. The smile that Sullivan remembered so fondly suddenly vanished. She could almost hear his heart stop.

"Another Sullivan? I like her already," replied Marti, oblivious to what was transpiring. "Well, I'll let the two of you talk." She gave her husband a peck on the lips. "I'll see you at home. It was nice meeting you, Sullivan. Tell that husband of yours I said hello."

"Yes, ma'am." Sullivan waited until Martina was out of earshot to speak. "I take it she has no idea who I am or that I even exist."

"No, she doesn't," answered Samuel, still shell-shocked.

"Are you still going to act like you don't know who I am?"

"I couldn't even if I tried, not when you're looking back at me with my own eyes." Samuel finally seemed to be jolted from his trance. "So that was you who called the other day."

She nodded. "I didn't know what else to do after you refused to talk to me on the phone. Please don't be upset with Charles for deceiving you about my visit. He only did that because he knew how much it meant to me to finally see you again."

"It's all right."

"I'm sure you don't know what to think with me showing up out of the blue like this."

Samuel's eyes began to water. "I must have imagined this moment in my head a thousand times. Each time I knew exactly what to say."

"And now?"

Samuel shrugged and sighed. "Now I don't have the first clue."

Sullivan inched toward him. "Maybe you should start with hello."

He smiled a little. "Hello, Sullivan."

"Hello . . . Samuel. I'm sorry, but I don't feel comfortable with calling you Dad, not yet, anyway."

"It's okay. I know I haven't earned that title from you."

"I want you to know that I'm not here because I want anything from you, except maybe a few answers. The Lord has blessed my husband and me with everything we could possibly ask for. I just wanted to see my daddy."

"Let me look at you. . . ." He stood back, taking it all in. "The last time I saw you, you were a little bitty ole thing, running around the yard in that yellow sundress with the tiny white polka dots going down the front."

Sullivan became overwhelmed with emotion. She pursed her lips together, fighting back tears. "I remember that dress. I can't say I remember that much about you, though. Only your smile. I remember that you smiled a lot."

"You made me smile, baby girl." He touched her face. "Now look at you! That little girl has grown into this beautiful young woman. It certainly warms my heart to see that you've turned out so well. You're the first lady of a thriving church. You have a good husband, although he's a little closer to my age than he is to yours."

Sullivan blushed. "He says I keep him young."

"I'm sure you do. I'm glad God has been so good to you, Sullivan."

"Yes, I've been blessed, but it hasn't always been like this. I spent a lot of years lost and ruining not only my life but also the lives of people around me. To be honest, it's pretty safe to say that I've been a mess for most of my life."

"I'm sorry." Samuel lowered his head. "I can't help but feel responsible for that. If I'd been around more, things might have been different for you."

"Maybe . . . maybe not. I'm not here to blame you for anything that's happened to me. If I've learned anything, it's that you can't spend your whole life dwelling on your mistakes or what might've been. Truthfully, I wouldn't change anything I went through if that's what had to happen for me to get to this moment. As long as I have God, my daughter, and my husband, I'm good."

"I see you have a kind heart too. I'm thankful for that." His eyes lit up. "So I have a granddaughter?"

"Yes, and she's a handful! I was born to be her mother. She means the world to me." Sullivan fumbled with her phone. "Look, here's a picture."

Samuel gazed down at the image captured on Sullivan's phone. "She's gorgeous. She looks a lot like you at that age." He pulled out a chair for Sullivan. "Please have a seat."

She sat down. "Thank you."

"How's . . ." Samuel gulped. "How's your mother?"

Sullivan sighed. "I assume she's a joy to be around when she's sober. Unfortunately, I don't get to see that side of her."

Samuel shook his head. "I'm sorry to hear that. She used to be so full of life and joy. She had the most melodious laugh. It was infectious."

Sullivan was baffled. "I don't think we're talking about the same person."

"Did she tell you anything about me?"

"No, nothing that didn't involve the words *liar* or *bastard*."

"I'm not surprised. Things didn't exactly end amicably between us." He was quiet for a few seconds. "So is there anything you want to know or want to ask me?"

"I have so many questions, I don't even know where to start," Sullivan blurted out.

"I've found it best to always start at the beginning."

"Okay." Sullivan loosened up some. "Why didn't you want me?"

Samuel sighed and reached for Sullivan's hand. "It was never like that, baby girl. I loved you very much."

"Is whatever it is that went down between you and Vera the reason you walked out of my life?"

Samuel struggled with how to respond to the question. "Things got so complicated with your mother. I imagine either she told you or you figured out that I was married at the time you were born."

"Yes, she made it very clear to me that you had another family."

"I did, and I won't sit here and blame Vera for my affair or anything that happened as a result of it. It was my decision to step outside my marriage and God's will. It was also my decision to stay out of His will."

"Well, if I know Vera, she wasn't entirely faultless."

"No, but I was the one who'd made that commitment to Marti and the kids, not Vera. Here I was, getting up in front of the church every week, telling them what God could do in their lives, but I never took the opportunity to allow Him to work a miracle in my own."

"Christians make mistakes too. Believe me, I know!" Sullivan shifted in her seat. "I've always been curious about something. Maybe now I can finally get the answer."

"What's that?"

"How did you and Vera meet? What was she like back then?"

He laughed a little. "She was a spitfire, I tell you! She was sweet, though."

Sullivan recoiled. "Vera was sweet?"

"Yeah. I remember the first time I saw her working in the bookstore—"

"She worked?"

Samuel laughed again. "That's how we met. I was in college and had a paper to write on Richard Wright. I went to the bookstore that day looking for *Native Son* and found the prettiest li'l cashier I'd ever laid eyes on. I think I found an excuse to go to that bookstore every day after that. She took my breath away."

"Are you sure you didn't mean to say she took your *wallet* away?"

"I promise you, she wasn't that way when we met." He paused. "Sullivan, I want you to know that I loved your mother. I really did. It just got to be too much on both of us."

"How so?"

"You see, my father was a respected judge and my mother was a teacher. Back then, guys of a certain stature in the community were expected to marry a certain kind of girl. Martina was that kind of girl. Vera wasn't."

"But you loved her. Shouldn't that have counted for something?"

"I loved Marti too. Marti and I had been together a year before I'd even met Vera. I was already committed to her."

"Did she know about my mother?"

"I'm sure a few members of the peanut gallery gave her an earful every now and then, but she never said anything to me. I guess it's fair to say I loved Marti too much to leave, and she loved me enough to stay."

"So what happened with Vera? What was the thing that finally broke the two of you up for good?"

"Sullivan, all I can tell you is that life happened. People grow apart. They change, and they fall out of love. There came a time when Vera wanted me to leave my wife and family, Sullivan." He shook his head. "I just couldn't do that. When I told her, she said to never contact either one of you ever again. The next thing I knew, she packed you up and moved away."

"Why would she do something like that? Why would she want to keep me from you?"

"Honey, we were young and didn't make the kind of choices we'd make today given the same situation. Don't fault your mother for being young and confused. I want you to know that in all these years, I never stopped thinking about you. I never stopped praying for you." Sullivan smiled. "Does that answer all your questions?"

"Do I have any brothers and sisters?"

He handed her a framed picture from his desk. "You have a younger brother, Thomas. He's in grad school.

He just got engaged to the girl he's been dating since his sophomore year in college."

"I can tell he's a heartbreaker," teased Sullivan. "He's very handsome."

Samuel passed her another picture. "You also have an older brother in California. His name is Daryl."

Sullivan stared down at the picture. "He looks like you."

"He's a television producer for one of the local news stations out there."

"Wow. That's impressive." Sullivan handed the pictures back to him.

"Yeah, Daryl's a good guy. He's married with two kids."

"So I'm an auntie?" asked Sullivan, cracking a smile.

"Yes. Your niece, Sage, is twelve and your nephew, Chance, is fifteen. Daryl's wife, Sharla, is sweet, real pretty like you. I would like for you to meet all of them one day."

"I would like that too. Do I have any sisters?"

"You did. Her name was Amber. She was killed in a car accident."

Sullivan felt for him. "Losing her must have been hard for you. I don't know what I'd do if anything ever happened to Charity."

"It was hard on both of us, but we survived."

Sullivan looked around his office, imagining the kind of life she might've had growing up with her father as opposed to Vera. "This still feels surreal to me," she confessed. "What about you? What's going through your head right now?"

Samuel exhaled. "I never should've let you go without a fight, but I was a coward, Sullivan." He folded his hands. "In a lot of ways, I still am."

"What does that mean?"

"I suppose that a real man would've told his wife the truth about you and your mother by now."

"Why haven't you?"

Samuel released a deep sigh. "Simply put, I like the way my family looks at me. I like that my wife looks at me like I'm God's gift to her. I like that my boys still look at me like I'm their hero. None of them will ever look at me the same way again once they know the truth. To be honest with you, I'd planned to take this secret to my grave."

"I think I'm more of my father's child than you realize." Sullivan could empathize in light of her own paternity situation with Charity. "There's nothing worse than seeing the look of disappointment on the face of someone you love."

Samuel's eyes fell. "It's hard for me to look at you, Sullivan. I can't imagine what you must think of me."

"I don't think anything right now. I don't know you." She hesitated. "But I'd like to."

Samuel nodded. "I think I'd like that too."

Samuel's administrative assistant buzzed into his office to alert him that his next appointment had arrived.

"Sullivan, I hate to kick you out, but I really need to take this meeting."

She stood up. "It's all right. I should be heading back, anyway. I've got a long drive ahead of me."

He caught Sullivan off guard when he reached out to hug her. "I'm so glad you came today. I really am. I've missed you for twenty-five years, and I thought I'd never get the chance to see you again." He released her.

Sullivan felt a sense of peace that she'd never had before. "Would it be okay if we exchanged contact information so we can keep in touch?"

"Oh, yeah, definitely." Samuel hurried to his desk to retrieve one of his business cards. "It has my direct line here and my e-mail address."

"Thank you." Sullivan scribbled her telephone number and address on the back of a receipt she found in her purse. "This is my info. Call anytime, day or night."

"I will."

"I'll be in touch soon." On impulse, Sullivan hugged him again. "You have no idea how much this day means to me."

Sullivan drove home on a high. All her life, she'd been able to snag any man she wanted. It was only now, at age thirty-three, that she had finally found the one man she'd always needed.

Chapter 17

"You sure know how to surprise a girl."
—*Angel King*

Fallen leaves from the live oak and palmetto trees crunched beneath Jordan's and Angel's feet as they toured the grounds of the quaint bed-and-breakfast inn that Jordan had reserved for their date.

"I must say, Mr. McKay, you sure know how to surprise a girl," said Angel as she and Jordan walked hand in hand, admiring the spectacular view of the Savannah River in the low-country marsh on Cat Island in Beaufort, South Carolina. "When you said you were taking me to breakfast, somehow I imagined us getting the pancake special at IHOP, not crossing state lines to come to a little piece of heaven."

Jordan laughed. "I'm pulling out all the stops to impress you, lady. I appreciate you being a good sport about it. All I told you was to clear your calendar for the day and bring an extra pair of clothes and a toothbrush."

"I wasn't worried. I trust you." Angel sighed. "Jordan McKay, I do believe that what we have here is the perfect date."

"It's not hard when you're out with the perfect woman."

Angel stepped ahead to get a closer look at an apple tree. "It's so beautiful here. I almost don't want to leave."

Jordan wrapped his arms around her from behind and kissed her on the cheek. "We don't have to if you don't want to."

"You promise?" She laughed a little. "It's like our own slice of paradise."

"It can be. In fact, I declare this to be our spot," he proclaimed.

"Oh? So how do we commemorate it?"

He faced Angel and kissed her. "Like this."

"We did that in Savannah . . . and on I-Sixteen . . . and when we stopped to eat at the border . . . and after we got here."

"So you're saying I've got to step it up, huh?"

"You do if you want to impress me."

"There's only one way I know to make this officially our spot."

Angel squinted her eyes. "I'm not doing that out here."

Jordan feigned being offended. "Angel King, is your mind wallowing in the gutter?"

She crossed her arms in front of her. "Is yours?"

"I plead the Fifth."

She playfully pinched him. "Jordan!"

"Actually, they weren't all gutter thoughts. I had something else in mind too."

"I'm almost afraid to ask."

"I think I could really fall in love with you, Angel."

She reached up and touched his face. "I was just thinking the same thing."

"So you're okay with spending the night up here?"

"Yeah, we have separate rooms. I think it'll be all right."

"You know, it gets kind of cold in these parts at night. What if it starts to get chilly in that bed of yours?"

"Then I'll turn up the heater."

He chuckled. "All right, I hear you. So how would you like to spend the day, Ms. King? A few rounds of golf? Hitting up some art galleries? I saw a few advertisements about the Beaufort Shrimp Festival, which is happening this weekend. We can check it out if you want to."

"It all sounds perfect, and I'm in excellent company, so I know whatever we decide will be fine."

Jordan pulled her closer. "Now that we've got the day covered, how would you like to spend the night?"

Angel kept him at bay by reciting, "Dearly beloved, I beseech you as strangers and pilgrims, abstain from fleshly lusts, which war against the soul." She said it not only for him, but also to keep her own hormones in check. There was definitely a war being waged on her flesh. She could only pray that her spirit would be victorious over her soul and body.

Jordan backed off. "Do you keep scriptures handy like mints?"

Angel laughed. "There's definitely a parallel between the two. You should keep them both on hand, because you never know when one is going to be needed."

"Don't you ever want to let loose sometimes and do something spontaneous without finding a biblical reason to justify it?"

"Yeah, I came up here with you, didn't I?"

"Yes, you did," he conceded.

"You seem to struggle a lot more with this celibacy thing than I do," noted Angel.

"Babe, I'm a thirty-four-year-old warm-blooded alpha male. Celibacy for me is way easier said than done, especially when I'm standing next to a sexy . . ." He kissed her on the lips. "Gorgeous . . ." He kissed her on the neck. "Vibrant . . ."

"See? Now you're trying to get me in trouble," Angel charged, momentarily indulging in his affection.

He nibbled her ear. "That's not all I'm trying to get into."

"Okay, I get it!" Angel declared, dragging herself away from him. "Maybe we should focus on some nice nonsexual activities for tonight."

"I'm sure there's a revival or a baptism going on that you'd like to take part in," teased Jordan.

She playfully yanked one of his dreadlocks. "Don't be cute . . . although that request would be nearly impossible for you to carry out."

"There you go, flirting with me again. You're very good at this whole sexy innocence thing." He smiled. "You know what else you're good at?"

"No. What?"

Jordan intertwined his hands with hers. "Making me happy."

"The feeling is mutual. I guess that's one more thing we have in common."

Chapter 18

"When you answer my question with a question, it makes me feel like you're trying to avoid the answer."
—*Lawson Kerry Banks*

The sight of Simone's Camry parked in her driveway never ceased to unnerve Lawson. Lawson knew that Simone was simply there to drop off or pick up her son, but it didn't make the scene less distressing.

Lawson crept into the house undetected. She spotted Garrett and Simone hovering over Simon, looking every bit the happy family. She hung back and watched as they marveled over Simon sitting upright by himself on the floor.

"Can you believe he's sitting up?" asked Simone. "Next thing we know, he'll be crawling."

"That's my boy!" exclaimed Garrett. Lawson had never seen him look so proud, and it had been a long time since she'd seen him look so happy. "He was a little wobbly with it earlier today, but he's mastered it now."

Simone scooped Simon into her arms and kissed him. "You're Mama's big boy, aren't you?"

"Hey, now, he's Daddy's boy too!"

"Yes, he is." Simone smiled and placed her hand on his shoulder. He didn't really seem to notice, but it irked Lawson that he didn't mind, either.

"I'm glad we were here to see it together," said Simone. "It seems like whenever Simon reaches a new milestone, either I see it and you miss it, or he's over here and I miss it."

"I know, but thank you for letting me spend as much time with our son as I can."

"Garrett, you're his father. I'm not one of those baby mamas who want to hold the kid hostage. Simon needs both of us, not just me."

"I want you to know how much I appreciate it." He lifted Simon into the air. "I love having this little guy around."

"I'm glad at least one of you does," grumbled Simone.

"Lawson will come around, Simone."

"I'm not holding my breath." She shook her head. "How can anyone, especially a professed Christian, hate a baby?"

"She doesn't hate him."

"Really?" Simone was doubtful. "Does she ever play with him or change him? I've never so much as seen her hold him. She didn't even bother to come to the hospital after he was born."

"It's tough on her, you know? She doesn't see Simon as my child or her stepson. To her, he's a reminder that I broke our vows. I'm not going to press her on the issue. She'll come around in due time."

"It's not fair to Simon, and it's certainly not fair to you. Does she plan to hold our fling against you forever?"

"Lawson is doing the best she can right now. I have to give her credit. A lot of women in her position would've bounced. She's hung in there with me. She's tried to be supportive."

"Supportive?" Simone frowned. "Is that what you call making you feel guilty for loving your son and for not acting like he doesn't exist? You'd never treat her son the way she's treated yours."

"It's different with Namon. She didn't cheat on me."

"Keep telling yourself that." Simone slipped Simon's shoes over his feet. "I've got to be honest with you, Garrett. I don't like Simon having to be subjected to this hostile environment that your wife has created. Babies can pick up on that kind of stress. It's not as bad now, because he doesn't understand, but what about when he gets older and it becomes obvious that she doesn't want him here?"

"I'm not worried about that. Lawson is an excellent mother."

Simone shook her head. "You'd think that knowing how much your son means to you would be enough to make her do better."

Garrett stood up. "All right, that's enough about Lawson."

Simone joined him. "What's the matter? Truth hurt?"

"No, I . . . I shouldn't talk about my problems with her with you. That's kind of how we ended up in this scenario."

She nodded. "I understand, but please know that I'm here for you to talk to or vent to, or whatever else you need."

"Thanks. I appreciate that."

"Oh, and before I forget, one of my coworkers invited Simon to her son's birthday party next Saturday. You can come with us if you'd like."

Garrett considered it but changed his mind. "I probably shouldn't."

"Why not?"

"It wouldn't look right, and it wouldn't be fair to my wife."

Simone sighed. "Somebody ought to tell that wife of yours how lucky she is." She reached up and kissed him on the cheek.

Garrett smiled. "I think she knows. Let me go back in the bedroom and pack up Simon's stuff."

"I'll come with you," Simone offered. "Four hands are better than two." Simone trailed Garrett to Reginell's old bedroom.

Lawson emerged from the shadows. Garrett had invoked her name at least five times, but if her friends and the Bible were to be believed, what a person said didn't matter. It was what was in his heart that counted, and it was there, she feared, that her name received no mention at all.

Simone and Garrett returned to the living room, armed with Simon's bags with toys.

"Hey, babe. When did you get here?" Garrett kissed her.

"Just now."

"We were just leaving," Simone explained, before making a quick exit with Simon.

"Was she in our bedroom?"

"No, of course not. She was helping pack up Simon's stuff, that's it."

"Garrett, are you still attracted to her?"

"Why would you ask that?"

Lawson huffed. "When you answer my question with a question, it makes me feel like you're trying to avoid the answer."

"No, I'm not attracted to her at all. She's Simon's mother, nothing more or less."

"Are you still attracted to me?"

"Absolutely. I love you, Lawson. You're the only woman I've ever truly loved."

He embraced her. Lawson wanted nothing more than to believe him, but it had been much easier to do so before Garrett gave her every reason to doubt him.

Chapter 19

"Don't you worry, baby. Juicy's still got it."
—Reginell Kerry

Reginell bowed politely as the sparse crowd applauded her before handing off the microphone to the emcee. It wasn't exactly Madison Square Garden, but she was grateful that her boss would let her perform during the last twenty minutes of her waitressing shifts on amateur night at Chase's Bar and Grill, where she worked.

As she darted off the small wooden platform that was a lame excuse for a stage, Reginell spotted Ray, her former singing manager and a strip club owner, lurking near the bar, with his full lips wrapped around a cigar. His eyelids hung low around his bloodshot eyes, as he was perpetually high on one substance or another. She tied her apron around her waist, grabbed her tray, and raced over to greet him.

Reginell plastered on a saccharine smile. "Hey, Ray, long time no see."

He poked his pudgy fingers into her apron pockets and spotted her tips earnings. "Is that all you've made in tips tonight?" he asked before taking a swig from the bottle of beer he was holding. "I remember when you used to make twice that with one table dance."

"I remember too." Reginell flashed the small wad of one-dollar bills. "This is barely enough to fill up my tank. On top of that, I've got to split it with two other waitresses."

Ray looked around at the badly lit, half-empty dive. "At least you know it can't get no worse than this."

"I guess waiting tables and splitting pennies is all a high school education will get you these days."

Ray rested his arm over his portly belly. "Tough breaks, kid."

"Yeah, well, I've got to make money some kind of way, unless, of course, you've got some news for me," she added anxiously.

"What kind of news? What you called me for, Reggie? So I could watch you get humiliated up close and personal?"

"No. What do you think about me getting my old job back?"

He alternated between his cigar and beer again before answering her. "I don't."

Reginell pursed her lips together and swallowed the remnants of pride she had left. "Ray, I know we didn't part on the best of terms, but if you give me another chance, you won't regret it."

He looked her up and down. "Shoot, you ain't got nothing I want, Reggie."

She tossed her braids back and stuck her chest out. "I used to."

"Yeah, but that was before you fouled up that video shoot I sent you to, and before you just up and quit the club with no notice or nothing. You didn't even bother to clean out your locker."

"Ray, that so-called music video shoot was an orgy waiting to happen! And the only reason I quit the club was that Mark didn't want me working there anymore."

"Did he change his mind?"

"No, but this ain't about him. This is about survival, and this right here"—she looked around at the restaurant—"ain't gon' cut it."

Ray grunted. "I might have something for you."

She squealed, "For real?"

"Yeah, we've got some big names coming through this weekend. I might be able to use you to work security or something like that."

Reginell stomped her foot in frustration. "Come on, Ray! *Security?*"

"Oh, you think you still got it? It's been a while since you've been up on that pole."

She gave him a coy smile. "Don't you worry, baby. Juicy's still got it."

"That remains to be seen. I'll tell you what. Come by next week, on New Booty Tuesday, and I'll see what you're working with. You've got to start from the bottom just like everybody else."

Reginell agreed with a pouty mouth. "That's fine. Maybe I shouldn't go in full throttle, anyway, just start with part-time and work my way back up."

Ray laughed. "That's what you say now, but I know you like the loot. When the fellas start popping those bands, you'll be ready to dance."

"Uh-huh. We'll see."

"Yes, we will." Ray slipped his fedora over his cornrows. "Seeing as how standing here talking to you ain't makin' me no paper, I need to get back to my money-making *chicas* down at Paramours."

"Yeah, you do that. Let 'em make all the money they can while they can, because once Juicy steps back on the stage, they're going to be driving home with a lot fewer coins in their pockets!" vowed Reginell.

Ray darted toward the door, crossing paths with an unwitting Mark on his way out. Reginell gulped when she saw the two of them within inches of each other.

Mark approached Reginell and kissed her on the cheek. "Hey, babe. You ready to go?"

"In a minute. I need to cash out and take a look at the schedule for next week."

Mark tilted her face toward him. "You all right? You look a little flushed."

Reginell forced herself to smile. "I'm fine, just tired. Thanks for giving me a ride home."

"Anything for you, you know that." He pecked her on the lips. "Say, who was the guy that just left out of here?"

Reginell swallowed hard. "Huh?"

"Big dude in the hat. I thought I saw him talking to you. He wasn't giving you a hard time, was he?"

"No, he's a customer who had one too many drinks and got a little friendly, that's all," Reginell lied. "Stay here. I'll be right back."

Reginell heard the lie again in her head as she made her way to the back of the restaurant. It was the first time she'd ever lied to Mark. Until she stacked the kind of money she needed to subsidize her living situation, she doubted that it would be the last.

Chapter 20

"How did we let this happen?"
— *Angel King*

Following a day of sightseeing, tearing along wooded trails on rented bikes, and nearly eating themselves into a coma, Angel and Jordan bid each other good night around midnight and retired to separate rooms across the hall from one another.

Angel had drifted off into a twilight sleep when she was awakened by a knock at the door. Clad only in her bra and panties, Angel wrapped the blanket around her body and switched on the lamp before answering the door. "Who is it?" she asked before unlocking it.

"Baby, it's me," Jordan replied in return.

Angel swung open the door, prepared to chastise him for waking her at two o'clock in the morning, but before she could say anything, he shut the door and covered her mouth with his and began kissing her passionately.

Angel broke away from him to catch her breath. "Wait a minute," she panted. "We shouldn't be doing this. It's late and we're away from home and we're in this bedroom together. . ."

Jordan cupped her face in his hands. "Angel, baby, I want you so bad. It's been driving me crazy knowing that you're right across the hall and I can't even touch you." He began devouring her neck and eased back her blanket.

Angel could feel herself swoon as he pressed his body firmly against hers. "It's tempting to me too, but we've got to do what the Word says—flee from sexual fornication."

Jordan peeled back the T-shirt he was wearing, revealing ribbed abs carved into his caramel complexion. "Is that what you want me to do? Flee?" He leaned down to kiss her again.

Angel's chest heaved rapidly. "I can't think straight. . . . Give me a second." Angel struggled to pull a scripture—any scripture—from her memory bank. Either her mind drew a blank or it was drowned out by her libido, driven to its peak by almost two years of celibacy. All she could come up with was, *Jesus wept.*

Jordan caressed her arms. "You're so soft and beautiful," he whispered in her ear. "I started falling in love with you the moment I laid eyes on you at the hospital that day."

Angel found herself returning his touches and kisses. "You're not playing fair, Mr. Jordan."

He ran his hand along her back until he reached the fastener on her bra. The hooks disengaged in his hand. "I can't help it. Of all the people and of all the places, we were at the same place at the same moment hundreds of miles from home. Don't you think God had a hand it that, baby?"

"Yeah, I guess."

A moan escaped Angel's lips as Jordan ran his hand along the contours of her body. "Don't send me back to the other room, Angel. I want you so bad, I'm almost ashamed of myself. I want to hold you. I want to taste you."

"I want you too."

"Just live in the moment, baby. We'll repent tomorrow."

Jordan hoisted her up and carried her over to the bed and turned off the light.

After the heated fervor and passion of their tryst, condemnation enveloped Angel as she lay naked in Jordan's arms. "How did we let this happen?"

Jordan glided his fingers through her disheveled hair. "I believe it was fate."

"I believe it was lust," she retorted. "I'm so disappointed in myself."

"Don't be. It was a romantic moment." He kissed her. "I don't want you to have any regrets."

"It's nothing against you personally, Jordan." She exhaled. "The only other man I've ever been with is my ex-husband, Duke. Even though I'm not a virgin, it was still important to me to save myself for the man I'm going to marry."

"How do you know I won't be that man, huh?"

She flashed him the side eye. "I just wish we had waited, like we said we were going to do."

Jordan sat up. "Hold up. I didn't force myself on you. You wanted it as much as I did. And if I can be honest, you seemed to enjoy it as much as I did too. Both times."

"I know that. Nothing happened that I didn't let happen or want to happen, but it made me feel like we had sort of a special connection through our celibacy."

"Now we have a special sexual connection," teased Jordan.

Angel turned her back to him. "It's not the same thing."

He held her. "I was kidding, Angel. We had a special connection before, and we still do now. Nothing about the way I feel about you has changed. If it has, my feelings have only gotten stronger."

Angel didn't say anything.

"Well, look, I know you're feeling a little let down, but at least you can take comfort knowing I didn't give you anything."

Angel sprang up. "What?"

"You know . . . an STD or something."

"Why would you bring that up at this moment, Jordan?"

"Relax. I said I *didn't* give you anything. I got my HIV results back yesterday. I'm clean as a whistle!"

"Huh?" was all Angel could think to say.

"You don't believe me? I can show you my papers," he offered.

"It's not that. It's just . . ." She couldn't even form into words what she wanted to say. "Were you at risk? Is that why you took an AIDS test?"

He shrugged. "Word on the street was that somebody I used to mess with had that die-slow, so I didn't want to take any chances."

"Had what?"

"You know, that die-slow . . . that package . . . the monster . . . HIV positive."

"Oh." Angel sank lower into the bed. Her biggest concern about their unprotected romp had been an unwanted pregnancy. Now even that paled in comparison to everything else Jordan might have given her. "I'm glad you tested negative, but you know you have to be tested again in a few months to be sure. Correction. I guess now *we* have to be tested."

"No, this was the second test. I'm not some shady guy, Angel. I didn't so much as touch a woman while I waiting to find out."

"Is that why you were celibate?"

He paused. "Well, yeah," replied Jordan, as if there was no other logical reason to abstain from sex.

"Here, I thought you were waiting like me, that sex was something you wanted to save for the woman you married."

"Babe, technically, I never said I was celibate. I said I was on a break. Now that my stuff is clean, the break is over."

"I don't believe this is happening."

Jordan kissed her on the cheek. "You're just tired. Go to sleep. You'll feel better in the morning."

"I'm serious, Jordan. We can never be this careless again."

"Will you stop talking like that? You're making me have regrets now. Trust me, when you wake up, you'll see that it's not even that big of a deal. Shoot, you'll probably want to go another round. Let's go to sleep. I'm beat."

With that, Jordan wrapped his arms around her and went to sleep.

Angel lay wide awake until the sun peeked through the blinds of her window. Even though she was securely in Jordan's arms, she'd never felt so alone in her life.

Chapter 21

"I've been waiting for this moment my whole life."
—Sullivan Webb

"So do you think I should call him Sammy or Dad or Pastor Sullivan?" Sullivan asked Charles as she set the table for dinner. Samuel Sullivan had called to make plans to see Sullivan again the next week and to meet her family. She had suggested dinner at her house, and he had agreed to make the journey to Savannah.

"I think you should call him whatever you're both comfortable with. Did he say anything about his wife coming or his other children?"

Sullivan shook her head. "He hasn't told them yet. He's waiting for the right time."

Charles stopped her. "Honey, are you positive you want to pursue this?"

"Yes, Charles, why wouldn't I? I've been waiting for this moment my whole life."

Charles kissed her on the cheek. "I just don't want to see you hurt or disappointed."

"I won't be," she assured him. "My father has missed me as much as I've missed him. If it wasn't for Vera practically kidnapping me like she did, we never would've been apart this long."

"I don't know if it's fair to put all the blame on Vera, sweetheart."

"That's because you see the good in everyone, but you don't know her like I do. Keeping me from my dad was probably her way of punishing him for choosing his wife over her."

"That may be true, but I want you to keep a level head and an open mind."

Charles's words were followed by a knock at the door.

"He's here!" Sullivan squealed with all the excitement of a ten-year-old. "How do I look?"

"Marvelous," said Charles.

Sullivan scampered to the door and greeted Samuel with a smile. "Hello and welcome to our home."

"Thank you for inviting me." He nervously extended a bouquet of mixed pink peonies. "I don't know much about flowers. The florist said you'd like these."

She accepted them. "I love them. Please come on in. Let me take your coat."

Samuel followed Sullivan inside her spacious contemporary Victorian home. "This is a nice home you've got here, Sullivan."

Sullivan set the flowers down and hung up his coat in a hall closet. "We've been blessed. We're living proof that God is good." She led him into their dining room.

Charles stepped forward and shook Samuel's hand. "It's good to see you again, Brother."

"Same here. I guess you're the one responsible for us all being here today."

"I don't take the credit. God has a way of placing us where we need to be and when we need to be there in order to carry out His divine purpose."

Samuel agreed. "It's kind of ironic. As her father, I gave Sullivan life and, by extension, gave her to you. Then you turned around and gave my daughter back to me."

Sullivan beamed. Seeing the two men who meant the most to her in the same room at the same time was something she had feared she'd never see unless there was a dead body and a funeral involved.

Samuel turned to Sullivan. "When do I get to meet this granddaughter of mine?"

Charles squeezed Sullivan's hand. "You stay here with your father. I'll go get her."

"Have a seat," offered Sullivan.

Samuel sat down. "I have to admit, Sullivan, I'm a little uncomfortable."

"Why?"

"I never thought I'd be here. I never thought you, and especially your husband, would accept me into your home knowing what I've done."

"Charles is very forgiving and understanding. So am I. We probably understand infidelity a lot more than you think we do." Sullivan broke into a huge grin when she saw Charity tottering into the room. "There she is! Hi, princess!" Sullivan scooped her daughter up and kissed her. "We have someone very special here today."

Charity began babbling in response.

"She's a beauty, like her mother," said Samuel.

Sullivan balanced Charity on her hip. "She's starting to talk now. She can say Mama and Daddy and ball. She also says something that sounds kind of like deuce or dice. We can't figure out if she's saying juice or diamonds. She's my child, so it could go either way. Would you like to hold her?"

Samuel warily approached them, barely inching out his arms. "Can I?"

"Sure." Sullivan transferred Charity to her grandfather's waiting arms.

Samuel held Charity close to his chest. "Hey, baby girl."

"Charity, this is your grandfather," Sullivan told her. "Can you say Grandpa?"

"It's been a while since I held a baby," said Samuel. "Am I doing it right?"

Sullivan stood back, watching them. "It's perfect."

"Let me get the camera," offered Charles, reaching into his pocket to retrieve his phone.

"Oh, yes, we need pictures!" Sullivan replied, remembering. She scooted in next to her father.

"Everybody say 'cheese,'" ordered Charles. "Better yet, everybody say 'family.'"

"Family!" said Samuel and Sullivan in unison.

After they snapped several pictures of Sullivan and her father, Samuel playing with Charity, and Samuel with Charles, Charles suggested that Sullivan show her father around the house while they waited for dinner to get finished.

Sullivan guided Samuel on a tour of the second floor of their house.

"This is all very lovely, Sullivan."

"Thank you. You ought to come back during Christmastime. I go all out with the decorations. In fact, we're having our annual Christmas social here the first weekend in December. You and Marti should come."

"We'll do that, Sullivan. Thank you. This artwork is very exquisite," Samuel said, observing the painting that hung in the hallway. "I don't think I've ever seen this kind of work."

"You haven't seen these anywhere, because I'm the one who painted them."

Samuel stopped and stared at her. "You, Sullivan?"

She blushed. "Yeah. I was an art major in college. Painting has always been kind of a hobby of mine."

"This is more than a hobby, sweetheart. This is a gift from the Lord. Where did you go to school?"

"I graduated from Howard."

"Howard, huh? That's mighty fine." Samuel's face saddened. "I didn't even attend your graduation."

Sullivan hugged him. "It's okay. You'll attend Charity's graduation."

Samuel pulled away from her. "You must think I'm a sleaze."

"Why would you say that?"

"Here I am, a self-proclaimed man of God who was cattin' around on his wife. I didn't just cheat on her. I had another family."

Sullivan didn't want to seem judgmental. "It happens, you know?"

"Your husband probably really thinks the worst of me."

"Charles isn't some sheltered, backwoods preacher. He knows what goes on in the real world."

"I guess you all see a lot of this kind of thing in the church, huh?"

"We have." She bit her lip. "We've seen a little of it in our own home too."

Samuel was shocked. "Charles?"

Sullivan shook her head. "No . . . me. It's probably safe to say that the apple doesn't fall far from the tree."

"What happened? The two of you seem so happy together."

"We are, but we hit a rough patch a few years ago. Charles was busy with his campaign for county commissioner, and I was a bored, self-centered housewife looking for some excitement. I found it in a twenty-three-year-old mechanic."

"A mechanic?" Samuel chuckled. "You seem more like the high-maintenance type."

Sullivan laughed. "Believe me, I am! But Vaughn and I clicked, and before I knew it . . ." He nodded, understanding. "The secret didn't stay a secret for very long, though. There was a huge scandal behind it. It cost Charles his election, caused a huge rift in the church, and nearly destroyed my marriage."

"It looks like you two survived. You're together, and you have that beautiful baby girl."

Sullivan looked down at the floor. "Yeah, that's another thing."

"What?"

"Charity." Sullivan took a deep breath. "My daughter might not be Charles's biological child."

Samuel's eyes popped. "Oh! Well, your husband handles it very well. You'd never know by looking at the two of them together and the way he interacts with her."

"That's because Charles doesn't know," she admitted.

"Do you plan to tell him or have her DNA tested?"

"I suppose one day I'll get the nerve to do it. So, you see, you're not the only one who has made mistakes and has been less than honorable in marriage. We all have skeletons."

Samuel took her hand. "Thank you for trusting me enough to confide in me, Sullivan. You don't know what that means to me."

"You're my father. If I can't trust you, who can I trust?"

"A lot of people would wonder why you trust me and why you aren't nursing a grudge."

"I know you didn't leave me because you wanted to. You were in an impossible situation. Besides, there may come a day when Charity finds out all my secrets, and I wouldn't want her to hold the past against me. When I think about how many times Charles has forgiven me after I've let him down, how can I do any less for my own father?"

He kissed her on the forehead.

"Do you think any less of me now that you know about Charity's DNA debacle?" she ventured.

"No, I think you're human. I also think you're incredibly brave and strong. I see why your husband adores you."

"I adore him too. I just took me some time to realize it."

Samuel nodded. "I know what you mean. I was the same way with Marti. Your mother, Vera, was vibrant and sexy and exciting, probably like your mechanic. Being with her was like a rush or an adventure. But Marti was this gentle, quiet, sweet spirit. It was years before I learned to appreciate it. Excitement is appealing for a season, but as you get older and start thinking about the kind of life and family you want, you gravitate toward the Charleses and the Martis of the world.

"I've learned so much about being a man, a husband, and a father from my wife. She's my partner in every way. As much as I cared for Vera, she couldn't give me what I needed. I don't think I was what she needed either."

"Well, Cliff certainly isn't what she needs," muttered Sullivan.

"Who's Cliff? Is he her husband?"

"He's her boyfriend. He's the living, breathing definition of *slime,* but he's a steady source of income, which is all that matters to Vera. She's let materialism reside where love and compassion used to live."

Samuel shook his head. "That makes me sad. It was always my wish that she'd fall in love and settle down with a nice man. It was my prayer that she'd have a good stepfather looking after you, being the father I couldn't be."

"That didn't happen. I spent a lot of my childhood being used and molested by the men Vera had in her life."

Samuel's face reflected the crushing blow the news was to him as a father. "Sullivan, you have no idea how much it breaks my heart to hear that."

"It wasn't your fault."

"I should've been there, though. I should've protected you."

"I had God protecting me," she told him. "Besides, I'm a survivor!"

"Baby girl, I missed the first half of your life, but I'm here now. If you'll let me, I want to be here for the second half of it."

"*If I'll let you?*" she repeated. "That's what I've wanted to hear my entire life! You're my daddy."

Samuel smiled. "I appreciate your confidence in me. I won't let you down, not again. You, me, Marti, and the boys will just have to figure out a way to make this work."

"I know we will."

Samuel embraced his long-lost daughter. Sullivan held her father, feeling for the first time that the missing piece in her heart was slowly starting to fill.

Chapter 22

*"You should've used your backhand. It would've
made it feel more like old times."*
—*Sullivan Webb*

Sullivan found herself traveling to St. Simons Island to see Vera for the second time in two months, which was twice as many times as she normally saw Vera per year. However, the circumstances warranted a personal visit, as opposed to a phone call or e-mail. It was rare that she got a chance to rub Vera's nose in anything, and she wanted to take full advantage of the opportunity.

"I just want you to know that you're completely wrong about him," Sullivan announced, sitting down across from Vera at the kitchen table.

Vera took a sip of her drink. "Wrong about who?"

"My father. He's nothing like the shiftless, lying, low-down scumbag you made him out to be."

"Says who? Him? You just met him, Sullivan. Give him a few months. The real Samuel Sullivan never fails to show up eventually."

"For all of your bad-mouthing about him, my father has never once said anything negative about you."

Vera appeared surprised. "Ain't that special?"

"Just admit you were wrong about him."

Vera jerked back. "Wrong about which part, Sully? That he's a cheating husband or a deadbeat dad?"

"Both. His marriage to Marti and his relationship with you were extremely complicated. He was conflicted because he loved both of you very deeply but differently. I've been there. I know what that's like."

Vera shook her head in disbelief. "He's even got you sounding like him. You're gullible enough to believe anything that man tells you, ain't you? How he's convinced you he's a saint is beyond me."

"I don't think he's a saint, but I don't think he's the horrible excuse for a human being that you described, either. Samuel Sullivan is a very gentle, caring man. You should see him with Charity. He's wonderful with her, and she adores him."

"What about his wife? Does Marti adore her grandbaby too?" Sullivan bit her lip. "Yeah, that's what I thought. She doesn't know that child exists any more than she knows that you exist. Wake up, Sully! This man is playing you, and you're just stupid enough to fall for it."

Sullivan could feel the rage rising inside of her. Vera never failed to bring out the worst in a person. "Even if I am stupid for believing him, I must say that it's very refreshing to have a parent who doesn't need to put me down to feel better about her own pathetic life."

"You can say whatever you want about me. I stopped giving a cat's behind about what you thought of me years ago. I'm trying to help you, and you're too foolheaded to even see that!"

"How is lying to me and withholding information from me about my father *helping?* I should've known that you couldn't be trusted to tell me the truth, but it doesn't matter. My father and I are developing a very good relationship without your assistance or interference. He's even coming over for our Christmas party this year, *and* he's bringing his wife."

"Sullivan, a mouth can say anything. Do you want to know the kind of man your daddy really is? Ask him about Amber. Then come back and tell me what a fine, loving Christian family man he is," Vera said, daring her.

"He told me all about Amber."

Vera was stunned and stopped short of bringing her glass to her lips. "What did you say?"

"That's right. He told me about the little girl he and his wife lost in a tragic accident and how it broke his heart. Only a sadistic moron like you would take his heartbreak as a sign of weakness or as some kind of proof that he's less than a man."

Vera slammed the glass down and began rocking back and forth and trembling. "That lying son of a . . ."

"He's told me everything, Vera. I know all about how you met, how he tried to love you, but your reputation had proceeded you, so there's no way he could introduce you to society without ridicule. Unlike you, he's been extremely forthcoming with all my questions."

"That man is still the same!" Vera uttered to herself. "He's the same low-down dog he's always been."

"What's the matter?" Sullivan taunted. "Are you mad because I finally know the truth about how you were too big of a whore for any decent man to marry you? Or that you tried to pressure him into leaving his wife and kids? When that didn't work, you snatched me away from the only parent I had who cared whether I lived or died. Was it not enough for you that he'd already lost one child? Did you have to make the devastation complete by taking me away too? And for what? Because he didn't want to keep slummin' with the likes of you?"

Without uttering a word, Vera struck Sullivan hard across her face.

Hot tears pricked Sullivan's eyes as she held her bruised cheek. "Is that all you got?"

Vera glared at her with intensity.

"Is that all you got, old woman?" Sullivan repeated. "I've had much worse from you. You should've used your backhand. It would've made it feel more like old times."

"You ungrateful, idiotic wench!" croaked Vera. "You ain't got the first clue as to who your daddy is and even less of a clue as to who Amber is! Amber was *my* baby, not Marti's."

Sullivan let her hand slide down her face. "What?"

"*I* was the one who carried that sweet child in my womb! You want to know what really happened? The real reason I *snatched* you away from your daddy, as you put it?"

"Wait . . . Amber was *your* child?" asked Sullivan, still trying to put the pieces together.

"Yes." Vera took a deep breath and calmed down. "I got pregnant with Amber when you were around seven years old. I had been with Samuel for about nine years, and after nine long years, he promised that we were finally going to be a family. He said his boys were old enough to where he could leave his wife, and he was going to ask her for a divorce. Months go by, and I'm steadily planning for our new baby. I started getting her room ready and buying pretty little clothes. I even picked out a name for her and everything. Amber Nicole." Vera smiled and held her stomach as she spoke, as if she'd been mentally transported to a happier time and place.

A flash of her eyes signaled a new, harrowing thought. "Six months go by, and Samuel starts coming up with every excuse in the book for why he still hadn't left his wife. After I have waited for this man all this time, he comes over one day and says he's decided to stay with his wife and family. Then he tells me that I can't have this new baby, because it'll ruin everything for him." Tears streamed down Vera's face. "I loved that man, and I would've done anything for him. But I had somebody who I loved more. I told Samuel that I was too far along not to keep the baby, and I threatened to go to his wife and tell her everything.

"Samuel then turns on the charm and says he's had a change of heart. He said I was the only woman he had ever wanted and that he was leaving Marti for real this time. In fact, he said we should go tell her together. To this day, I don't know why I believed him. I guess what folks say is true. Love makes the obvious invisible."

Sullivan moved in closer, rapt by the story.

Vera continued. "So I dropped you off next door and got in the car with Sammy. I know that man must've driven the road from my house to his a million times, definitely enough to know every curve and bend in that road." Vera started wailing hysterically. "He did it on purpose, Sullivan! He wanted to kill me and my baby! I know he did!"

"Did what?" queried Sullivan. "What did he do?"

Vera pulled herself together. "He careened that old Mercedes of his right into a tree. I don't think he even cared about killing himself at that point. He just wanted me and that baby out of his way." Sullivan covered her mouth in repulsion. "And that's why I took you and left without telling anybody where we were going, and that's why we never stayed in one place too long. He'd already succeeded in killing one child by causing me to have a miscarriage. I wasn't going to stick around long enough for him to try again."

"Vera, do you know what you're saying? What you're accusing him of is murder!"

"That's exactly what I'm accusing him of, and I'll believe it till they put me in my grave. Samuel Sullivan purposely rammed that car into a tree and killed Amber, and he wouldn't have hesitated to kill me too if I wasn't too stubborn and ornery to die!" Vera gulped down her drink. "Nothing was ever the same after that."

Sullivan vehemently shook her head. "I can't believe this. I can't believe any of this, Vera! The man I know would never do anything as cruel and vicious as that."

"What man do you know, fool? You haven't met the real Samuel Sullivan. You just met his representative. The real Samuel is ruthless and cold and has a dark side to him that not even the devil wants to get on. Yeah, he can be charming, but cross him and see what happens. If a man would stoop to killing his own unborn child, there ain't nothing else he won't do!"

Sullivan exhaled. "With all due respect, I believe that you believe everything you just told me. I have no intentions of trying to change your mind or question your truth, but personally, I don't think he tried to kill you. He loved you, and he loved me. What was there to gain by taking that kind of risk?"

"It ain't what he had to gain. It's what he stood to lose by everybody finding out that he had not one, but two babies by the woman everybody had decided was the town whore. He wasn't going to risk his reputation, his ministry, or his family's name like that."

"If my dad says it was an accident, I believe him. He's been honest about everything else, so he has no reason to lie about this."

"Wake up, child!" Vera whacked the back of Sullivan's head. "He's been playing you all along. Are you that desperate for a man to love you that you'll believe anything one tells you?"

Vera's words cut Sullivan to the core. "How dare you question anything about me when you know the kind of hell you put me through as a child? If I have issues with men, it's probably because my own mother pimped me out to them from the time I was fourteen years old until I left to go to college. And if I am a whore or any of the other labels you like to put on me, never forget that I learned by watching you!"

"Then learn this by watching me. Stay away from Samuel Sullivan! I'm telling you, he ain't no good, Sully. He's going to hurt you."

"So what?" Sullivan shrugged her shoulders. "My parents have been hurting me my whole life. What can he possibly do to me that you haven't already done?"

"Why do you think I'm the way I am today, huh? That man took everything about me that was sensitive and hopeful and kind and squeezed out every drop. This bitter, tired old woman is all that's left."

"That'll never happen to me," vowed Sullivan. "I'll never be you, Vera."

Vera laughed a little. "That's the same thing I said when I saw it happening to my mama. Sullivan, you're more like me than you want to admit. And just like me, loving Samuel Sullivan is going to end up costing you way more than you can afford to pay."

Chapter 23

"All of your dirty little secrets are safe, at least for this weekend."
—*Kina Battle*

Reginell looked outside of Lawson's living room window at the rain pouring down in buckets. "Can you believe that in two days we're going to be laid out on the beach on Grand Bahama Island, looking at the aqua water while some sexy, rude boy named Dexter St. Jacques serves us drinks?"

"Not if we don't get through this checklist first." Lawson closed the blinds, disrupting both Reginell's view and her fantasy. She pulled out her clipboard and stuck a pen behind her ear.

"Lawson, must you treat everything like a covert military operation? We're going away for the weekend, not plotting a coup," said Sullivan. "You're taking all the fun and spontaneity out of it."

"Sullivan, you already know that I'm type A. I have to have everything methodically planned out, including my spontaneity, and there's nothing *fun* about getting stopped by airport security or not making it through customs." Lawson clicked her pen and began marking off items on her checklist. "Did everyone print a copy of the TSA regulations I e-mailed you? If not, I printed out extra copies."

"Yes, Lawson." Reginell groaned and perched herself on the arm of the sofa.

Lawson jotted something down. "Kina, do we have your word that there'll be no filming on this trip?"

"Absolutely. I've given Chris this week off, so all your dirty little secrets are safe, at least for this weekend."

Lawson released papers from her clipboard and began issuing them out. "I took the liberty of researching activities for us to do while we're there." She stopped when she got to Angel, who was dozing off. "Am I boring you, Miss King?"

Angel yawned. "No, I'm just tired. I think my iron is low. My energy level has been shot lately."

"That's because you've been working too much," Kina told her, diagnosing the problem. "You definitely need to get some rest while we're in the Bahamas this weekend. I'm sure Lawson scheduled some nap time for us."

Lawson handed Kina an itinerary. "As a matter of fact, I did."

Angel scanned the list. "Do you all know that this is the first weekend I've had off in almost four months?"

"You look a little peaked too," noted Kina. "Are you sure you're not coming down with something, Angel?"

"I don't think so."

"You better make an appointment with your doctor as a precaution," said Lawson. "The last thing you need is to be sick on vacation."

"And the last thing we need is to be stuck in close quarters with you if you're contagious," pointed out Sullivan.

Kina passed around her iPad. "Here are some pictures of the villa. Isn't it gorgeous?"

Lawson scrolled through the snapshots of the lavish property. "It looks heavenly. I may get over there and not want to leave, which might not be such a bad idea."

Sullivan took possession of the iPad. "Are you and Garrett still on the outs?"

Lawson shook her head. "I wouldn't call it the *outs*. We're very cordial and polite to each other, but we talk only when needed. I think we're both afraid that one careless word will cause an avalanche that ends in divorce court."

"Are you worried about him seeing Simone while you're away this weekend?" asked Reginell.

"If Garrett wants to cheat again, he'll cheat whether I'm in the Bahamas or in his back pocket," Lawson responded. "I can't drive myself crazy worrying about it anymore."

Angel's cell phone rang. "Hold that thought. It's my mom." Angel answered the phone. "Hi, Ma. What's going on?"

"Do you have a minute?" asked her mother Ruby.

"Yes, I'm just here talking to the girls, trying to get this trip to the Bahamas sorted out. What's up?"

"I saw one of your high school classmates at the gym a little while ago."

"Who?"

"Crystal Pennymon. You remember her, right? Little scrawny thing with long hair."

"Yeah, we were in a lot of the same clubs together. How is she?"

"Oh, she's fine. She asked about you, and I told her that you were living in Georgia now and had recently started dating another one of your classmates, one named Jordan."

"I bet she was shocked to hear that," said Angel with a giggle.

"Yes, she was shocked, but not for the reasons you might think."

"What do you mean?"

Her mother hesitated. "Well, she was shocked to hear that he was out."

"Out of what?" Angel asked in horror. "Out of the closet?"

"No, sweetie. Out of jail."

Angel's jaw dropped. *"Jail?"*

"Angel, baby, I'm so sorry to have tell you this. Apparently, Jordan got caught up in some duplicitous check scheme at the bank he was working at a few years ago. He was cashing fraudulent payroll checks for one of his friends. They got away with about a hundred thousand dollars of the bank's money before getting caught."

"Maybe Jordan didn't know the checks were fake," suggested Angel.

"Honey, if that was the case, he would have gotten fired, not arrested. The police, the DA, the bank, and everyone else seem to think he was in on it."

"I can't believe this." Angel shook her head. "There's got to be a logical explanation for all this. I know Jordan. He's not the kind of person who'd steal that kind of money. Besides, I'm sure he would have told me if he'd been locked up before, especially if it was recently."

"Well, you know everything's on the computer these days. Why don't you do a little research and see what you can find out?"

"I will."

"I know this is probably difficult for you to face, but it's better that you find out now, before you start to really fall for this guy."

Lawson rushed to Angel's side as soon as she hung up the phone. "What's wrong? Is your mother okay?"

"Yeah. She said she bumped into one of my old classmates today. When my mom told her I was seeing

Jordan, she revealed to my mother that Jordan had been locked up recently for check fraud or something like that."

"Are you serious?" Sullivan asked. "Has Jordan ever mentioned anything about it?"

Angel shook her head. "Not a word."

"Do you think that's why he left D.C.?" Lawson flung her hand over her heart. "Oh, my God. You don't think he's on the run, do you?"

"I don't know. I was about to check online to see what I could find out."

"Wait here a minute." Lawson disappeared into her bedroom. She returned with her laptop in tow and popped it open. "Here. Do a search for his name with the word *fraud* and see what you find out. Better yet, there's the Web site my students are always on to find out who's been locked up. I think it's Bust-a-Mug, or something like that."

Angel found the Web site and typed in Jordan's name. His mug shot appeared on the screen. "Yep, that's him, charged with fraud," Angel affirmed and lowered her head. "God, how could I have been so stupid?"

"What's the main newspaper in D.C.?" asked Lawson. "Go to their Web site and see if you can find some more information about it."

After a brief search, Angel found an article about the incident archived on the newspaper's Web site. Angel's heart sank when she saw his picture under the headline BANK BRANCH MANAGER CHARGED IN CHECKING SCHEME. "I guess this makes it official."

Sullivan started reading the article. "Well, wait a minute, Angel. It says here that he denies knowing that the checks were fraudulent."

Lawson scrolled farther down. "Oh . . . but here it says he pled guilty. That's probably not something an innocent man would do."

Angel couldn't bear to read any more. "We've talked about our lives and our past. Why wouldn't he tell me about that?"

"I hate to say it, but it sounds like Jordan might be a con artist," concluded Lawson. "I wouldn't be surprised if he's been gearing up to make you his next mark."

"Lawson, don't scare the poor girl like that!" admonished Sullivan. "He was probably ashamed to tell you, Angel. I know firsthand what it's like to want to keep your past behind you."

"Now that you know, what are you going to do about it?" asked Lawson. "Are you going to confront him? Is this a deal breaker for you?"

Angel sank down in the sofa and exhaled. "I don't know. I'm so confused right now that I don't know what to do or to think. If Jordan could keep something like this from me, what does that say about him? How can I trust him?"

"I wouldn't go jumping to any conclusions until you've heard his side of the story," cautioned Sullivan.

"He's been misleading her for weeks," said Lawson. "How can she believe anything that comes out of his mouth?"

"I say listen to what the man has to say and give him another chance," Reginell volunteered. "Besides, Angel needs a little thug in her life."

"It's that kind of logic that has pushed the number of female inmates to a record high," Lawson declared.

Kina sat down next to Angel. "Are you in too deep with this guy to just end it?"

"It's hard to say. I care about him, but I feel like I don't half know him at all."

"Okay, we know that he was locked up, but he's out now. He's paid his debt to society," Sullivan argued. "If you feel that strongly about him, maybe you ought to consider letting him explain what happened and giving the relationship an honest chance."

"What bothers you more? The fact that he has a record or that he didn't tell you about it?" asked Kina.

"Both are equally undesirable, Kina," answered Angel.

Lawson closed her laptop. "I say cut your losses. You haven't been seeing each other that long. You're not obligated or tied to him in any way."

Unless you count being soul tied, thought Angel, remembering Mark 10:8, which said that after sex, "And they twain shall be one flesh: so then they are no more twain, but one flesh . . ."

"I don't think I'm even going to bring it up until we get back from this trip," Angel said, having decided what to do. "Perhaps then I'll be more focused and can come back with some answers."

"And don't forget about that checkup before we leave," Lawson reminded her.

Angel nodded.

"But you *do* need to forget about your troubles, your stress, your bills, and all that other drama," said Reginell. "Because we're going to the Bahamas, baby, and ain't nothing stopping us from having a ball this weekend!"

Chapter 24

*"If we're going to keep it real, we're going to keep it
one hundred all the way."*
—*Lawson Kerry Banks*

After a two-hour flight, Lawson, Sullivan, Reginell,
Angel, and Kina found themselves sunbathing on one
of the powdery sand beaches in the Bahamas. After
a lazy afternoon spent on Grand Bahama Island, the
ladies retreated to their secluded, luxuriant four-
bedroom Bahamian villa for dinner, prepared by the
personal chef Kina had hired.

Reginell looked over their veranda facing the beach
and took in the salty sea air. She released her breath.
"Now, this is the life!"

"Indeed it is," Angel agreed, sliding her feet into the
sparkling swimming pool. "I didn't realize how badly I
needed this vacation."

Kina began distributing the frozen cocktails that
she'd whipped up in the kitchen while they waited for
the food to be served. "I think we all did. I don't know
about you, but I'm starting to have a real appreciation
for the good life."

Reginell tossed back her pineapple and banana dai-
quiri. "Dang, Kina, you didn't spare any alcohol, did
you?"

Angel shook her head, mixing the drink as Kina approached her. She watched the sun set over the ocean,

leaving streaks of orange and purple painted across the sky. "This place is so beautiful. How can anyone look around at all of this and not believe there's a God?"

Sullivan donned her sunglasses and stretched out on a lounge chair. "I've seen better, but it'll do."

Lawson lifted a frothy glass from Kina's hand and joined Angel at the pool. "Are you going to be a sourpuss all weekend? If that's the case, we could've left you in Georgia."

Sullivan lowered the brim of her oversize hat to block out the sun. "Fine. This place is amazing. Is that what you wanted me to say?"

"It's a start," Kina mumbled, flopping down on one of the plush chairs outlining the swimming pool. "Dinner will be served in about twenty minutes. He's cooking curry chicken, fresh steamed vegetables, and island-style rice. It smells incredible!"

"Twenty minutes, huh?" Reginell reached into her bag and pulled out a marijuana cigarette. "Perfect timing. The munchies will start kicking in around then."

Lawson winced. "Reggie, please don't tell me that is what I think it is."

"I don't know what you *think* it is, but one of the locals was kind enough to hook a sister up!" Reginell lit up the blunt and took a pull from it.

"A local? Well, that sounds safe," retorted Sullivan.

"Reggie, why are you reverting to your old habits?" Lawson scolded her. "This is beneath you, both as a Christian and an engaged woman!"

Reginell blew out the smoke. "Chill out, Lawson. I'm on vacay. Everybody in the Caribbean smokes weed. It's probably not even illegal over here."

"You're a Christian," repeated Lawson. "You don't have the luxury of doing what everybody else does."

"Whatever," grumbled Reginell. She offered the joint to Sullivan. "Do you want some?"

"Do you honestly think I'm going to put my mouth on anything your mouth has been on? I have to kiss my husband and daughter with these lips." She flung her hand. "Go smoke over there somewhere so I don't have to smell it."

"And you already know better than to ask me," asserted Lawson.

Kina spoke up. "I'll try it."

"See? Now, there's an adventurer!" Reginell passed the blunt to Kina.

Kina examined it, trying to balance both the drink and the blunt. "Goodness, I haven't smoked so much as a cigarette since I was seventeen years old."

Reginell smiled. "I promise that this is a little more grown up than Uncle Tommy's cigarettes you used to sneak and smoke behind the house."

Kina inhaled the drag she took.

"Wait. . . . I've got to get a picture of this!" Reginell rushed to grab her camera.

Kina blew out the smoke. "Don't be posting this online, Reggie!"

"Really?" Sullivan smirked. "Don't you think the fans would get a kick out of seeing the head Christian in charge blaze one up?"

Reginell snapped a picture. "No worries, mon. What happens on the island stays on the island."

Lawson shook her head. "Kina, you're a mother. Is this the example you want to set for Kenny?"

Kina passed the blunt back to Reginell. "I just wanted to try it, Lawson."

"And you're about to become a mother too," Lawson pointed out to Reginell. "Mark has two impressionable teenagers. Do you think he'd approve of this?"

Reginell was undeterred. "You're such a buzz kill. Mark ain't here. Neither is Mariah and neither is Namon, and what they don't know won't hurt them."

Lawson frowned. "You're the one I'm worried about getting hurt, li'l sister."

"You want to hit this?" Reginell thrust the joint in Angel's face.

"Do you think the quintessential health nut is going to defile her body that way?" Sullivan joked.

"Don't be such a prude. Weed is from the earth," Reginell said, quoting, then inhaled.

Sullivan raised an eyebrow. "It's never a good sign when you have to resort to quoting Smokey from *Friday* in an argument of persuasion."

Angel shook her head and shooed Reginell's hand away. "I can't. I think the smell alone will send me heaving to the nearest toilet."

"Come on, everybody. Lighten up," Kina implored the others. "This weekend is supposed to be about all of us fellowshipping and reconnecting and trying to reestablish some of the bonds that have been severed due to time and distance, lack of communication, or—"

"*Betrayal,*" Sullivan said, chiming in.

Kina sighed. "Or betrayal. Sullivan, part of the reason I wanted you to come is that I want us to get back to the closeness we had before everything got all crazy."

Sullivan sat up. "*Everything* didn't get all crazy. *You* got all crazy, Kina! How could you do that to me?"

"Sully, do you really want to do this right here, right now?" asked Lawson.

Reginell finished her drink and held up her empty glass. "If you are, it sounds like we're going to need some more of these!"

Sullivan looked Kina squarely in the eyes for the first time in over a year. "Yeah, Kina, let's do this right here and now. I want to know how one of my friends—one of my best friends, at that—could try to ruin my marriage and destroy me life."

Lawson jumped into the conversation. "Sullivan, you're the one—"

Sullivan held up her hand to shush Lawson. "Stay out of this, Lawson! I want Kina to answer."

"I'm not going to sit here and let you attack my cousin."

Sullivan contorted her face. "Lawson, why don't you go on the beach and pick some coconuts or something? This is between Kina and me, not Kina, Sullivan, and Lawson!"

"It's all right, Lawson. I can handle it." Kina took a deep breath and a sip of her drink. "There's no one answer I can give you, Sullivan. There's certainly not an answer to justify what I did to you and Charles. All I can tell you is that I was really, *really* messed up after E'Bell died. Yeah, I was glad that the abuse had stopped, that the name-calling and insults had stopped, and that I didn't have to walk around my own apartment in fear anymore, but nothing prepared me for how alone I felt."

"Kina, you weren't alone. You had us," Angel told her.

Kina took another sip, building the courage to be honest with each swallow. "Not really. At that time, you had just gotten engaged to Duke and were trying to build a life with him and the girls. Lawson and Garrett had just gotten married. Sully and Charles were busy trying to pick the pieces back up after the whole Vaughn fiasco, and Reginell was off somewhere, doing her own thing. Once I came home from work, I didn't have anybody. I was so lonely, but I couldn't tell anyone. I mean, how could I admit to all of you that I actually missed the guy who had beat on me for breakfast, lunch, and dinner?"

Lawson's heart went out to Kina. "Kina, you could've told us that. We wouldn't have judged you."

"I didn't want you to know, just like when E'Bell was abusing me. When you're in that kind of violent situation for so long, you get very good at hiding the truth and perfecting whatever image you want people to believe in, even those closest to you."

"Was loneliness the reason you got involved with Joan?" posed Angel.

Kina nodded. "You know, being with Joan was never about whether I was really gay or straight. She was someone who was there, showering me with the attention and affection I needed. God knows she treated me better than any man ever did, but in the back of my mind, I always knew that she wasn't what I was looking for."

"And that's when you decided to go after Charles," Sullivan said, surmising Kina's motivation.

"I was so thankful to him for giving me a job at the church, and he was so supportive and caring. He loved the Lord, and it seemed like he knew everything about life and God and how to treat people. I'd never met a guy like that before, and I couldn't help myself. I convinced myself that God wanted us to be together because he was the kind of man I'd prayed for my whole life."

"Yes, but he was *my* man!" bellowed Sullivan.

"Now, Sullivan, if we're going to keep it real, we're going to keep it one hundred all the way," began Lawson, now fueled by liquid courage. "Everybody here knows that for years, you treated Charles like crap with all your running around and flirting, withholding sex when you felt like it, and only God knows what else you've done and haven't told us about. A lesser man would've left your butt a long time ago. Your only saving grace is that Charles loves the Lord more than he loves you, and he tries to do what's pleasing to God. Charles must know that you'd be an even bigger mess without him. So before you start hollering about how Charles is *your man,* think about how much love and appreciation you've shown to *your man.*"

Sullivan rolled her neck around to address Lawson. "I doubt that you want to go there with me, Lawson. If you knew that much about being a good wife, Garrett wouldn't have been in the bed, folding Simone up like a basket of laundry, would he?"

Lawson narrowed her eyes and hissed, "That was below the belt, Sullivan."

Sullivan gave Lawson the once-over. "The truth hurts, doesn't it?"

Kina went on. "I wasn't trying to hurt you, Sully. Truth be told, I really wasn't even thinking about you. The only thing I could see was that Charles was a good man, and I needed a good man. I guess once you got pregnant and we were all convinced that the baby was Vaughn's, I took it as a sign from God that Charles and I were meant to be together. When I told him how I felt and he continued to profess his love for you, I just snapped."

"But why?" asked Angel.

"I guess because it seemed like no matter what Sullivan did to him and no matter how much she hurt and humiliated him, Charles still wanted her. I thought if he knew about Vaughn and the baby, it could be the one thing that could make him take the blinders off and see Sullivan for who she really was." Kina faced Sullivan. "I regretted telling Charles right after I blurted it out, but by then, it was too late."

"So you don't think I deserve a man like Charles?" charged Sullivan.

"No, you don't," answered Lawson. "There . . . I said it."

Sullivan glared at Lawson, then took in a mouthful of her cocktail. "So I'm not good enough for Charles, huh?"

Kina, Reginell, and Angel braced themselves for what might come next, not knowing who among them would be the recipient of Sullivan's rage. When Sullivan was mad while sober, she was unpredictable. Who knew how she'd respond under the influence of alcohol?

"Don't you think I know that?" Sullivan added after a few moments of silence. "I know I don't deserve a man like him, who's kind and decent. I know he deserves much better than me—a woman who wasn't even in love with him when we got married. I was a lazy twenty-three-year-old who didn't want to work and knew I needed to find a man rich and gullible enough to subsidize my lifestyle. Charles fit the bill perfectly."

"So that's all he's ever been to you? A paycheck?" asked Angel.

"No." Sullivan began tearing up. "Look, you've got to understand that where I come from, men don't love women. They use them. They hurt them. The trick is to get everything you can out of a man before he ups and leaves. For a long time, I didn't care how I treated my husband. I just knew that I had to use him as much as I could before he left me. After a while, however, I saw that he wasn't trying to leave, that he genuinely loved me—even being the screwup that I am. That's when I knew that it was safe to love him, and I cherish that love. It's the same way with you all." She looked around at her friends. "Like Charles, you loved me and stayed

by my side no matter how many times I self-destruct-
ed. I value this friendship we share almost as much as
I value my relationship with Charles. I thought you all
felt the same way."

"We do," Lawson assured her. "Sullivan, you're our
sister."

"Admittedly, I'm a screwup. I find a way to destroy
anything I touch, but when I met you all and you accepted me just as I was, I made darn sure I wasn't going to screw up being a real friend to you. That's what
made it hurt so much, Kina. You know, I can handle
you catching feelings for Charles. Why wouldn't you?
You were working closely with him, he's a good-look-
ing man, and he's the sweetest thing that ever walked
this earth. You're not the first or the last woman at
Mount Zion to fall for my husband. I would've understood had you come to me and told me how you felt
about Charles. I wouldn't have liked it, but I would've
understood. I would've even understood you telling
Charles about Vaughn and the pregnancy if you did it
out of love and concern. But no, everything you did was
solely out of spite and jealousy. Our friendship, which
meant everything to me, meant so little to you that you
could betray me without so much as a second thought.
That's the part that hurts, Kina! It was never about you
and Charles. This was always about you and me."

"I'm so sorry, Sullivan," replied Kina, sobbing. "I've
been a terrible friend."

"Yeah, you have." Sullivan cracked a smile. "But I've
been a terrible wife, so I guess we're even."

"Neither of you are a terrible anything," said Angel.
"Don't even joke about that. The Bible says you shall
have whatever you say."

Kina wiped her eyes. "Can we try to be friends again,
Sully? I love you, and I miss our friendship. I really
want to put this behind us."

"We can try," conceded Sullivan. "Baby steps, though. You can start by refilling my drink."

"Baby step your way to the kitchen to fill mine up too," added Reginell.

Kina laughed. "Sure. I'll check on dinner while I'm at it." Kina collected the empty glasses and headed toward the kitchen.

Angel got up to pat Sullivan on the back. "I'm very proud of you, Sully. You let Kina say what she needed to say without going off the deep end."

Sullivan reclined on the lounge chair. "Yeah, yeah, yeah. I'll smile and play nice this weekend, but I still don't trust Kina as far as I can throw her."

Chapter 25

"God isn't obligated to take care of anything He didn't ordain, and I don't believe He sanctioned me doing the nasty with Jordan."

—Angel King

"It's about time you decided to join us," Lawson said to Reginell, who dragged herself to join them for breakfast by the pool the next morning. "You were supposed to join us on the jetty for a sunrise prayer session."

Reginell yawned and sat down next to Kina. "I guess the thought of waking up at six to watch the sun come up didn't satisfy me like the thought of spending a few extra hours in the big, comfortable bed."

"It's too bad you missed it," said Kina, slicing her French toast. "It was beautiful. The weather was just perfect. It was warm, with a nice balmy breeze coming through."

Reginell reached for the pitcher of orange juice in the center of the table. "I'm sure Lawson will tell me all about it."

Lawson set her fork down. "What's going on with you, Reggie?"

"What do you mean?"

"The smoking, the drinking—"

"You were drinking last night too," protested Reggie.

"I had one drink! You practically downed a whole bottle by yourself. Lately, you've been hanging out more. You've all but abandoned the Diamond Butterfly Ministry you started to help other young women caught in the sex industry. Namon says you're not around as much when he goes to see his dad. Is everything all right between you and Mark?"

"Dang, Lawson, can I live? Everything is fine with Mark. This is just who I am. I like to drink. I like to party. Every now and then, I might blaze one with my girls. What's so wrong with that?"

"It just doesn't seem like the kind of thing a Christian should do."

"Well, I guess I'm not as saved as you." Reginell grabbed a plate and looked over at Angel's meager breakfast of pineapples and sautéed plantains. "Is that all you're eating?"

"You should try some of this French toast," Kina suggested to Angel. "It's delicious."

"I can't. Just looking at it is making me queasy."

Sullivan piled some slices on Angel's plate. "The health police can't fine you way down here. It's okay to live a little and eat something that's not grown organically."

Angel pushed the plate away. "No, seriously, *I can't*."

"Are you all right?" asked Lawson, concerned. "You were kind of withdrawn and quiet all night. You even kept to yourself the whole time we were at the beach this morning."

Angel poured some juice. "I guess there's no point in keeping it a secret. You all are going to find out eventually."

Reginell reeled back. "What? You and Jordan tying the knot?"

"I wish it was that simple." Angel took a deep breath. "I went to see my doctor yesterday. He found something in my stomach that wasn't supposed to be there."

"Oh, God, is it a tumor?" asked Kina in a hushed tone.

"No, it's a baby. I'm pregnant."

"Shut the front door!" exclaimed Sullivan, spewing her food. "Are you serious?"

Angel nodded.

"But are you *positive* you're pregnant?" Lawson asked, grilling her.

"Lawson, I'm a nurse. I know the signs, and I've been pregnant before. Plus, my doctor confirmed it before we left to come here. I'm about four weeks along."

"Wow . . . I'm speechless," said Kina.

"Me too. I didn't even think you and ole boy were getting it on!" admitted Reginell.

"Obviously, they weren't getting *everything* on, or she wouldn't be in this situation," mumbled Sullivan.

"It was one time," claimed Angel. "All right, twice, but I never expected this to happen. Reggie, I guess you're not the only one whose sins have found you out. Y'all, *I'm pregnant!*"

"Well, I suppose we ought to congratulate you before we start humiliating you. I know it wasn't planned, but I know how long you've wanted a child of your own."

Angel shook her head. "Not like this, though."

"Does it really matter how the child was conceived?" asked Sullivan. "I mean, this is the baby you've wanted since your miscarriage ten years ago."

"Yeah, but Jordan and I aren't ready to be parents. We're barely even speaking these days."

"Thankfully, God is giving you almost a year to get ready. You'll be fine by the time the baby gets here."

"Were you and Garrett?" Angel shot back. "I'm sorry, Lawson. That was mean. I'm hormonal, okay?"

"Clearly!" said Lawson, perturbed. "Does Jordan know?"

Angel shook her head. "I literally just got it confirmed right before I met you all at the airport."

"Wow . . . Do you think he's going to be cool with it?" asked Sullivan.

"Like he has a choice!" exclaimed Lawson. "Regardless of what happens with their relationship, he has to help her with that baby."

Sullivan brought her glass to her lips. "That's almost funny coming from you, seeing as how you'd like nothing more than for Garrett to check out of Simon's life."

"I never said I didn't want Garrett to help with Simon. I said I didn't want him to help himself to Simone."

"I have no idea how Jordan's going to react." Angel paused. "How messed up is it that I don't even know this guy well enough to know how he'd react to us having a baby?"

Lawson wrapped her arms around Angel. "No matter what happens, you know we'll all pitch in and support you."

"You're not in this by yourself. You know that!" said Sullivan.

"I barely had the time to spend the weekend down here. How am I going to be able to make time and space in my life for a whole other person?"

"The same way we all did," replied Kina. "You figure it out as you go."

"You will be an awesome mom. I know if I can do it, you can."

"I know. I just don't know if I'm ready to be a mother."

Reginell nodded. "I know how you feel."

Lawson flung her hand over her chest. "What? You too?"

"No . . . *geesh!* I meant about having to change my life and become a wife. Y'all make married life look so boring. I don't know if I'm ready to stop having fun."

Sullivan reached for another slice of turkey bacon. "Marriage is as fun or as boring as you make it."

Kina turned to Angel. "Do you think you and Jordan will get married?"

Angel shook her head. "I can't even think about marriage right now. The more I get to know him, the less I want to be in a relationship with him."

"But you have this baby to consider now. Are you prepared to raise him or her as a single parent?"

"I don't know!" shouted Angel. "Now, enough with the questions! I don't know what I'm going to do about any of it, all right? All I know is I'm pregnant, out of wedlock. I don't know how I'm going to take care of a kid when I barely have enough money to take care of myself. I don't know what's going to happen between Jordan and me, and I don't know what I was thinking when I lay down with him and conceived this child. Now, I know you all have a ton of questions and opinions. I love you for that, but I can't handle it right now. That's why I waited so long to tell you all I was pregnant. I need time to process it without your voices drowning out my own."

Kina apologized for all of them. "We're sorry, Angel. None of us want to make you feel any more pressure than you're already feeling."

"Thank you."

"But you are keeping the baby, though, right?" Kina asked.

Angel withdrew from the table. "Depends on how you define the word *keep.*"

Kina's mouth dropped. "Angel, you don't mean—"

"That's enough. I'm tired." Angel pushed her chair into the table. "No more questions."

***

After no one had seen or heard from Angel in more than an hour, Sullivan tiptoed to Angel's bedroom and knocked on the door. She poked her head inside. "Can I come in?"

Angel wiped her eyes and turned over in bed. "Sure, come in."

Sullivan sat down on the bed next to Angel. "Aww . . . Are these tears?"

Angel sniffed. "I don't know if I'm depressed or hormonal."

"So there's really a little baby growing inside of there?" squealed Sullivan, pointing at Angel's stomach.

"Yeah, I guess so," said Angel, passing her hand over her belly. "Who would've thunk it, right?"

Sullivan laughed a little. "I've been where you are. You know I'm here for you if you need to vent, scream, cry, whatever."

Angel gave her a weak smile. "Thank you."

"We're going to town to do some shopping. You feeling up to it?"

"I think I'm going to just hang out here, maybe walk down to the beach later. It's not like I can really afford to go shopping anyway."

"While we're on the subject, do you know what the best part of having a best friend who's a fashion maven is?"

"Enlighten me please."

"Hand-me-down maternity clothes that are some of the most fabulous and chic maternity clothes Savannah has ever seen! Since I can't get any use out of them—not for a while, at least—you might as well."

Angel's eyes were downcast. "That's really generous of you, Sully. Thanks."

"You don't look too happy for a girl who just got promised a brand-new wardrobe. Honestly, Angel, most of the stuff I have is cuter than all that Bohemian crap you wear on a daily basis."

"It's not that. I appreciate the gesture, especially since it's so rare that you do anything for anyone else that's not self-serving in some way. I'm just . . . I don't know . . . confused about this baby, I guess."

"I don't know why. You'll be a fantastic mother," Sullivan assured her. "And if I was able to raise a kid without DFCS being called to the premises once a week, surely you can."

Angel laughed. "Amen to that!" She turned serious again. "I'm not questioning my mothering skills, just questioning whether or not I want to be a mother."

"Really?"

Angel sat up in bed. "Sully, can I be candid with you? Don't get me wrong. I love Kina and Lawson, but . . ."

"Sometimes they make it hard to be real without feeling like you're going to hell for having a thought that's not in the Bible," Sullivan said, filling in the blank.

Angel nodded.

"You know you can, and I won't judge you. That's the best thing about having a best friend who's a screwup. I'm in no position to condemn you!"

Angel leaned in closer to Sullivan and spoke in almost a whisper. "I know children are supposed to be a blessing, but, Sully, this couldn't have happened at a worse time. My business is suffering, I'm working two jobs, and my relationship with Jordan is in disarray."

Sullivan patted her hand. "I understand. I was scared to death when I found out I was pregnant."

"That was different. You were afraid because you didn't know who the father was, but you knew you wanted your baby. I can't say for sure that I want mine."

"I wanted her, true enough, but I still had my doubts, and not just about Charity's paternity, either. As much as I love that little girl, there are times when I miss my old pre-Mommy life. I miss being able to take romantic weekends with my husband and being able to go shopping on a whim. But I wouldn't trade Charity for anything in this world. I know that I was born to be her mother."

Angel hugged the pillow close to her body. "Do you ever think about the babies you aborted?"

"Every day," admitted Sullivan. "But I did what I felt was right at the time."

"Yeah, but you were a kid when you got pregnant. I'm a grown woman. I should know better. I'm a nurse, for Christ's sake! If anyone ought to know how not to get pregnant, it's me!"

"Angel, let's be genuine for a minute. How many people are there in the world who were actually planned for? I'm sure there are far more 'surprises' than not."

"I know, but you kept Charity knowing that it could cost you your marriage, your lifestyle, and everything else if Charles found out that the baby could be Vaughn's. It feels like I have no right to feel this way about my child when women in far worse circumstances keep their babies."

"Honey, don't compare yourself to me. My situation is totally different from yours. You have a right to feel whatever it is that you're feeling. I have a husband and money and an excellent support system and access to resources that you don't have."

"What if . . . what if I can't take care of this baby?"

"I'm no expert on the Bible, but I do know that in Genesis it says, 'Now therefore fear ye not: I will nourish you, and your little ones.' Maybe this is one of those times where you just have to trust God and trust that

He loves you enough to make sure you and this baby are taken care of."

"It feels wrong to even ask God for help," Angel said, confiding in Sullivan. "God isn't obligated to take care of anything He didn't ordain, and I don't believe He sanctioned me doing the nasty with Jordan."

"Child, God hasn't sanctioned and ordained ninety percent of the stuff I've done! But you know what? He always finds a way to let it work out for my good. You're not the first unmarried woman to get pregnant, and you certainly won't be the last. You can get through this. It's just hard right now."

Angel threw her head back. "*Ugh!* Why me? Why now?"

"Why *not* you, Angel? Stop stressing out. The baby doesn't need that, and neither do you."

Angel exhaled. "What am I going to do, Sully?"

"I don't know, but whatever it is, let it be your decision, not mine, not Lawson's or anybody else's. This is between you, God, and Jordan. Pray for discernment and wisdom in this situation, and cast your cares onto Him, because He cares for you," Sullivan said, paraphrasing one of the Psalms, and rose. "Now, get your rest. You're going to miss this luxury once there's an infant in the house."

"Thank you for talking to me and being honest."

Sullivan smiled. "Always. Enjoy your nap."

Angel buried her head in the pillow. She dozed off, hoping against hope to wake up and discover that her unwanted pregnancy was nothing more than a bad dream.

Chapter 26

"Nice girls finish last. I know because I used to be one of them!"
—Kina Battle

At dusk the ladies sat in a deserted corner of the beach, watching their last sunset in the Bahamas.

"I'm a little sad that it's our last night," said Kina, digging her toes in the sand. "We should do this more often."

"Yeah, we should come to the Bahamas at least once a week," remarked Angel.

"I have an idea." Reginell reached into her bag and pulled out a notebook and pen. "You all up for a game?"

"I'm not engaging in any activities that you and your little stripper friends used to do," Sullivan warned her.

"Sullivan, with your track record, I'm sure the strippers could probably learn a few tricks from you. Okay, the only rule to this game is to answer honestly," Reginell stated as she distributed small slivers of paper to everyone that evening. "Write a question down that you want one of us to answer."

"What kind of question?" asked Lawson.

"It can be anything, but try to avoid yes-no questions. It should be something you have to think about." Reginell found enough pens in her bag for everyone. "Write your questions on the paper, fold it up, and drop it into this cup." She pointed to a coffee cup.

The ladies scribbled their questions and deposited them as instructed. Once everyone had contributed, Reginell shook the coffee cup and passed the questions back out. "Make sure you don't have your own question."

Sullivan unfolded her paper. "I don't."

"Me either," said Lawson.

Reginell sat down. "Good. Who wants to go first?"

Kina raised her hand. "I will. My question is, what is something you've done that you'll never do again?" Kina crumpled the paper. "Outside of letting my weight get back up to three hundred pounds, I'd have to say I'll never let people walk all over me again. That's something I've always done, even as a kid. I never spoke up for myself or fought back, but being on *Lose Big* forced me to fight for what I wanted and to take ownership of my life. I could never go back to being that weak person I was a year ago."

"We liked that Kina," said Lawson. "Not to say that we want you to be a pushover, but it was nice being able to talk without having to schedule an appointment with your PR team or having a conversation that isn't scripted or taped."

"I think you just need to balance both sides of your personality," Angel advised her. "You can be strong without being a witch, and you can be nice without being a lackey."

"If I was worried about being nice, I never would've won the competition," argued Kina. "Nice girls finish last. I know because I used to be one of them!"

"All right, Sully, you're up," said Reginell.

Sullivan unfolded her question. "What do you need more of right now? Let's see . . ." Sullivan tapped the side of her head. "Shoes . . . sex . . ."

"You won't be getting any of that here with us this weekend, ma'am!" Angel told her.

"Maybe that's what you should've told Jordan," noted Lawson.

"What I really want more of right now is time with my father," replied Sullivan. "We've missed out on so much time and so many years, which are gone forever."

Lawson patted her on the back. "In Joel, the Bible says the Lord will restore to you the years that the locusts have eaten."

Sullivan raised an eyebrow. "Is *locusts* how we're now referring to Vera?"

"Sully, that was mean," Lawson chided.

"You're right," Sullivan replied. "I'm being way too hard on the locusts."

"I think you're being way too hard on your mother," said Angel.

Sullivan gawked at her. "Are you kidding me? Angel, you know better than anyone what a nut job she is! Calling her a locust is really a compliment."

Angel gave in. "Vera has her issues. I'll give you that. However, I wouldn't go putting Samuel Sullivan on a pedestal yet. Say what you want about your mother, but she stuck around. She didn't abandon you. Your father did."

"Yes, and whose fault is that?" Sullivan asked.

"I'm sure there's enough blame to go around," conceded Lawson. "But the fact still remains that your father bailed on you. You said yourself that he'd planned to take that secret to the grave. He never would've reached out to you if you hadn't forced his hand."

"Who's next?" Sullivan blurted out, unwilling to entertain negative talk about her father.

"I'll take a gander at it," ventured Angel. "Fill in the blank. Love is . . ." She thought it over. "Love is . . . elusive. It is for me, anyway."

Lawson wrinkled her nose. "Why do you say that?"

"Look at my track record. When is the last time I had a relationship that was actually productive?"

Sullivan proceeded gingerly. "Well, Angel, sometimes you have to look at the common denominator."

Angel frowned. "What's that? That all the men I chose are incapable of being in a committed relationship?"

"No, that they all dated you. You're the common denominator," said Sullivan.

Angel pointed at herself. "So you think I'm the problem?"

"*Problem* is a strong word," Lawson told her. "I think you should reevaluate not necessarily the men, but the choices you make in your relationships."

Kina nodded. "She's got a point, Angel. When you fall in love, you fall hard and you fall quickly."

"If you keep falling headfirst, you're bound to crack your neck sooner or later," quipped Sullivan. "I don't think you give yourself enough time to explore the relationship and get to know the men before you start professing your love for them."

Angel pouted. "That's not true."

"Isn't it? Take a look at your relationship history. You met Duke in college, claimed love at first sight, and married him a year later," Lawson said, recounting the events.

"Sullivan married Charles six months after they met," countered Angel.

Sullivan refuted the comparison. "That's different. I was broke, and Charles was horny. It was a mutually beneficial arrangement."

Lawson went on. "You were engaged to Duke again six months after his wife died. Then you dove in headfirst with his cousin, only to discover that he was a pervert with a porn addiction. I warned you about taking your time with Jordan, and what did you do? You slept with him on your second date, and now you're pregnant by a man who you barely know at all. Had you taken your time before giving your whole heart, those relationships might have turned out differently."

Angel was stuck. "I either move too fast, and I end up hurt, or I move to slow and end up alone. How do I fix that?"

"It's like we told Kina," Lawson replied. "You've got to find a balance."

"All right, I'll go next," Reginell said, volunteering. She silently read her question and frowned. "Who came up with this question?"

"What is it?" asked Angel.

"What did you want most as a child that affects you as an adult? I don't even think I know what that means."

"I've taken enough psych classes to know that as adults, we are shaped by things that happened or didn't happen in our childhood," explained Lawson.

"I guess we know whose question that was," Sullivan noted.

Lawson rolled her eyes at Sullivan. "I didn't have a lot of structure and stability in my life as a child, so I'm very anal about that kind of stuff now. Sully didn't have a father, so she's always gone after older men."

Sullivan broke in. "Wait . . . you think I have Daddy issues?"

"I think you have *several* issues, and *Daddy* is definitely one of them," Lawson asserted. "All right, Reggie, answer the question."

Reginell thought it over. "The only thing I wanted as a child that affects me as an adult is having the opportunity to sing. It's the only thing I've ever been good at or that made people pay attention to me other than taking my clothes off."

Kina elbowed her. "Why are you always so down on yourself, Reggie?"

Reginell exhaled. "I'm a realist. I know I'm not like y'all. I don't have my dream career like you, Lawson, or my own business like Angel. I'm not a TV star like Kina or even pretty like Sullivan. I'm just . . . I don't know . . . *basic*. Without singing, I'm nothing, and since no one will let me sing . . ."

"Reggie, I hate to hear you talking like that," lamented Lawson. "Do you really think that stripping is the best God has planned for you? If you would turn your life over to Him, you could live a life better than you ever imagined."

"I've tried that. Nothing ever really changes for me, though."

"Don't minimize the miracles God has already done in your life. Reggie, you have a man who loves and treasures you. He accepts you completely as you are. Do you know how many women spend their lives searching and praying for that?" asked Angel. "Not to mention that you have friends, a loving family, and a God-given talent to sing. A lot of people would kill to be in your shoes."

"All right, Lawson, it's your turn," noted Kina.

"My question is, are you happy?" Lawson sighed. "At this moment, yes. It's hard not to be when you're in this fabulous place with no worries and no drama and no baby mamas."

Kina leaned forward. "What about when you get home?"

"Home is a whole other matter entirely. It's not up to my husband to make me happy. It's my job to do that, because happiness is a choice, but Garrett plays an undeniable role in that. At this point, I really don't know what to do to fix my marriage or be happy in it."

Sullivan reclined on her beach towel. "Why don't you stop trying to fix things and let God do it?"

"Normally, I wouldn't advocate taking marital advice from Sully," began Angel. "But she has a point. Honey, at some point, you have to turn this thing with Simon and Simone over to God."

Reginell shook her head. "How is it that y'all have advice for each other but can't figure out your own lives?"

Angel laughed. "Now, that's a darn good question. Maybe if we took our own advice, our lives would be perfect."

Kina stood up and dusted herself off. "I think I'm going to walk on the beach one last time. Anybody want to stroll with me?"

"Pass," said Sullivan.

"Yeah, me too, cuz," replied Lawson. "I'm heading back to the house in a few minutes to start packing."

Angel staggered to her feet. "I'm heading up to the house now. My stomach hurts."

"What's wrong? You must have a baby in there or something?" Sullivan teased her.

"Ha-ha!" Angel hurled a towel at her head and went back to the house.

"I'll go with you, Kina." Reginell caught up with Kina. "I can use the exercise."

"Have fun," Lawson called after them.

"So what's been going on with you, girl?" asked Reginell once they'd gotten some distance from Sullivan and Lawson. "We haven't even really talked since you've been back."

"It's been crazy! You know I'm not used to getting invited anywhere. Now I'm getting asked to make appearances at all kinds of parties and events. I'm meeting a bunch of different people. It's great."

"I'm sure it is! What about men? Are you meeting any of them?"

Kina blushed. "Reggie . . ."

"You can tell me, Kina. Lawson is the one ready to hurl the Word at you, not me."

"I've been a good girl." She raised her right hand. "Scout's honor."

Reginell stopped and looked at her suspiciously. "Kina . . . tell the truth and shame the devil."

Kina laughed. "Okay, there was this one guy," she revealed.

"I knew it!" exclaimed Reginell. "Who is he?"

"This rapper dude named Calin."

Reginell's mouth dropped. "Cut 'Em Cali! Kina, you smashed off Cut 'Em Cali?"

Kina tried to quiet her. "Keep it down, Reggie. You never know who's listening."

"What happened? How did you meet him?"

"We were both at a For Sisters Only event last week. We ended up having lunch together, and he took me out for drinks. Then one thing led to another."

"Girl, how was it?"

Kina's face turned sour. "It wasn't good, Reggie. I'm not the type to have sex in a nameless hotel room with a man I have no spiritual or emotional connection with."

"You don't think he's going to tell anyone, do you?"

Kina shook her head. "I doubt it. I asked him about that. He said he doesn't hit and tell. Plus, he said he wouldn't get any props for sleeping with a reality show church chick."

Reginell made a face. "That's harsh!"

"It's just as well. I hope I never have to see him again. It would be embarrassing. Now, I want you to tell me something. What's all this I'm hearing about you having money problems?"

"Lawson talks too much, but I'm good."

"Are you sure? You know I'd loan you some money."

"Thanks, Ki, but it's handled."

"Handled how?"

Reginell looked away.

"Reggie?"

"I got a new job. . . . Well, I got an old job."

"What do you mean?"

"Ray hired me back at Paramours."

Kina was disappointed. "Dang, Reggie, why would you do that?"

"Kina, don't judge me. I needed the money. Waiting tables wasn't paying the bills."

"Couldn't you do something else?"

"Nothing legal," Reginell replied. "Look, it's temporary. I need to catch up on some bills and pay for this wedding. That's it."

"Does anyone else know?"

"Does Jesus count? Please don't tell anybody, Kina."

Kina hooked her pinkie with Reginell's. "Cuz, you keep my secrets, and I'll keep yours!"

Reginell smiled. "Deal!"

They pinkie swore and looked at each other warily, remembering that the last time they promised to keep each other's secrets, neither of them held up their end of the deal.

Chapter 27

"I don't think I'm ready for this."
—Angel King

"I see you're finally back on U.S. soil," said Jordan before hugging Angel.

"Yes, we landed a couple of hours ago."

"I'm glad you called me. Come here." He kissed her. "I've missed you."

"Have you?" She rebuffed his attempt at becoming more affectionate.

"Yeah, I've been missing you for a while. We haven't spent as much time together as I'd like since we got back from Beaufort."

Angel exhaled. "I wish we had spent more time together."

He reached out for her. "Me too, baby."

"No, I wish we had spent more time talking. If we had, you probably would've gotten around to telling me about the two years you spent in prison for fraud."

Jordan pulled away. A look of shame washed over his face. "How did you find out about that?"

"Jordan, that's irrelevant. What matters is that I didn't find out from you."

"Baby, I wanted to tell you. No, I take that back. I knew I *needed* to tell you, but I didn't want you to rush to judge or think any less of me before getting to know me."

"I get that part, but the more time we spent together—"

He cut in. "The more time we spent together, the more I realized I was falling for you. Then I was afraid to tell you because I didn't want to lose you, Angel."

"Jordan, I really need to understand these charges. What happened?"

"Baby, I've missed you, and you just got back. Do we really need to get into this right now?"

Angel crossed her arms. "Yes."

Jordan sat down. "All right. I was the branch manager for a bank back in D.C. One of my homeboys came through to cash a thirty-thousand-dollar check from his job's account. He didn't have all the documentation the teller needed, so he asked to speak to me. I knew the guy, so I gave her permission to cash the check. He gave me a few Gs for helping him out. He came in a couple more times to cash more checks. I didn't really think anything of it. Maybe I should've asked more questions, but I didn't. I found out later that one of the secretaries was forging the checks for him. Apparently, the bank and his company were on to what was happening. One day he came in to cash another check. The next thing I knew, I was in handcuffs."

"So you didn't know what was going on?"

"Like I said, I didn't ask questions."

Angel buried her head in her hands. "I honestly don't know what to think or how to feel about all of this, Jordan."

"Don't think about it. It's over. I did my time, and I've put it all behind me."

"I have to be real with you," began Angel. "I haven't felt the same way about you since we spent the night together. I feel like you misled me about being celibate and accepting my position on celibacy, and now this. I think we moved way too fast in our relationship."

"If that's how you feel, we can slow things down if you want. I still think you're overreacting about that night, though. We made love. So what? If it's that big of a deal and you don't want it to happen again, it won't, okay? You'll have to throw me down, get buck naked, and force yourself on me before I even touch you again."

She laughed a little. "I'm going to hold you to that."

"That's fine, as long as you allow me to still hold you sometimes."

"You're going to be holding more than just me, Jordan." She raised her eyes to meet his. "I'm pregnant."

He sprang back. "You're what?"

"I'm pregnant. My doctor confirmed it a couple of days ago."

His lips spread into a smile. "Wow. We're having a baby?"

"This isn't cause for celebration to me."

"Are you kidding? This baby is a tremendous blessing!"

"I think, in general, babies are a blessing. Unfortunately, I don't feel very blessed at this moment. I can't afford a child right now. I don't have time for a child right now. No one knows what's going to happen between you and me." She shook her head. "I don't think I'm ready for this."

"We've got nine months to get ready, Angel." He hugged her. "My first child . . . I can't believe it!"

Angel couldn't believe it, either. She was carrying a child that she wasn't sure she wanted and that she knew that she couldn't afford by a man she hardly knew. This was no time for celebration.

Chapter 28

*"Even if it was only for a moment, you wanted her
more than you wanted me."*
—*Lawson Kerry Banks*

The vibe between Garrett and Mark had always been
somewhat tense due to the fact that Mark was envious
of Garrett's bond with Namon and Garrett was intimidated by Lawson's relationship with Mark. They tried
to keep the tension at bay for Namon's and Lawson's
sake, but it wasn't uncommon for egos and testoster-
one to take the place of serenity and sound judgment.

"So what's good here?" asked Reginell, scanning the
Bayou Café's menu. She, Mark, Lawson, and Garrett
had met up for dinner to discuss Namon's pending college plans.

"The Cajun dishes are excellent," said Garrett.

"Can you believe it'll be Thanksgiving in a couple of
weeks, then Christmas?" Lawson said. "This year has
truly flown by!"

"While we're talking about the holidays, Lawson,
what do you think about me surprising Namon with a
car for Christmas?" asked Mark.

"We checked out some cars last weekend," interjected Reginell. "We saw this cute black Escape that we
think Namon will love!"

Lawson cleared her throat. "Well . . ." She cut her
eyes over to Garrett.

Garrett set his menu down. "Actually, Lawson and I have been talking about giving my truck to Namon and buying something bigger that'll fit the whole family."

The waiter came and took their orders and left.

"No offense, Garrett, but your truck is kind of old, right?" Mark drank some of his water. "I want my son to have a car fresh off the lot."

"My truck is fine."

"Yeah, in town maybe, but Namon is going off to college in a few months. He's going to need something reliable going up and down that road."

Lawson spoke softly to Garrett. "Baby, we should probably consider taking Mark up on his offer. You can still get the car you were planning on buying, and we'll have your truck as a backup in case we need it."

Garrett breathed heavily. "Fine."

Lawson smiled. "Thank you for doing that for Namon, Mark."

"Our son deserves the best. There's nothing I wouldn't do for him."

"We all want the best for Namon, Mark, not just you," added Garrett.

"I can't believe my little nephew is about to go off to college," said Reginell.

Lawson set down her glass after taking a sip. "Mark, you know that Namon is bound and determined to attend Grambling in the fall, but I want him closer to home. I think he should look more closely at the schools around here. Georgia Southern is an excellent choice, and so is Valdosta or SSU."

Mark nodded. "I agree. I went to school out of state. It can be overwhelming if you're not ready for it."

"I say let the boy go where he's going to be happiest," suggested Garrett.

"Happiness stretches as far as my bank account does!" retorted Lawson. "If he goes to school in Louisiana, there are out-of-state fees, in addition to tuition and the added expense of traveling back and forth."

"He's trying to earn a band scholarship, though, right? That'll help out on that," Garrett replied.

Lawson shook her head. "If it was an academic scholarship, that would be one thing, but I don't want him to feel pressured to stay in the band, especially if those long practices and games start to interfere with his studies."

Mark spoke up. "Garrett, I don't know if you can relate, but participating in extracurricular activities like that becomes like a second job. For me, it felt like football first, then the classroom."

"Just because I didn't go to college doesn't mean I can't relate," snarled Garrett.

"No, baby, he didn't mean it like that," explained Lawson.

"Are you the authority on what Mark means and feels? Shouldn't that job go to your sister?"

Reginell's head popped up. She'd been staring down at her phone, texting. "Huh? How did I get in the middle of this argument?"

"Nobody's arguing," insisted Lawson. "We're here for a family dinner, so let's table this discussion for later. Mark, we can talk about it at work tomorrow."

"Oh, because I'm not the biological father, I don't have any say-so in Namon's future?" asked Garrett. "I've raised that kid for the past twelve years."

Mark grunted. "How many times are you going to bring that up? Everybody at this table knows you raised Namon, but everybody also knows I didn't even know he existed until three years ago. Otherwise, your services wouldn't have been needed."

"*My services?*" Garrett snapped.

Lawson laid her hand on top of her husband's. "This is not the time."

"Yeah, your services, but I forgot," sneered Mark. "You've been donating your services to more than one woman these days."

"Mark!" exclaimed Reginell.

"Babe, some things are between my son's mother and me. Your brother-in-law needs to stay out of it." Mark raised his eyes toward Garrett. "Stay in your lane, homeboy."

"Or what?" Garrett growled. "Have your baby's mama watch you get beat down again?"

Lawson nervously looked around the restaurant. "Where is that waiter with our food?"

Mark tossed a few dollars on the table. "You know what? I'm not even hungry anymore." He grabbed Reginell's hand. "Come on, Reggie. Let's go."

"I haven't gotten my food yet," Reginell whined as she was being led out by Mark. "Can we at least stop by Popeyes on the way home?"

"That went well," mumbled Lawson once Reginell and Mark were gone. "You didn't have to go there, you know."

"Go where?" Garrett frowned. "Forget that. Why do you always take his side?"

"I don't always do anything."

"Whenever Mark comes around, it's like the twelve years I've spent raising, loving, and being a father to Namon don't even matter to you."

"Garrett, you know I don't feel that way."

"How am I supposed to know that, Lawson, when you're all on this guy's sack?"

"Excuse me?" scoffed Lawson. "Before you try to go *there* about Mark, I don't see you running up and consulting with me about Simon."

"That's because I don't see you making an effort to even acknowledge that he exists!"

"And let's not forget *why* he exists," shot back Lawson.

Garrett was irked. "So you're back on this Simone bull?"

"I believe you were the one who was backed up on Simone."

Garrett stood up and slid Lawson the car keys. "This is for the birds. I'll catch a cab home. I'm out."

"I'm not blind or stupid, Garrett," Lawson remarked.

"What are you talking about?"

Lawson gave in. "Simone is beautiful, and she obviously has something that you like, or you never would've been attracted to her."

Garrett calmed down and returned to his seat. "Lawson, I was wrong. There's no other way to put it. But you know we were going through an awful period in our marriage during that time. I desperately wanted a child with you, my wife. Every day that's what I was praying for, and every month I'd get my hopes up and have them crushed. I thought you were feeling the same hurt and disappointment I was. I thought sharing that made us closer. Then to find out that you'd been taking birth control pills all along, that you'd been playing me for a fool, was devastating. I was hurt. On top of that, I had to deal with you being jealous of Reggie dating Mark. You made me feel like I was nothing, Lawson. It wasn't right, but it was very easy to turn to Simone. She was there, building me up, stroking my ego. She was doing all the things you wouldn't. I got caught up."

"If you didn't have Simon, I could pretend it didn't happen, but it did happen. You touched her. You kissed her. Even if it was only for a moment, you wanted her more than you wanted me. You wanted her bad enough to gamble this life that we'd spent ten years building together. You didn't even think enough of me or yourself to slap on a condom and make sure we were protected. You risked not only your life but mine too."

"I wasn't thinking clearly. All I could see was feeling like a man again and getting back at you for hurting me. It was stupid and careless and dangerous, but I can't do anything about that now, Lawson, except be a better husband to you going forward."

"But now the two of you share this awesome bond with Simon."

"You share the same bond with Mark," he pointed out.

"It's not the same. Mark and I didn't bond together over Namon. You and I did. But as much as I loved you, I was willing to at least consider marrying Mark, who was a virtual stranger to me, in order to protect and retain custody of Namon when he threatened to seek full custody. I would've done anything to be with my child. I'm sure you'd sacrifice anything for your child too, including our marriage."

"It'll never come down to that, Lawson."

"But I don't know that, and that's what I live in constant fear of. I don't know if you'll have a moment of weakness and cheat on me again or if you'll decide you want to be with her and Simon. There's nothing about this situation that's within my control." Lawson shook her head. "My God, what have we become?"

"I don't know."

"We've gotten so far from how close we used to be. When I think about us, I just don't know anymore. . . ."

Her real concern was that pretty soon, they wouldn't care anymore.

Chapter 29

"I risked everything . . . just so I could feel loved for a few moments."
—*Angel King*

Angel slipped into a pair of beige yoga pants. Then she remembered the receptionist's warning on the phone. There could be a lot of blood following the procedure. Angel decided to go with a black sweat suit.

"Might as well," she concluded. "Black is what you wear to a funeral."

Angel flopped down on her bed. She had come to the harrowing decision to terminate her pregnancy after much thought and many sleepless nights. Angel reflected on a conversation she'd had with Lawson two days earlier.

"What was it like to be a single parent?" Angel had asked her.

"It was hard, Angel. I'm not even going to lie to you," Lawson had told her. "It's the hardest thing I've ever done, but being a mother is also the most rewarding. I love Namon more each day that passes. I can't begin to describe the joy I feel watching him grow into a young man. Sure, for a hot second, I did consider not having him, but even at sixteen years old, I knew my baby deserved a chance at life. I've never regretted it."

Angel also recalled Kina's caveat, which was simply, "God said, 'Thou shall not kill.'"

Eventually, it was Sullivan's advice that won out. Angel had to do was what best for her, not everyone else, and she'd decided that what was best for her was terminating the pregnancy.

She rubbed her hand over her stomach. Her stomach was still relatively flat and showed no evidence of the life growing within, and there would be no life there after the next few hours. She decided to talk to her unborn child for the first and last time.

"I'm sorry you weren't blessed with a better mother, little one. You deserve so much more than I can give you. I really do believe that all life is precious, including yours—*especially* yours. I know you shouldn't have to suffer for my sins and my bad decisions, but I don't know what else to do. I feel like such a failure and a disappointment to you and to God, who warned us not to arouse or awaken love until it so desires. I didn't listen. I risked everything for a man who turned out to be nothing like the partner I've been praying for or the kind of man I want to be your father, just so I could feel loved for a few moments.

"I'm scared, but you don't have to be. The Lord will watch over you, and you won't be alone. I'm sure your brother or sister will be there to watch over you as well. Maybe I'll get the chance to finish raising both of you when I get to heaven . . . if I get to heaven."

Angel lay back on the bed, unable to stop the tears from flowing. "Lord, forgive me," she prayed aloud. "I just don't know what else to do."

Although she was exhausted both physically and emotionally, Angel forced herself out of bed and finished preparing to undergo the abortion.

She lifted her eyes toward heaven. "God, I know I have no right to ask this, but let this procedure go smoothly. Guide the doctor's hand as he . . ."

She stopped mid-sentence. How could she ask God to guide the doctor's hand to execute a perfect baby killing? Angel scooped up her bag and keys but was startled by a knock at the door.

"What now?" she groaned, walking to the door. The last thing Angel needed at that moment was to deal with anyone selling cookies, magazines, or religion.

"What are you doing here?" asked Angel, more relieved than surprised to see Lawson and Sullivan at her front door.

Sullivan pulled Angel in for a hug. "Come on, did you really think we'd let you go through something like this alone?"

Angel bit her quivering lip. "To tell you the truth, yeah."

Lawson squeezed Angel's hand. "Angel, you know where I stand on abortion. I don't agree with what you're doing at all, but you're my girl and I love you. We stick together. That's what friends do."

"Thank you."

"If you get there and decide you want to run back home, we've got your back for that too," added Sullivan.

Angel hugged them both. "You're more like family to me than my real family."

"We're sisters," affirmed Lawson. "We just have different parents."

"All right, grab your stuff," commanded Sullivan. "We'll meet you in the car."

Sullivan and Lawson sat on each side of Angel at the clinic while they waited for Angel's name to be called. A melancholy chill hovered over them as Sullivan and Lawson attempted to calm Angel's anxiety.

Minutes and seconds seemed to crawl by. Angel rubbed her hands together. They were clammy, and she could feel her heart accelerating. Angel was barely cognizant of the women being summoned behind the white doors. The ones in the waiting area looked as dejected and pensive as she did.

"Being in here is really creeping me out," disclosed Sullivan, who looked rather uncomfortable. "I hate this place."

"I'm nervous," Angel admitted, her right knee bobbing up and down.

"That's normal," Sullivan assured her. "You'll be okay. Within the next couple of hours, you'll be back home in your own bed, and you can put all of this behind you."

Angel let out a deep breath. "I just want it to be over with, you know? Every second I'm out here is like torture. It's agonizing. I wish it was tomorrow already. I want this whole nightmare to be over."

"It will be very soon," said Sullivan.

"What if I hate myself for this in the morning?" Angel shook her head. "I still can't believe that I'm here, that it's really come down to this."

Lawson draped her around arm Angel. "It hasn't come down to anything yet. You still have a choice. You don't have to let those people kill your baby."

Sullivan huffed. "Lawson, you're not helping. You're only making her feel worse. Angel, don't listen to her. Heck, don't even listen to me! You've got to do what you feel in your heart is best for you. You're the one who has to live with the consequences of your decision, and there will be consequences whichever way you choose."

"What is Jordan saying about this?" questioned Lawson.

Angel was drenched in guilt. "He doesn't know that I'm here. I couldn't bring myself to tell him." Angel closed her eyes. "I can do this," she told herself. "I just need to get through the next few minutes."

"We'll be here for you when you come out, and we'll be here for you and the baby if you decide not to go in there at all," said Lawson.

"Thank you," said Angel. Angel's confidence began to falter. She turned to Sullivan for perspective. "Does it hurt, Sully?"

"I was knocked out, so I really don't know. But some women I know stayed awake during the procedure. They said it feels more like pressure than pain."

Angel's eyes fell downward. "Some people believe that the baby can feel it." She shook her head. "I don't want my baby to feel that. I told them I wanted to be put to sleep. I don't want to see it or hear some machine sucking the life out of me."

"Sweetie, why don't you take another day or two think about it?" suggested Lawson. "We can still leave. We can get up and go to the car right now if you want to."

"What difference will another day make? I'll still be totally unprepared to take care of this baby. The father of my child will still be a thief and an ex-con." Angel shook her head. "Another day would give this baby more time to develop and make what I have to do that much harder."

Sullivan squeezed Angel's hand. "We'll support whatever it is you want to do."

Angel turned to Sullivan. "How did you feel afterward?"

"I was fine, just some cramping and bleeding, but it goes away after a few days."

"No, I mean did you feel differently, like you'd literally had the life sucked out of you? Did you feel . . . empty?"

"Like a part of me was missing?"

"Yeah."

Sullivan thought back. "A little bit, but to be honest, I mostly felt relieved."

"Your situation was different from hers," Lawson pointed out. "You were just a kid."

"Do you ever regret going through with it?"

Sullivan sighed. "At the time, no, but having Charity has made me reflect on that decision. Sometimes I wonder how I could've done that to my baby, especially when I think about how much I love my daughter." Sullivan reached for Angel's hand. "But don't compare yourself to me or anyone else. You're the one who has to live with your decision, not me or Lawson or anybody else."

"But you *will* have to live with it," added Lawson. "Can you live with yourself if you decide to go through with this?"

Before Angel could answer, a nurse came into the lobby. "Angel King?"

Angel gulped. Sullivan hugged her. "It'll be fine."

"It's now or never," Lawson said. "Once you walk through that door, there's no turning back."

Angel forced her body out of the seat. She took a few steps forward, then looked back at her friends. Sullivan nodded her head toward the nurse. Lawson mouthed, "Don't do it."

Angel took a deep breath and ambled toward the nurse. Her heart bolted toward the exit. She didn't know whether or not her feet would follow.

Chapter 30

"I'm not going to try to OD, like I did after my divorce and miscarriage. I've lost my will to watch TV, not my will to live.."

—Angel King

Lawson draped a quilt around Angel's body and sat down next to her on the sofa. "Can I get you something? Tea or maybe a bite to eat?"

Angel drew her knees to her chest and rested her chin on them. She shook her head. "I'm not hungry, just tired."

"Are you in pain?"

Angel's eyes looked vacant. "I don't feel anything."

Lawson handed Angel the remote control, hoping to distract her. "Why don't you watch some TV? I'm sure there's a wonderfully horrible movie on that'll cheer you up a little." She offered a weak smile.

"Maybe later."

Sullivan rubbed Angel's back. "Are you sure you don't want us to stay?"

"No." Angel stretched out on the sofa. "I want to be alone. I need to sleep."

"Don't forget about the food we picked up on the way here. It's in the fridge when you get hungry. The doctor said there's no reason why you shouldn't eat."

Sullivan scooped up her purse. "Can we get you anything before we go?"

"Can you get me a bottle of water out the refrigerator? I'll need it to take my pills later."

Sullivan hesitated.

Angel knew what she was thinking. "Don't worry. I'm not going to try to OD, like I did after my divorce and miscarriage. I've lost my will to watch TV, not my will to live."

"I know. I just want you to promise that you'll call if you start feeling too sad."

"I'll be fine once I get some rest and a little time to myself." Angel turned her back to them, and Sullivan and Lawson tiptoed out.

"Do you think we should leave her by herself with a bottle full of painkillers?" whispered Lawson.

"I don't know. I don't think she's suicidal, but I didn't think she was the last time, either."

"This is such a disaster!" declared Lawson. "You know she should've kept that baby, Sullivan."

Sullivan dug into her purse for her car keys. "What I know is what's done is done. All we can do now is pray for Angel and keep an eye on her."

"We can't monitor her twenty-four-seven. What happens when she's alone and that guilt really kicks in, or when she starts missing her baby?"

"I can't answer that," said Sullivan. "I don't think any of us can."

Angel didn't want any visitors that afternoon, least of all the man whose baby she'd aborted, so she didn't hide her annoyance when Jordan dropped by unannounced. She let him in without speaking and resumed her spot on the sofa.

"I guess you're still mad at me," Jordan said, joining her on the sofa.

"Why do you say that?"

"You haven't said two words to me since I told you about the charges."

"You didn't *tell* me anything, Jordan. I found out and confronted you with it."

"Okay, well, you haven't said two words to me since I *admitted* to it. How about that?"

Angel turned her back to him and hunkered down beneath her blanket. "You should just go."

"Angel, I'm sorry. I don't know what else to say, but I want to make it up to you if I can. I want to make things right between us again."

"You can't make this right."

"Honestly, babe, I think you're overreacting."

Her eyes narrowed into slits. "What?"

"Yeah, I mean you're lying up here in the dark, moping and depressed. It's not even that serious."

"Jordan, you have no idea what's going on or what you're even talking about. The best thing you can do for both of us is just leave."

"Angel, I'm not leaving you like this, not until you tell me what's really got you so upset."

Her eyes began to water. "I said I don't want to talk about it. I don't want to talk to you. Leave me alone, okay?"

"I would if it was just about you, but you're carrying my baby in there. Whatever is going on with you affects our son or daughter, so I think I have a right to know what's up with you."

"Please stop talking about the baby," she whispered.

"Sweetheart, what's wrong?" Jordan made her face him. "Are you having complications with the pregnancy?"

"Not now." She paused. "I'm not pregnant anymore."

"What do you mean?"

She couldn't look him in the eyes. "The baby is gone."

"You, um . . ." Jordan's voice cracked. "You lost the baby?"

"Yes."

Jordan's face went pale. He looked as if he'd had the wind knocked out of him. "When? Why didn't you tell me?"

Angel bit her lip and remained silent.

He sighed heavily. "Baby, come here." He folded her into his arms. "I'm sorry this happened to you . . . to us."

Angel succumbed to the tears she'd been holding back. "I'm sorry too."

Jordan kissed her cheeks where tears had fallen. "Why didn't you call me? I would've come to the hospital or done something. I would've been there for you and our child."

"It's okay. There's really nothing you could've done."

Jordan pulled away from their embrace and reached for Angel's hand. "What did the doctor say? Do they know what caused you to miscarry?"

Angel's eyes fell downward. For a moment, she considered letting him believe she had had a miscarriage. It would certainly go over better than admitting that she had aborted his only child without telling him, but she felt like he deserved to know that truth, even if he might hate her for it later. "It wasn't a miscarriage, Jordan. I had an abortion."

The news pierced him, cutting to the core. "You did what?"

"Please don't make me say it again. It was hard enough the first time."

"Oh, I'm sorry. Am I making this hard for you?" he asked in an icy tone that almost frightened her.

"You have every right to be mad. I should've told you."

"Now you remember I have rights too—after the fact, of course! How could you do that without so much as telling me you were even thinking about it? It was my baby too." He backed away. "Or was it?"

"Of course it was your baby!" she asserted. "What kind of tramp do you think I am?"

"I don't know what to think of you right now, Angel. You killed my baby. You didn't even give me the courtesy of a phone call to let me know."

"Jordan, we are nowhere near ready to have a kid together. In your heart, you had to have known that."

"I didn't care about that! This was my first child, Angel. I wanted to be this child's father regardless of whether or not I was your man!"

"I'm sorry, Jordan. I really am. I don't know what else I can do or say. It's done now."

"You're right." He rose. "I ain't got nothing else to say to you, either."

"Jordan . . ." She reached for his arm, but he snatched it away from her.

He turned around. "No, I take that back. I do have something to say to you. You're cold, Angel. I know I've done my dirt, but I never killed anyone. I've never taken a man's child away from him. I know you're supposed to be a holy-rolling Christian, but you're one of the vilest human beings I've ever met. I hope you rot in hell for this!" Jordan stomped out, slamming the door behind him.

Angel had thought she couldn't possibly feel any worse than she did leaving the abortion clinic. Jordan McKay had proved her wrong.

Angel then remembered the prescription for hydrocodone she had filled on the way home. She read the bottle. "Take one tablet by mouth every four hours as needed for pain," she read aloud. Despite what the doctor had prescribed, Angel took four tablets, figuring she needed at least that many to cope with her pain.

Chapter 31

"You've been delivered. It's time you started acting like it!"

—*Kina Battle*

Kina, swathed in what could only be described as a burgundy choir robe, stood before a small crowd on that brisk November night, armed with "The Romans Road to Salvation" and hidden cell phone cameras.

"Okay, does everybody have their Bibles?" Kina asked the bevy of supporters gathered that night. They all nodded. A few shot their Bibles into the air for proof. "Good, good," said Kina, nodding. She turned to her camera crew. "Now, make sure you get the outside of the club first so everybody will know the name, and be sure to capture every moment on film. I've been promising the viewers something big all week, so I expect us to get a lot of hits on the Web site tonight, especially once word travels."

"We're ready to upload to all the major social net-working sites as soon as you give us the go-ahead," the cameraman replied.

"Great." Kina gave her face a quick glimpse in her compact. "All right, let's do this!"

Kina and her band of merry men and women began charging toward the entrance of Paramours. As they approached the entryway, everyone could hear the bass thumping and laughter emanating from the modest hideaway strip club. The unpaved parking lot was lined with everything from broken-down Hondas to Hummers.

They were stopped at the door by the club's bouncer, a mountain of a man, who brandished the gun and holster beneath his jacket. "Where do you think y'all are going?"

Kina was ushered to the front of the pack. "We're going inside. There's no law saying you can deny us entry. We come in peace."

"Around here, *I'm* the law, and I'm telling you to get outta here!"

"You come with guns and brass, but we come in the name of the Lord!" proclaimed Kina, paraphrasing David in his standoff with Goliath. Her followers cheered her on.

"Hey, y'all got to take this somewhere else," directed the bouncer.

"Or what?" Kina demanded, getting in his face. "Are you gonna hit me? Are you gonna shoot a woman?"

"I'm telling you," he warned her. "You better get out of my face and take all this foolishness back on across the road somewhere."

"We want to see the owner!" yelled Kina.

The bouncer crossed his beefy arms in front of him. "He ain't here."

"Well, we want to watch the strippers," Kina said, bargaining with him.

"Look, I'm giving you five . . ." The bouncer's attention was diverted by an altercation between two men in the parking lot. "Hey! Hey!" he called to them and brushed past Kina and her crew to intervene in the fight. Kina and her followers squeezed through the door and into the club.

When they stepped into the darkened club, they stumbled upon a topless dancer breezing freely throughout the establishment. Hordes of other naked and scantily clad women were posted up in various areas of the room, all vying for the attention and dollars of the club's patrons. Lap dances were in as great abundance as the large trays of food and alcohol. Kina wrinkled her nose at a man she recognized from church. He was seated with a dancer, who looked to be no older than age eighteen and straddled his lap. Food and bodies occupied almost every available space in the room. Loud bass music echoed throughout. Paramours appeared to be the working man's Xanadu.

"This is a disgrace," decreed Kina as she watched one girl lift a leg over her shoulders while gyrating for a group of men, much to their delight.

"What do you want us to do?" asked one of Kina's supporters. The music was so loud that they practically had to yell in order to hear each other.

"Start handing out Bibles and witness to those who'll receive the Word."

As the group began to disperse, an obviously intoxicated dancer strolled up to one of Kina's team members and kissed him on the cheek. "You want a dance?" she whispered in his ear and licked his lobe. The middle-aged man in his wrinkled suit was flustered.

"No," Kina countered and shoved a small Bible into the woman's hand. "What he wants, and what we all want, is for you to live up to your full potential. God formed you in His own image. He created you to be so much more than this. Sweetheart, when you get home and put on some clothes, I want you to read Ezekiel sixteen. 'Thus says the Lord God, because your lust was poured out and your nakedness uncovered in your whoring with your lovers, and with all your abominable idols, and because of the blood of your children that you gave to them . . . They shall strip you of your clothes and take your beautiful jewels and leave you naked and bare.' But there's another way. There's hope for you in the Lord."

The woman balked. "Who is you?"

"I'm just a servant of the Lord, sent here to show you a better life and a better way of doing things."

The woman seemed more spooked than redeemed. She let the Bible fall to the floor.

Kina shook her head and began scanning the room. Her eyes landed on a woman standing across the room, having a drink and laughing with two men. She was wearing a black halter top, high-heeled black boots, and a thong. It was Reginell. Kina didn't want to humiliate her cousin, but not even family could get in the way of soul saving . . . and ratings.

Kina signaled to her cameramen to go ahead of her. As she beelined toward Reginell, Kina waved her Bible in the air. "See, this is what I'm talking about!" cried Kina. "My own kinfolks trapped in Satan's lair! I demand you come out of this club right now, Reggie! You are the righteousness of God, and my Jesus did not die on that cross so you could throw it back in His face this way. You've been delivered. It's time you started acting like it!"

Reginell was filled with horror at the sight of Kina, knowing her ever-present camera could not be far behind.

"What are you doing?" screeched Reginell.

"I'm saving you from yourself, my sister. God has a bigger and better plan for your life than this. Pick up your cross and follow Him!" One of Kina's crew zoomed in on Reginell to capture her expression. "First Corinthians six, nine and ten. 'Do you not know that the wicked will not inherit the kingdom of God? Know ye not that the unrighteous shall not inherit the kingdom of God? Be not deceived: neither fornicators, nor idolaters, nor adulterers, nor effeminate, nor abusers of themselves with mankind, Nor thieves, nor covetous, nor drunkards, nor revilers, nor extortioners, shall inherit the kingdom of God.'"

"If you don't get that doggone camera out of my face!" Reginell threatened through clenched teeth.

"I'm trying to help you, sister." Kina outstretched her hands. "I'm trying to help all of you. You're lost, but God's grace is sufficient." Her street team began distributing small leather Bibles. "It's not too late to turn your life around. It's never too late. God is waiting for you with open arms. He never left you. You left Him. Now it's time to come on back home."

"Ain't that the chick from that reality show?" questioned one of the dancers.

"Yes." Kina faced the camera head-on. "I'm *Lose Big* winner Kina Justine Battle. Just like the Lord gave me victory over my hardships and circumstances, He can do the same for you."

Witnessing the commotion, Ray pounded his way to where they were. "What's going on in here?" he barked. "Is there a problem?"

"Yes, there is a problem," declared Kina. "This demonic playground is an abomination to the Lord! You're no better than a common pimp, selling off the souls of these women for a few measly bucks. You should be ashamed."

Ray beckoned his security team. "Hey, get these cameras, these Bibles, and this crazy broad up out of here!"

"Jesus is coming back! Your soul is condemned to hell if you don't do something about it!" Kina cried as she was being escorted out by a bouncer. "'So are the ways of every one that is greedy of gain; which taketh away the life of the owners thereof!' Proverbs one, nineteen!"

Ray responded with a string of expletives.

Kina wriggled out of the bouncer's grip and grabbed Reginell. "Reggie, you're coming with me! I can't save everybody else in here, but I'll be shot dead before I allow any cousin of mine to wallow in Satan's playpen."

Ray raised an eyebrow toward Reginell. "Oh, she's with you?"

"She's my cousin, but I didn't know she was going to do this."

"Go to hell and take your cousin with you!" ordered Ray.

Reginell was mortified and attempted to plead with him. "Ray—"

Ray pointed toward the door. "Both of y'all, go! I knew I should've never let you back in here, Reggie. You're more trouble that you're worth."

Reginell and Kina were very unceremoniously shoved out into the dark night along with the rest of Kina's party.

Reginell pounced on Kina the moment they were kicked off the premises. "What is wrong with you, Kina? What did you do that for?"

"I did this for you, Reggie, for your soul."

"That's some bull, Kina. You did this for you and that stupid reality show you're trying to pitch. How could you sell me out like that?"

"I was trying to help you by bringing you out of darkness and into the light."

"The only light you care about is the one attached to that camera!" Reginell accused. "You can't post this online, Kina."

"It's too late," Kina informed her. "It was a live stream."

"What if Mark sees this, Kina?"

"And that's my problem?" Kina replied, firing back. "You shouldn't have gone behind his back and kept this a secret from him, Reggie. What does the Bible say? Everything done in the dark will be brought to light!"

"You've got some secrets you don't want to come to light either, cuz. How would you like it if I started shedding some light on you?"

Kina exhaled. "I know you're upset now, but you're going to see that I did it for your own good. You're going to thank me one day. Eventually, you'll see that I did you a huge favor."

"I'll thank you when hell freezes over, Kina, and stop acting like you're trying to look out for me. We both know exactly why you did this." Reginell shook her head, as hurt as she was angry. "I can't believe you sold me out like that—your own cousin."

"You sold yourself the minute you started taking off your clothes for chump change. You were sold to the devil and to the world a long time ago."

With her entourage in tow, Kina sashayed off to her next scheduled event.

Reginell stood alone outside in the cold with nowhere to go. She couldn't go back inside Paramours. Ray probably wouldn't let her past security, and she couldn't face the other dancers. She couldn't go home. Mark might be waiting there, demanding an explanation or, worse, his engagement ring back. There was nothing to do but wait for her world to come crashing down around her once again. Only this time, she wasn't going down alone. Reginell was determined to bring Kina Battle down with her.

Chapter 32

"I've wanted to be a mother for as long as I can re-member, but not like that, and to be honest, not with him."

—*Angel King*

Du'Corey "Duke" King hugged Angel, happy that in spite of their complex and often painful relationship history, they were still able to be friends, and that she was still active in his daughters' lives. "Thanks for coming over to spend time with the girls. They love it when you come over for dinner like this."

"It's Miley's birthday. I wouldn't have missed it for all the tea in England . . . or is it China?" she joked. "Of course, it appears that my presence can't compete with a shiny new American Girl doll. They haven't come back downstairs since opening it after dinner."

He smiled. "Not even my presence can compete with that, but Morgan and Miley really do miss you."

Angel picked a doll up from the floor. "I miss them too."

"They're not the only ones who miss you," Duke revealed.

"I don't want Miss Morgan to feel left out since I bought out the whole store for Miley's birthday. Do you mind if I pick her up from school one day next week? I want to take her to that yogurt bar she loves so much."

"That would be great. Call me and we can set it all up."

Angel smiled a little. "Dinner was fantastic, by the way. You've gotten much better in the kitchen, I see."

"I didn't have much of a choice! After you left, I had to do something. A kid can only live on a Happy Meal diet for so long."

Angel held the doll a moment before setting it on the coffee table. "Duke, do you ever think about the baby we lost?"

"Yeah. I don't think it's the kind of thing you *cannot* think about. But I'm thankful for Miley and Morgan, and I try to focus on the two children I have who are alive."

Angel nodded. "You're blessed to have such beautiful, amazing little girls."

"You'll have kids of your own one day, Angel," he reassured her.

Angel shook her head. "I don't think God is going to bless me that way, not again."

"Just because it hasn't happened yet doesn't mean it's not going to happen."

She looked up at him. "Do you think that I'm cursed or that I bring bad luck on myself?"

"What?" He chuckled. "No, I don't think you're cursed. Besides, the Bible says, 'The curse causeless shall not come.'"

"What if I've done something to cause it?"

"What do you mean?"

Angel sat down. "Duke, I did something so terrible. I don't know if I'll ever . . ." Her words trailed off.

"What did you do?"

"I had an abortion," she said, confiding in him. "I killed my baby."

Duke was taken aback. "When?"

"A few weeks ago."

"I'm sorry to hear that." He hesitated. "I didn't realize you were dating anyone."

"What you mean to say is that you didn't realize I was sleeping with anyone, right?"

"Yeah, that too," he admitted. "So what happened? Why didn't you keep the baby?"

"My life was falling apart," revealed Angel. "My business was suffering, and I didn't have any money. The guy and I hadn't even been dating that long. Then I found out that he'd done time and had these charges he didn't tell me about. It was one thing after another. I felt trapped. I did what I thought made the most sense."

"I'm speechless, Angel. I had no idea you've been going through anything this heavy. Why didn't you come to me for help?"

"Duke, I'm not your problem or your responsibility anymore."

"You're not a problem, and I'll always feel some sense of responsibility for you. You were my wife, and you're my friend. Don't ever hesitate to call me for anything you need. I don't care if it's money or advice or a ride to pick up some chicken. You call me, you hear?"

"I hear you." She was grateful for the support. "At the time, I couldn't think about anybody but myself, which is part of the problem. What I did was so selfish. I only thought about me and what I wanted and what I had going on in my life. I never stopped to think about anyone else."

"Do you mean the baby's father?"

"Yes."

"How did the guy feel about you being pregnant?"

"He was ecstatic. Meanwhile, I was downright depressed. I had so many mixed feelings about the baby.

I've wanted to be a mother for as long as I can remember, but not like that, and to be honest, not with him." She and Duke locked eyes. "It probably sounds stupid, but you're the only man I've ever envisioned myself having a child with."

He laughed a bit. "Yeah, I always thought we'd have that cottage on the beach with the houseful of kids that we used to talk about." His mood became pensive. "I suppose some fantasies are meant to remain just that."

"It sure looks that way. Nothing in my life has turned out the way I planned it."

"Join the club. Do you think I planned to be raising two daughters as a single parent? If things had gone according to plan, we would've celebrated our first anniversary a few months ago."

"Yes, we would've," Angel replied, remembering.

"My grandmother used to say that we make our plans and God laughs at them. Sometimes, you gotta roll with the punches, kid, and have faith that it'll all work out in the end."

"I wish I could do that."

"Angel, between the two of us, my screw-ups make yours look tame. Life isn't about rehashing everything we've done wrong, and I don't believe God wants you to keep feeling guilty about what happened. The key is to learn from it and move on."

"What's the point in learning from it when I can't do anything about it? I can't undo the abortion or sleeping with Jordan. I can't undo the pain I've caused him. There's absolutely nothing I can do to make this situation right. That's the part that's eating me up inside."

"Then if you can't make it right, all you can do is ask God to forgive you and go on with your life."

Angel exhaled. "I would if I had the first clue about how to do that."

Chapter 33

*"If I'm so great, why did my husband go out and
sleep with someone else, huh?"*
—*Lawson Kerry Banks*

"I thought I'd find you here," Lawson said to Mark,
joining him on the bleachers on their school's vacated
football field after school had let out. "How are you doing?"

"You don't really want me to answer that, do you?"

Lawson winced. "That bad, huh?"

"Nothing can spoil a day quite like finding out the
woman you love has been showing the goods to any
man with a few dollars to spend on a lap dance. Adding
insult to injury is having your mother tell you that it's
posted on the Internet." He blew out a breath. "Suffice
it to say I've had better days."

"Have you talked to Reggie?"

"She's avoiding me. She did send a text to say she
knows she screwed up, but that's it."

"Mark, I don't know what to say. I won't pretend to
know how you must be feeling right now, but I do know
that Reggie loves you. She just doesn't think sometimes."

"It's obvious she wasn't thinking about me or our
relationship. Did you know she'd started back stripping?"

"You know my sister doesn't volunteer to give me any info about her personal life. I usually have to drag it out of her. I didn't know for sure if she'd started back at the club, but I knew something was up."

"You could've told me."

"Mark, if there's one thing we don't do in our group, it's blabbing about each other's business to other people. Whatever happens in the sister circle stays there, at least it did before Kina and her film crew intervened."

"I admire your loyalty. I wish some of that would rub off on your sister."

She placed her hand on top of his. "You have to remember that Reggie is still young. She just turned twenty-five. She's going to make mistakes."

"Lawson, a mistake is dialing the wrong number. My fiancée was living a whole other life that I was clueless about."

"Would it help if I told you she was doing it for you? The last thing Reggie wants to be to you is a financial burden. I think she would've done whatever it took to be an equal contributor to this wedding and in your life together."

"I never asked her do that. Equal and fair are not the same thing. I have a pretty good idea how much waitresses make. I didn't expect her to be able to contribute the same amount that I do. It hurts that she didn't trust me to take care of us."

"No, she didn't trust God to take care of her and let Him, in turn, take care of the two of you."

Mark nodded. "Yeah, you're right. Why does she do things like this, Lawson? Doesn't she know how disrespectful it is to me as her man?"

Lawson sighed. "My sister is a lot like a student name Terrance who I have in my first-period class. Terrance has had a rough life, been in and out of foster care since he was a baby. Many of the places he lived in were abusive, and he was never really nurtured as a child. All he knows about the world is that it beats him up. Knowing this, I always go out of my way to make a big deal about it if he does well on a test or shows kindness to someone else. Whenever that happens, it never fails that the very next day Terrance will do something totally disapproving, like cut class or cuss one of the students out or start a fight or do anything that will land him back in trouble. He doesn't know what to do with himself when someone shows him any love or appreciation. It doesn't make sense to him, because he's not used to it. Degradation, punishment—that's what makes sense, because that's all he knows.

"I think Reggie is like that. She's not used to being loved and accepted for who she is. She doesn't feel like she's good enough for you, so she acts out. I don't think she even realizes why she does it."

"Is this how I'm supposed to spend my life? Waiting for her to act out and self-destruct?"

"Only you can answer that."

Mark dropped his head. "Sometimes, I wish . . ."

"Wish what?"

He looked up at Lawson. "Sometimes, I wish Reggie was more like you."

Lawson laughed. "No, you don't! Trust me."

"I'm serious. You're principled, and you stand up for what's right. You're committed and loyal. You're comfortable in your own skin. I admire that."

Lawson's disposition shifted. "If I'm so great, why did my husband go out and sleep with someone else, huh?"

"That's because Garrett is a fool!" opined Mark. "He didn't realize or appreciate what he had at home."

"I guess the same could be said of my sister."

"Don't let what your husband did make you second-guess who you are for one second. I think you're amazing, Lawson. I always have. I couldn't have asked for a better role model and mother for my son."

Lawson was flattered. "Wow . . . Thank you."

"I mean it." He turned her face toward his. "You're something special."

It could've been the fact that they were both hurting or that there had always been chemistry lying dormant between them. Whatever the case, at that moment, Lawson and Mark were drawn to each other, and it culminated when. Mark leaned in, gently placing his lips on hers. Lawson briefly closed her eyes and kissed him back.

Lawson wiped her lipstick off his lips with her thumb. "I bet you've wanted to do that again for seventeen years," she joked.

He chuckled. "Seventeen years ago we did that and a whole lot more, La-la! That's how Namon got here."

Lawson reached for his hand. "We make a great parenting team, don't we?"

"Good coworkers too. Don't forget that."

"And we're friends," she added. "I really value our friendship, Mark."

"So do I."

She released his hand. "So that's why . . ."

Mark nodded. "Yeah, I know. We don't need to cross that line ever again."

Lawson concurred. "It would be a catastrophe. Plus, I know your heart is with my sister. Any fool can see that."

"And any fool can see how much you love your husband."

Lawson sighed and rested her head on his shoulder. "Mark, what are we going to do about them?"

"Your guess is as good as mine, but you're right about one thing. I do love her, Lawson."

Lawson sat up. "Then tell her, and do it quick, before she starts acting out again!"

"I'll do my best, but you know your sister has a mind of her own."

"Be patient with her, Mark. Reggie really is a good girl."

"I know she is."

"All right, you've sulked long enough." She yanked him up. "It's time to get your woman back!"

Mark dusted off his pants. "Reggie is a great woman, and so are you." He kissed her on the brow. "I don't want you to forget that."

Lawson smiled. It was nice to be reminded of that, even if it was from her sister's fiancé. Her smile faded, however, when she realized how quickly a person could give in to temptation. If she, with all her high moral standing, could succumb to kissing her sister's fiancé, how much quicker could Garrett be seduced by the woman who bore his child?

Chapter 34

"I'm not going to apologize for being blessed."
—*Kina Battle*

"This was certainly sweet of you," Angel complimented, sitting down to the Sunday dinner that Lawson had prepared for her, Kina, Sullivan, and Reginell.

"It's a little more than a dinner, Angel," Lawson revealed, setting a pitcher of tea down on the table. "It's an intervention."

"For who?" Sullivan asked, helping herself to the garden salad.

"For Kina. I'm starting to get worried about her."

"I'm not. If I know one thing for sure, it's that money brings out what's really in the heart of a person," attested Sullivan. "This behavior has always been inside of Kina. She was just waiting for the opportunity to bring it out."

Angel agreed. "I was a little concerned about the way she was spending money and hauling those cameras around everywhere, but what she did to Reggie, exposing her like that, was taking it too far."

Lawson prayed aloud over the food before fixing her plate.

Angel panned the room. "Where is Reggie, anyway?"

"She didn't want to come. I hope she's with Mark, and they're sorting through this mess," Lawson said.

Sullivan raised her eyebrow. "Is that what you really hope?"

Lawson had a flashback to her and Mark's kiss but refused to indulge in the thought. "Obviously, I want my sister to be with the man she loves. I also want my son's father to be happy. He and Reggie belong together."

"Keep telling yourself that," muttered Sullivan.

Kina breezed into the house, unannounced, with her filming entourage in tow. "The door was unlocked, so I let myself in." Kina took time to go around the table to hug and kiss everyone before taking a seat. "I'm here. The party can start now!" Kina pulled out a bag from a take-out restaurant. "I hope you don't mind, but I brought my own dinner. I had a craving for sushi."

Lawson noticed that she was under the cameraman's ever-present and watchful eye. "Can you turn that thing off for a minute? This is kind of private."

"He's supposed to be capturing my life as it happens, Lawson. That also includes moments like this."

Sullivan spoke loudly into the camera lens. "Okay, Kina, tell us about the thug you've been running around town with. Would you like to have that discussion in front of the camera as well?"

Kina's olive skin reddened. "Can you give us a minute, Chris?" He shut off the camera. "Was all that necessary, Sullivan?" hissed Kina.

"Yes," replied Lawson. "Threats seem to be the only way we can get through to you without there being a camera involved. Kina, I hope that you receive what I'm about to say in the spirit of love that's intended. Remember the Word says, 'He is in the way of life that keepeth instruction: but he that refuseth reproof erreth.'"

"Meaning?" demanded Kina.

Lawson responded, "Namon found some pictures of you online today."

Kina raked the contents of her take-out box onto one of Lawson's plates. "If this is about me hanging out with Cut 'Em Cali the other night, I can explain that. We happened to be at the same function, and there were people taking pictures. There's nothing more to it than that."

"You being splashed all over the blogs, posing with some misogynist rapper, is only part of it," replied Lawson.

Kina beamed, proud to have been featured. "Great photo op, wasn't it? Everybody's talking about it. I've had people calling up, asking if we're a couple."

Angel shook her head. "Why would you be posing it up with a documented wife beater, of all people? Especially after everything you went through with E'Bell."

"It was just a picture, Angel, but you've got to admit posing with him has caused a nice little buzz."

"Yes, but for all the wrong reasons," Lawson pointed out. "People are starting to talk, Kina, and not all of it is good."

"The only bad press is no press, Lawson."

Lawson frowned. "So you care only about your name being in the news cycle for another fifteen minutes?"

"Don't be so dramatic, cuzzo. It's not like I'm trying to marry the guy, but that one picture got me two radio interviews, a mention on Celebonies.com, and another five hundred hits on my Web site."

"Hits . . . now that's something both you and Cut 'Em Cali have in common," Sullivan noted.

"See? That's what I'm talking about! One minute it's all about Jesus. The next it's, 'Oh, I got a million hits on my Web site today!'" Lawson backed away from the table and stood up. "If I can paraphrase Paul in Corinthians, I don't say these things to make you ashamed, but to admonish you as my beloved sister. I'm not coming to you with a rod but with love in a spirit of gentleness."

Kina squinted her eyes, confused. "What are you talking about, Lawson?"

Lawson sat down. "We, or at least *I*, think you're letting fame go to your head."

"I know I've changed on the outside, but inside I'm still your favorite cousin. I just know who I am now, and I finally took hold of all that confidence you all have been trying to get me to latch on to for years."

"It's not that, Kina. You've been making some questionable decisions recently," Angel divulged.

"What's wrong with me wanting to be successful? Kina Battle isn't just a person anymore. I'm also a brand."

"I had a different *b* word in mind," grumbled Sullivan.

Angel attempted to reason with her friend. "We don't want to see you go down a dangerous path, Kina, that's all."

"What?" asked Kina, wide-eyed and innocent.

"Was putting Reggie on blast like that really called for?" charged Lawson.

"So my crime is trying to show a bunch of lost women, your sister included, another way of living and telling them about the goodness of God's grace and love? You should be applauding me for putting forth the effort."

"And I would if I felt like you had pure motives," explained Lawson. "But you did it primarily for ratings."

"Says who?" scoffed Kina.

Sullivan rolled her eyes. "Kina, when is the last time you *didn't* do something for ratings? You're no different from those dirty politicians who were following me and Vaughn around and posting pictures online to ruin Charles's campaign."

Kina sighed. "I think I see what's going on here. People warned me this would happen."

Lawson breathed a sigh of relief. "Thank God! I'm glad you have people around you who don't mind letting you know when things are getting out of hand."

"No, what I was warned about are friends who might become jealous and start to resent my success."

"Huh?" Sullivan furrowed her brow.

"Look, I know it's hard for you to see me in a position of power, especially since you all saw me being E'Bell's doormat for so long. It's not hard to understand how suddenly seeing me with fame and money can inspire envy."

Lawson shook her head. "That's not what's going on here."

Kina patted Lawson's hand. "Lawson, it's okay. I realize that your life kind of sucks right now, and it's not easy to see someone else be happy."

Angel voiced her opinion. "Kina, we're all very happy for you and all the success you've had. We've always been your biggest supporters. We just think you're losing sight of what's important."

"How can you say that when everything I do is done to glorify the Lord and expose the world to His goodness? What's wrong with that?"

"Nothing," replied Angel. "Like Lawson said, no one is questioning the message, just the motive."

"Be honest, Kina. Not everything you've done has been in the name of spreading the gospel," Lawson asserted.

"I'm not going to apologize for being blessed, for having a great life, or for having nice things," Kina responded. "God's favor ain't fair."

"No one is asking you to apologize. There's nothing wrong with you having nice things, but there's definitely something wrong with nice things having *you!* You've turned into a person we hardly recognize anymore," said Lawson

Sullivan set her fork down. "This is a waste of time. This woman's head is stuck too far up her who-ha for her to listen to anybody who's not willing to do her bidding."

"I think I've lost my appetite." Kina gathered her things. "I never thought I'd see the day that my own kinfolks and the people who call themselves my friends would be too envious to be happy for me." Kina stormed out, with Chris trailing her with his camera.

"Good riddance!" Sullivan muttered.

"Ladies, maybe we shouldn't be too hard on Kina," said Angel. "If someone put enough money in our faces, we'd probably act the same way. No person can know for sure how they'd behave in any given situation. We could all find ourselves doing things we swore we weren't capable of doing."

"Are we still talking about Kina here?" Sullivan asked.

Angel didn't reply.

Sullivan went on. "Angel, please don't start drawing comparisons between your abortion and Kina's diva antics, because there are none!"

Angel frowned. "Aren't there? We both were too caught up in ourselves to worry about how our actions might affect someone else."

"Angel, you've got to cut yourself some slack," Lawson advised her. "I know I was completely against you having an abortion, but it's done. It's time that you forgave yourself."

"That's easy for you to say. You weren't the one who killed your own child."

"No, but I was the one who lied to my husband about wanting one, and it almost cost me my marriage. I had to get over it, though. I asked for God's forgiveness, and then I forgave myself. Colossians one, thirteen and fourteen says, 'Who hath delivered us from the power of darkness, and hath translated us into the kingdom of his dear Son: In whom we have redemption through his blood, even the forgiveness of sins.'"

"Try telling Jordan that. He thinks I'm a monster. He won't even talk to me now."

"To that I say, 'Hallelujah and kick rocks!'" proclaimed Sullivan. "Jordan is a jerk. Don't squander another single, solitary thought on him."

"He really wanted his baby."

Sullivan chortled. "I'm sure the people he stole from *really wanted* their money. You *really wanted* a man who wasn't a fraud and a criminal. People don't always get what they want."

Angel checked the time. "I need to get out of here if I don't want to be late for work."

"Are you going back to work? You just got off," asked Lawson.

"And now I'm going back," snapped Angel.

Lawson shook her head. "So you punish yourself for sleeping with Jordan by having an abortion, and then you punish yourself again for actually having the abortion by working yourself to death."

"Working is the only time I don't have to think about what I've done. Nothing happens by accident. God had a plan and a purpose for that child. Who knows what his or her future held?"

"Honey, don't you think God knew this was going to happen long before you did?" quizzed Lawson. "He's the author and finisher, the beginning and the end. Your pregnancy was a surprise to you, not Him. Neither was your abortion."

"You can't let this guilt eat you alive," urged Sullivan. "It happened. There's nothing you can do about it except move on and try not to let it happen again."

"It doesn't seem right to just go on like nothing happened."

Sullivan was stumped. "Why not?"

"This guilt is with me all the time. If I laugh or see something interesting or have a good feeling, I remember that my baby will never get to experience that, and it's because of me and my selfish decision."

Sullivan shook her head. "Let me tell you something, Angel. I had an abortion. Heck, I had two, but I go on with my life every day the same as every other woman. I'm not saying it's right by any means, but I don't think that God has condemned me to spend my life in my own personal hell, worrying about it. Do you honestly think that walking around here, looking pitiful, working yourself to death, carrying all this guilt is going to sway the Lord one way or the other? If anything, you carrying on like this is an insult to Him."

"How so?"

"It's an insult to the blood His son shed for our sins. When Jesus was nailed to that cross and said, 'It is finished,' that's what He meant! Condemnation, conviction, guilt—they were all finished. He died for all past, present, and future sins. Your acting like this is tantamount to saying Jesus's blood wasn't strong or good enough to cleanse your sins. Think about everything He endured on that cross—the nails, the degradation, the thorns, the stripes, having God turn away from Him. Are you saying that all of that wasn't enough to cover you having an abortion?"

Lawson's eyes bulged. "Wow . . . When did you go and get so smart, Sully? That almost sounded like preaching!"

Sullivan smiled bashfully. "I read my Bible and listen to my husband every once in a while."

Angel still wasn't convinced. "I've got to go. Thank you for dinner, Lawson."

Sullivan hugged her. "Think about what I said."

Angel nodded and walked out.

"Once again, I've managed to clear a room," Lawson concluded, looking around at the empty seats.

"I'm still here."

"Yes, you are." Lawson smiled. "So what's going on with you and your father?"

Sullivan sighed. "I don't know. Vera told me something very disturbing about him, but I have to consider the source before I take it seriously."

"What did she say?"

"She claims that my father tried to kill her and that he actually did kill their unborn child."

"Really? Why would he do that, or why does she think he did that?"

"She said he did it to keep the truth about their relationship from coming out, but, Lawson, the man she describes isn't the man I've gotten to know."

"Then again, how well do you know him? Vera was booed up with the man for several years, so she probably knows him better than anybody. Your mother is a lot of things, but I've never known her to be a liar."

"I've known her to be vindictive and evil," said Sullivan.

"True, but that's not the same thing as being a liar."

Chapter 35

"You've got to trust me. I have everything under control."

—Kina Battle

Lawson knocked on the door to Kina's hotel room. She had decided that the fighting and discord had gone on long enough, and that the two of them would have to put an end to it one way or another.

Kina opened the door and blurted out, "I'm sorry for the other day. Please forgive me."

"I'm sorry too." They broke into laughter at the same time.

"Girl, come on in," Kina said, allowing her to enter. "You can help me finalize plans for my grand opening."

"Are you excited?"

"I am. My publicist sent out a press release about it a couple days ago, so I've been fielding calls all week from people who want to support the store. A lot of churches are planning to come. News outlets are going to be there. The crowd for the ribbon-cutting ceremony will be massive," Kina commented, making assumptions. "You're going to be there, right?"

"You know I will, Kina. We're family. I don't want you to think we're not proud of you or don't support you. We just don't want to see you get in over your head."

"And I love you for it, but you've got to trust me. I have everything under control." Kina's cell phone rang.

"This is my PR team. Probably more requests for the grand opening."

Before Kina could say hello, her publicist, Christa, began to rant. "Kina, what in the world is going on? Who is this Joan person?"

The color washed from Kina's face. Kina clutched the phone, flustered. "Why? What have you heard?" If her publicist had gotten word about her ex-girlfriend Joan, nothing good could follow.

"Kina, what's wrong?" whispered Lawson. Kina shooed her away.

"This Joan person is conducting an exclusive tell-all interview as we speak, and she's claiming that the two of you were lovers. It's going viral. I'm sending you the link."

"Why would she do that?" asked Kina, more to herself than to Christa.

"Is it true? Were you involved with this woman?" Christa demanded to know.

"It . . . it wasn't even that long or that serious," Kina stammered. "It happened right after my husband died. I was lonely and confused."

"That's great. This is a public relations nightmare, Kina! Your Christian fan base is going to be livid," Christa remarked, predicting the outcome. "I've got to start working on an official statement for you. In the meantime, don't answer the phone, don't respond to any e-mail, and for Christ's sake, don't post anything online until I tell you to!" Christa hung up.

Kina turned to Lawson, rattled. "Joan did an interview. She told everyone about us." Kina gathered her thoughts. "Hand me my laptop."

Lawson grabbed it from the table and passed it to her. Kina's hands trembled uncontrollably as she tried to type.

Lawson took the laptop from her. "Kina, you're shaking. Let me do it. What are you looking for?"

"I need to find this interview. Do a search for Kina and Joan." Lawson began pecking at the keyboard. Kina stopped her. "No, wait. Christa said she was sending me a link. I need to pull up my e-mail account."

Kina accessed her e-mail and followed the link to the interview. There, on the monitor, was her jilted ex-lover, Joan Dunlap, sitting across from a popular celebrity reporter.

"Hello, my name is Keydra Parks and welcome to Celebonies.com. My guest sitting here today is Joan Dunlap from Savannah, Georgia. We all cheered along with *Lose Big* contestant Kina Battle as she inched her way to victory to become this season's winner. She especially received support from the Christian community, and she became as famous for her relationship with Christ as she did for her phenomenal weight loss. Lately, there have been different reports about Kina living a secret, not so Christian life once the cameras are off. My guest today is here to shed some light on who Kina Battle really is." The reporter turned to Joan. "Welcome and thank you for coming on the show."

Joan smiled. "Thank you for inviting me."

"Joan, we all know Kina Battle as the winner of *Lose Big,* but you knew her before the fame. What can you tell us about Kina?"

"First off, let me say that Kina is a beautiful spirit. I care about her very deeply, and I'd never do anything to intentionally hurt her. However, when I heard some comments she recently made about the LGBT community, I felt like I had to say something."

"Now, Joan, you're a lesbian. Is that correct?"

"Yes."

"And you've been open about your sexuality for a while, right?"

"Yes, I came out in college. Everyone who knows me knows that I'm a lesbian. I'm not ashamed, and I don't try to hide it."

"When did you meet Kina Battle?"

Joan shifted in her seat. "We met at the gym a couple of years ago. We had an instant connection. It was kismet."

"Was Kina aware of your sexuality?"

Joan nodded. "I told her I was gay the day we met."

"What was her reaction to that?"

"She was fine with it. She had a lot of questions, like when did I know I was gay and how did I think God felt about that, but overall, she was very accepting of my lifestyle."

"Joan, tell us . . . what was the extent of your relationship with Kina?"

"Kina and I were a couple," confessed Joan. "We were falling in love, at least I was."

"So this was a real, bona fide relationship?"

"Yes. We were dating. We spent time together, we went on dates, and we talked about the future. I've kissed her. I've held her. We know intimate things about one another. It was a relationship."

"What happened? Why did it end?"

Joan shrugged her shoulders. "I'm not sure. She said something about not wanting to have to explain our relationship to her son and feeling like God's plan was for her to be with a man. But I have no doubt that she cared about me, and if Kina had *her* way—as opposed to the church's way—we'd still be together."

"Is Kina a lesbian, Joan?"

"Only Kina can answer that. All I can tell you is that I am, and that Kina was my girlfriend."

"Have you talked to her since the breakup?"

Joan shook her head. "No, Kina cut me out of her life. I don't know if it's because she wanted to or because she felt she had to, but I've respected her decision and kept my distance."

"Do you miss her?"

"Yes. I'm still in love with her."

Keydra looked at Joan with empathy. "What would you want to say to Kina if she's listening right now?"

Joan faced the camera. "Kina, I want you to know that I know you, and this person that I see on TV is not the real you. You know that what we shared was real. It may not have been conventional, but you and I were happy. I don't understand why you want to deny it now. It's a part of your story. It's a part of who you are. When we were together, you were finally living on your own terms and being your own woman. Now you're just some media puppet. I miss that woman who I used to hold late at night and share coffee with. She's lost. I need you to find her again."

"Well, you heard it here first on Celebonies.com," Keydra Parks said, wrapping up. "Thank you for your time and your candor, Joan. To find out more about Joan and her passionate affair with Christian reality star Kina Battle, go to our Web site and follow us on social media. This story is only going to get bigger, folks, and we will keep digging until we find out all there is to know about your favorite carnal Christian, Kina Battle. If there are any other friends, foes, or lovers who want to call in or come by to set the record straight, no pun intended, about Kina, hit us up on our Web site. Of course, we'll be on-site for the grand opening of Ki-Ki's Tees. We'll be there, but will anyone else? Log on to Celebonies.com to find out!"

Lawson and Kina were both numbed into silence.

Lawson spoke first. "I don't know why Joan would go and do something like that," she raged. "I thought she was your friend."

Kina exhaled. "Who knows? It wasn't exactly an amicable split. I suppose I'd be a little salty too if the person I loved was ashamed of our relationship. I never thought she'd take it this far, though."

"Do you think that's why Joan did it? You think she wanted revenge?"

"I never saw her as the vengeful type, but I guess people are capable of anything when properly motivated."

"Okay, granted, it looks bad, Kina, but who really looks at the celebrity blogs, anyway?"

"My fans, for one. That interview makes me look like a total fraud!"

"You don't have to let the media define you. Take control of this story and tell your side of it."

"My publicist has issued a gag order. She doesn't want me to say anything to the press." Kina buried her face in her hands. "Oh, God, Lawson, what am I going to do?"

"You're going to do what Isaiah seven, four, tells us to do. 'Take heed, and be quiet; fear not.'" Lawson took her hand. "This too shall pass."

"That's great in theory, Lawson, but what am I going to do if another person decides to jump on the 'kill Kina's career' bandwagon?"

"Then you do something you probably haven't done in a while, Kina. You need to let go and let God."

Chapter 36

*"This ain't nothing compared to the real story behind
Kina Justine Battle."*
—Reginell Kerry

"Okay, Lawson, what's the big reveal?" asked Sullivan once Lawson let her into the house. "Make it quick, because I have a facial in an hour."

"I'm as much in the dark as you are," confessed Lawson. They were joined by Kina and Angel.

Sullivan sat down. "I got a text from Reggie saying there was some kind of emergency and to be here by four forty-five."

"We all got the same text from Reggie," said Angel.

Sullivan looked around the living room. "So where is she?"

"I don't know." Lawson looked down at her watch. "I thought she'd be here by now."

"Do you think this has anything to do with her and Mark?" asked Kina.

Lawson shook her head. "I have no idea."

Sullivan stood up. "This is obviously some kind of hoax. Lawson, your sister has way too much time on her hands. You might want to encourage her to find a hobby."

At that moment, all of their phones began vibrating or ringing.

Angel looked down at her phone. "It's another text from Reggie. She wants us to go to some Web site."

Lawson wrinkled her brow. "Isn't this the same Web site that Joan was on, Kina?"

"Oh, no," groaned Kina. "Who has a tell-all interview about me this time?"

"I guess we have to log on to find out," Angel concluded.

They logged on to the Web site. Keydra Parks was in the middle of promising another salacious interview with someone else in Kina's inner circle. The ladies watched with a mixture of shock and revulsion as Reginell appeared on the monitor, sitting on the sofa in the living room in her apartment.

"What the heezy!" exclaimed Angel.

"Oh, my God," cried Kina. "Lawson, call her. You've got to stop her!"

"Don't worry, Kina. I'm calling her now!" Lawson frantically dialed Reginell's number. "Shoot! It's going straight to voice mail."

"Ladies and gentlemen," began Keydra, "we're continuing to follow this story about *Lose Big* winner Kina Battle as new details about the reality star's private life emerge. She presented herself to the nation as the all-American Christian girl. Our hearts went out to her as we learned about her struggles as a single parent and a former teen mom who finally found her voice and inner strength after surviving an abusive marriage. Conversely, the more we get to know Kina, the more we realize there is a lot more to her story than what she's shared with the world. Today as our guest, joining us by Skype, we have dancer—"

"Singer, songwriter," Reginell interrupted.

"I stand corrected," said the interviewer. "Exotic dancer turned singer and songwriter Reginell Kerry. Miss Kerry, how are you?"

"I'm great. Very excited to be talking with you to-day!"

"Miss Kerry, you were one of the dancers at the club that Kina Battle bombarded a few nights ago, right?"

"Yes, I was there."

"And you're the cousin of reality star Kina Battle, correct?"

"Yes, first cousins. We practically grew up in the same house."

The camera panned to an enlarged picture of Reginell and Lawson playing together as children.

"So I guess it's safe to say you know Kina very well."

"Oh, yes, definitely."

"Take us back to the night at the club." Keydra showed a clip taken from Kina's Web site of the raid at Paramours. "What was going through your head when you saw Kina come in with her army and video cameras?"

"Well, first I thought it was wrong, because a lot of the women in the club don't want their business out there like that. A lot of them have other jobs or kids at home and don't need to be exposed like that. Some of the men in there have wives or professional jobs too. They come to the club to relax and chill out for a minute, not to have a bunch of crazy, Bible pushers all in their face."

"Your cousin said her only mission was to lead people to Christ. Is there anything wrong with that?"

"It's all in the way you do it. She didn't have to come bust in there like that. Just because somebody's in the strip club, that doesn't mean they're not saved or that they don't love the Lord. Everybody ain't on the same level with that, so I don't think she has the right to judge them."

"You've come here with some very strong allegations against your cousin. Tell us what's going on."

"Basically, I just want everyone to know that Kina isn't as sweet and innocent as she wants everyone to think she is. I love her and everything, but it's time for the truth to come out."

"Can you elaborate?"

"Yes, I can," asserted Reginell. "Ever since she won that reality show, she's been acting brand new, but we all know the truth, Kina!"

"Are you saying that fame has gone to her head a little bit?"

Reginell was riled up. "*A little?* Listen, the Kina who came back here is not the Kina who left! I ain't hatin' on her. We're all glad she won and got her body tight and right, but she's changed. Kina doesn't care about anything except getting her shine on. She doesn't care who she hurts in the process."

"My producers tell me that you've brought some pictures with you."

"Yes, I have." Reginell turned to the enlarged screen projection. Pictures of Kina smoking in the Bahamas flashed on the screen.

Kina groaned and dropped her head. "Why didn't she delete those pictures?"

"Why did you let her take them?" asked Lawson.

"Yeah, America," Reginell declared, "that's your holier-than-thou weight-loss princess right there with a blunt in her hands."

Keydra feigned outrage. "Is that marijuana?"

"She ain't sucking on a Tootsie Roll like that."

"Wow . . . I'm speechless. When were these taken?"

"A couple of weeks ago down in the Bahamas. You can't really tell in the picture, but she has a drink in her other hand. You know, she's been going around telling people she don't contaminate her body with alcohol, but she was contaminated like a mug while we were down there."

"Are you willing to go on the record and say these pictures are authentic?"

"Shoot, yeah! I'm the one who took them! That's not all, either. Little Miss Perfect, Kina Battle, has been getting it in with rapper Cut 'Em Cali. She told me that herself."

"Reginell, there are going to be some people who question your motives for exposing Kina. Some might consider this to be payback for her outing you at the club or might think that you're capitalizing on your relationship with Kina for your own personal gain. What would you like to say to those people?"

"Let me clear this up right now. I love my cousin, and I love her son. I would never maliciously put anybody on blast like this, but I can't stand fake people, and right now my cousin is being fake. I just think everybody who supports her or who is trying to emulate her ought to know the truth."

"Almost every day there seems to be a new scandal released about Kina Battle. Are there more skeletons in her closet, or have we seen the last of them?"

"Honey, this ain't even half of it!" Reginell answered. "If you really want the dirt on Kina Battle, ask Sullivan Webb. Ask her why Kina stopped working at the church. Ask Sullivan what really happened the night her husband had a stroke and what it had to do with Kina. Just ask her."

Sullivan stared at the screen in disbelief. "No, this heifer didn't . . ."

"These little pictures—they ain't nothing compared to the real story behind Kina Justine Battle," declared Reginell.

"I am going to kill my sister," vowed Lawson. "What was she thinking?"

"You know, it's one thing for my dejected lesbian lover to drop me off on Front Street, but Reggie is my blood. I knew she was upset, but she didn't have to get me back like that." Kina shook her head. "I feel so betrayed right now."

Sullivan crossed her arms. "It's not a good feeling, is it?"

"Sully, this is not the time. . . ." warned Lawson.

"Kina, you and Lawson shouldn't be all that surprised. You know how Reggie gets when someone crosses her. You gave Reggie the ammo and the motivation."

"But why did she have to go dragging my name in it?" whined Sullivan. "I'm the subject of enough gossip as it is. I don't need this drama too!"

Kina winced, looking down at her vibrating phone. "That's my publicist. I'm not even going to answer. No doubt she's seen Reggie's little exposé, along with the rest of the world. I already know she's going to go ballistic on me."

"Yeah, she did a number on you! How do you think it's going to affect Ki-Ki's Tees' opening this week? Do you think it'll have a negative impact on the store opening?" asked Angel.

Kina slapped her hand against her forehead. "I didn't even think about that. Ki-Ki's Tees opens in a few days. This is the last thing I needed right now." Kina collapsed on the sofa. "This is a catastrophe. I should probably just call the whole thing off."

"You can't. You've invested half of your savings in it," Lawson reminded her.

"I don't know." Kina sighed. "I won a lot of money, but who knew the price of fame was going to be this high?"

Lawson patted her on the back. "Don't let this get you down, Kina. We'll figure something out. You've got a whole team of people on your payroll who are paid to handle this sort of thing."

"It's not just the bad press. This is going to kill any chance I have at endorsements and speaking engagements, not to mention the reality show I've been trying to pitch."

"Y'all, maybe we need to pray," Angel suggested. "Kina needs the Lord to intercede quick, fast, and in a hurry!"

Lawson said, "Ladies, you know the drill." Kina, Sullivan, and Angel joined hands with Lawson. "Lord, we come to you standing on the promises of Jesus. We receive your Word and profess our faith right now. God, we know that there are people out there looking to stop your Word from being spread throughout the world. They want to taint it, and they're using your servant Kina to do it—even my family members. But, Lord, we claim that no weapon formed against her shall prosper. God, we trust in you, and we know that you won't let us be put to shame or let our enemies triumph.

"God, at the same time I ask that you let Kina be sensitive to the promptings of the Holy Spirit, because you said that when we lose all sensitivity, we give ourselves over to sensuality so as to indulge in every kind of impurity. Give Kina a pure heart. Don't let her succumb to the ways of this world. Forgive her for the times she's tried to please man instead of please you. Surround her with godly counsel so she can make wise decisions. Touch and rebuke Reginell for what she's done, because you show your love through your rebuke and discipline. Help us to be the kind of friends Kina can lean on, and show her how to use this platform you've given her in the way you intended. In Jesus's name, amen."

"Well said," Sullivan remarked, complimenting Lawson.

"Thank you, cuz." Kina hugged Lawson. "Can I use your computer for a second? I need to check my account online. I may have to write Christa an extra-large check this week to keep her around."

"Sure. Go ahead."

"Thanks," said Kina, sitting down at the computer, then logging on to her bank account. She scrolled through the numbers, dumbfounded. "What the . . ."

Lawson frowned. "What's wrong?"

"Twenty thousand dollars! My money is gone!" Kina looked up at her cousin. "Lawson, I'm almost broke!"

Chapter 37

"You have to be whole alone before you can become someone's other half."
—*Reginell Kerry*

"So you've finally stopped avoiding me, I see," Mark commented as Reginell joined him at their restaurant table after finally agreeing to meet with him following two weeks of dodging him.

"I couldn't face you," she admitted. "The only reason I'm doing it now is that I miss you so freakin' much. I had to see you, even if it's for you to say good-bye."

"I've missed you too, probably more than you realize."

"Mark, baby, I'm so sorry. I should've told you I'd started back dancing. Better yet, I shouldn't have done it at all. I know that now. I hope that you can forgive me."

He reached for her hand. "Reggie, tell me why you started back stripping. Why didn't you think you could tell me about it?"

"I started back for the most obvious reason. I needed the money."

"I would've helped you out with the bills if you'd asked me to."

"I know, but I didn't want your money. I wanted to be able to pull my own weight in this relationship, not depend on you for everything."

"It's not about what's yours and what's mine. We're supposed to be a team."

She looked down. "The money wasn't the only thing, though. Mark, do you remember that night when we went to that retirement banquet?"

"Yeah."

"I felt so out of place there. I've never felt like that before, and I never want to feel that way again."

"Reggie, I told you not to worry about what those women had to say."

"But it wasn't about them. This was about me not accomplishing anything in my life worth talking about. One thing I do know is that I'm a good stripper. Dancing makes me feel like at least I've accomplished something. It might not be much in anybody else's eyes, but it's all I've got. It's the only time people pay me any attention."

"You've got your singing."

"Have you been to open mic night, Mark? Nobody is paying much attention to that, either."

"Your time will come, babe."

"I know, but it won't if I don't start making some changes first. When I was stripping back in the day, it really didn't bother me too much . . . didn't bother my conscience, I mean. This time was different."

"What do you mean?"

"It just felt like it was beneath me, like I can do better than that. I don't want to have to strip or wait tables or live below my potential. I need to get out and make something of myself. My career in music may take off. It may not. I've got to have something else to fall back on. I think I should start by going back to school. I applied to college today."

"That's awesome, Reggie. I'm proud of you."

"I said I *applied*. That doesn't mean I'm going to get in," she pointed out.

"Yes, you will. I know it."

Reginell smiled. "You've always had more confidence in me than I have in myself."

"That's because I see what the rest of the world doesn't. Reggie, you've got potential you haven't even dreamed about. You just have to go for yours and not let anybody, including yourself, stop you."

"You're right. Before, I didn't understand why Lawson told Garrett no the first time he proposed. She kept saying she needed to find Lawson before she could be Mrs. Banks. I think I get it now. You have to be whole alone before you can become someone's other half."

"Those are some wise words, Miss Kerry, and I'm not saying that because I'm madly in love with you."

"After all this, you still love me?"

"I will always love you, Reggie."

"I love you too, Mark. I love you enough to want to be a better person for you." She slipped off the princess-cut solitaire engagement ring Mark had given her. "I should give this back to you until I'm ready to be a wife and until I can present myself as the kind of woman you deserve and can be proud of."

"Reggie, that's your ring."

"Oh, I know!" she stated. "I'm just letting you hold it until I'm really ready for it."

"So you're not breaking up with me, then?"

"Not unless you're breaking up with me."

Mark leaned across the table to kiss her. "Not a chance, woman, but I want you to be happy with yourself. If this is what it takes, this is how it'll be for a while."

Reginell checked the time on her cell phone. "Well, you still have about an hour of the old Reginell left. What do you want to do with her?"

Mark grinned. "I can show you better than I can tell you! Let's go."

Chapter 38

*"It wouldn't be Christmas without Vera
ruining it for me."*
—Sullivan Webb

"Oh, that's perfect!" Sullivan remarked to her professional tree decorator. It was costing her two hundred dollars to have the florist do what she could've done with minimal effort and ingenuity, but tonight had to be perfect, from the food to the professionally decorated tree.

Sullivan sauntered around the house, making sure every bow and bough of holly was in place. It was going to be the first holiday party she and her father had ever shared together, and the first time he brought Marti into their home. Sullivan suspected that this would be the night that Samuel introduced her to the world as his daughter.

At six o'clock that evening, Sullivan, decked out in a strapless red peplum gown, began receiving their guests. Within the hour, the house was overflowing with guests. Sullivan checked the time and watched the door. Her father had yet to arrive.

"He'll be here," Lawson assured her, sensing Sullivan's uneasiness.

"I know. He's probably held up in traffic or something."

"But if he doesn't show, it'll be all right."

Sullivan forced a smile. "Don't be silly, Lawson. He's going to show up. He wouldn't let me down, not again." Her heart leapt when she heard the doorbell ring. "See? That's probably him."

Sullivan hurried to the door, disappointed to find a couple from the church.

"He'll be here," Sullivan insisted, dashing past Lawson. "I'll be back. I'm going to check on the food."

Sullivan found a quiet corner and silently prayed, *Lord, please let him show up.*

Sullivanwas relieved when she returned and found Charles greeting Samuel and Marti at the door. She joined the three of them.

"Pastor Sullivan, it's good to see you and your lovely wife again. Thank you for taking the time to come and fellowship with us tonight," said Charles.

"We wouldn't have missed it," replied Samuel. "We would've been here sooner, but we had to check into our hotel first."

"It's not a problem." Sullivan extended her hands to them. "Please, come in and make yourselves at home."

Sullivan rushed to find Lawson, who was eating hors d'oeuvres with Angel and Reginell. She pointed at Samuel, across the room. "I told you he was coming!"

"He's a nice-looking man," observed Angel. "When do we get to meet him?"

"I'll introduce you before the party is over."

"Sullivan, you've really outdone yourself this year," said Lawson. "Everything is beautiful."

"Thanks. I had to. I wanted it to be perfect, because I think my dad is going to make an announcement."

Reginell mishandled the fennel slaw on her crostini. "About what?"

Sullivan showed off a wide smile. "I think he's going to tell everyone that I'm his daughter."

"Sullivan, he hasn't even told his wife," Lawson pointed out. "What makes you think he's going to announce it to a room full of strangers?"

"It's just a feeling I have," Sullivan said. "Call it women's intuition."

They were interrupted by the loud sounds of a commotion coming from the foyer.

"What's going on?" Sullivan made her way to the uproar. "Oh, no," she groaned, mortified.

Disheveled, Vera staggered across the foyer, knocking over decorations, visibly inebriated. Because she was drunk, it also meant she had the potential to be volatile.

Sullivan angrily approached her. "Vera, what are you doing here?"

"Hey," crowed Vera, sloppily kissing Sullivan on the cheek. "Merry Christmas, baby!"

"What are you doing here?" Sullivan repeated. "I've been living here ten years, and you pick today, of all days, to show up?"

Vera cackled. "You know I'm never one to miss a party, Sullivan."

Sullivan yanked Vera's arm and started shoving her out the front door. "You need to leave *now!*" she demanded through clenched teeth.

Vera began to get louder. "Oh, I can't come to your Christmas party? I ain't invited?"

"No, you're not!"

Vera broke away from Sullivan. "So you 'shamed of me, right? You got all your fancy, high-saditty friends around you, so you're gonna act like you don't know nobody."

"Vera, don't make a scene! Please don't do this," Sullivan pleaded, hoping to calm or at least quiet her mother.

"Don't do what?" Vera's eyes settled on Samuel. "Oh, now I see why you don't want me here." She pushed Sullivan away and marched straight toward her ex-lover. "I bet I'm the last person you expected to see, ain't I?"

Samuel stiffened and clung to his wife.

"You gon' act like you don't know me, Sammy? Huh?" charged Vera.

Samuel whispered to Marti, "I think we should leave now."

"Oh, no, don't leave on my account, not before introducing me to your lovely wife," Vera said, slurring.

"Samuel, do you know this woman?" asked Marti.

"*This woman?*" Vera repeated with indignation and clamped her hands on her hips. "I got a name!"

"I'm calling the police," Sullivan uttered, looking around. "Where's Charles?"

"He went upstairs to check on the baby," answered one of the deacons. "He's coming, Sister Webb."

"You gon' do that? You gon' call security on your mama?" Vera turned to Samuel. "You gon' let her call the police on your baby's mama?"

"What?" gasped Marti.

Vera stared Marti down. "That's right. I'm Samuel's baby's mama, or didn't he tell you we have a child together?"

Marti whirled around, facing her husband. "Sam, what is she talking about?"

"This heifer is going to stop talking about me like I ain't in the room!" Vera spewed in a raised voice. She positioned herself in between Samuel and Marti. "You might think you know this man, but you don't half know him at all. Go on. Tell her, Sammy. Tell her about all the years you were taking care of my bills, my home, my lifestyle, and my child. You were Mrs. Samuel Sullivan on paper, but *I* was Mrs. Samuel Sullivan in every way that mattered. He might've been married to you, but I was his wife for eight years."

"Is this true?"

"Marti, I . . ."

"What's going on here" Charles demanded, rushing to the side of his humiliated wife.

"We're having a li'l revelation party, Pastor. The Bible says, 'Wherefore putting away lying, speak every man truth with his neighbor: for we are members one of another.' I bet you didn't think I remembered that, did you, Sammy?" Vera crossed her arms in front of her, pleased with herself. "Yeah, I remember every single thing you did, everything you said, every promise you ever broke, and every lie that came out of your mouth. I remember it all."

Charles intervened. "Vera, this isn't the time or the place for this."

"Naw, preacher, this is *exactly* the time for it. Now you and everybody else can see that Sister Sullivan here didn't just get all her whore-mongering ways from me. The good pastor's hands are just as dirty. Matter of fact, his hands are dirtier than mine, because they got blood on them!" Vera's face contorted, and her lips trembled. "They got blood on them, don't they, Sammy? Because you killed my baby, and I know you killed her! Sullivan wasn't our only child, was she? You remember Amber and how you drove your car through a tree so you could kill her. You would've killed me too if the devil had let you!" She began crying hysterically. "You're a baby-killing, lying, son of a witch! I hope that lightning strikes you dead!"

"That's enough, Vera. Let's go," said Charles. He ushered her out of the living room as quickly as possible.

Sullivan locked eyes with her father and Marti, not knowing what to say.

"Come on. Let's get out of here," Samuel muttered to Marti, practically dragging her out of the house to spare her any further disgrace.

Lawson rushed to Sullivan's side. "Are you all right?"

Sullivan was in a daze. "Sure. It wouldn't be Christmas without Vera ruining it for me, though I must say, she's gotten more creative in her tactics." Sullivan stepped forward to speak over the murmuring. "Please, everyone, carry on. Continue to enjoy the food and fellowship." She signaled to the waitstaff to serve more food and drinks. People gradually began socializing again.

Sullivan hurried away from the questions and the stares and stomped down the hall, looking for Vera. She met Charles as he was coming out of one of the guest bedrooms. He barred Sullivan from going in.

"Let her sleep it off, sweetheart."

"Don't worry. She'll be able to sleep for all of eternity when I get through with her!"

Charles grabbed Sullivan's hands. "Sullivan, there ain't no point in you charging in there like a banshee. Let it go."

"You can't be serious! Did you see what she did and hear the things she said about my father? Look how she humiliated him and his wife!"

"It was no more than he's humiliated her. By no means do I condone what Vera did, but she didn't say anything about the man that wasn't true. Your mother has been deeply wounded by that man, and she's been carrying that hurt around for over thirty years."

"Admit it, Charles." Sullivan folded her arms. "You don't like him, do you?"

"Sullivan, don't turn this around and make it about your father and me."

"I knew from the moment I brought him back into my life, you had an issue with it. The fact that you'd go so far as to defend Vera, of all people, shows how little you care about him or his having a relationship with me."

"I'm sorry, but I don't respect the man," admitted Charles. "I'm not saying the man has to be perfect, but being up in that pulpit requires a certain a degree of principles and morals. I can't say for sure he has any. When a man falls short—and we all do—he should own it, especially if he's a man of God. You can't be up there, leading God's people, while living the kind of life he does."

"You don't know anything about him, Charles. You met him what? Twice? I've spent time with him. I know his heart."

"You're right, Sully. I may not know him as well as you do, but I know that First Timothy five, eight says, 'If any provide not for his own, and specially for those of his own house, he has denied the faith, and is worse than an infidel.' You don't abandon your child or her mother for your own reputation and self-preservation. I've seen firsthand how much it's scarred you and your mother. I can't respect somebody who'd do that."

"Well, Charles, you can stay right here with your self-righteousness and your drunken, wounded mother-in-law. He's my father, and he's welcome in this house and in this family, certainly more than Vera. Now I'm going to find my father and try to fix this."

Charles stopped her. "Wait a minute, Sullivan. What you're not going to do is let that man's problems become *our* problem. No joker you've known two minutes is going to come in here and cause a rift between us. I don't care who he is."

The urgency in Charles's voice let her know that he meant business. Sullivan backed down. "I don't want him to think I tried to set him up by having Vera show up and show out."

Charles wrapped his arms around Sullivan and pulled her into a hug. "I'm sure he knows better than that."

"Charles, I just got him back in my life. I don't want to lose him again."

Chapter 39

*"You better pray that there isn't a cozy corner in hell
with your name on it."*
— *Sullivan Webb*

Sullivan felt compelled to apologize the moment
she saw her father the next morning. He'd asked her
to meet him at a park near his and Marti's hotel room.
Sullivan could only pray that he knew she had nothing
to do with Vera's antics and that he wouldn't hold it
against her.

Sullivan hugged him. "I'm sorry about the Christmas
party."

"It wasn't your fault." Samuel pulled away. "I don't
want you blaming yourself for what happened."

"How's Marti?"

"We had a long talk about it last night." Samuel
paused, pensive. "Marti made me take a hard look at
some things."

"Like what?"

"Like my place in the church and in the community
and how it would affect Daryl and Thomas if this got
out."

"*If?* My mother announced to everyone at the party
that I was your love child. I think it's safe to say that the
word is out now."

"Not necessarily," Samuel said. "There weren't that
many people at the party, maybe thirty or forty people,

and none of them know Marti and me or live in Atlanta."

"Yes, but what about when I come to visit? Won't
people start asking questions about the young woman
who is staying at your place or sitting with your family
at church?"

"They won't ask, because you won't be there." Samuel held her hands in his. "Sullivan, baby, we just don't
think it's going to work."

Sullivan was genuinely confused. "What's not going
to work?"

"You know . . . having you in my life and all."

She snatched her hands back. "What?"

"Sweetheart, I have a family already. I have a life. I
have responsibilities, and I've worked too hard—"

"Too hard for what?" she interrupted. "You've worked
too hard for everyone to realize what a liar and a fraud
you really are?"

"It's not like you're a kid anymore, Sullivan. You
don't need me."

"I *do* need you," she cried, her voice going up an oc-
tave. "You're my daddy. I don't care how old you are.
Every girl needs her daddy!"

"You've got a husband. Charles is a good man. He'll
look after you just like I would. You've got your own
family. You don't need me."

Sullivan backed away from him. "So she was right.
Vera told me not to get my hopes up. She told me not
to trust you, but I didn't listen. I wanted it so badly. I
wanted you, my father, to be a part of my life and my
daughter's life so badly that I couldn't see the writing
on the wall."

"Baby girl, you're young. Just keep living. After a
while, it'll all make sense to you."

"I just got you back in my life!" Sullivan threw up her hands. "How can you walk out of it again? How can you walk out of your granddaughter's life? Is that the image of a man you want her to have?"

"Sullivan, you're a preacher's wife. You know better than anybody how this works. You know what this kind of scandal can do to a ministry."

"Yes, I know exactly what it can do and how it can divide a church. I've lived it, but we got through it both as a church and as a family. Not only did we get through it, but it made us stronger."

"I can't take that chance." He lowered his head. "It's like I told you when you first came to me. I'm a coward, Sullivan. I don't deny it."

Sullivan could feel her heart breaking. "I thought you loved me. You said you wanted us to be a family and get to know one another again."

"I do, but there's too much at stake for that to happen right now. Maybe one day, but not now."

"So this is it? You called me out here to say goodbye?"

Samuel hugged her. "It's not you, baby girl. Don't ever think this has anything to do with you."

She sprang away from him. "This has *everything* to do with me! This isn't the fifties. So you had an affair thirty years ago. What does that matter now? Who cares?"

"It matters to a lot of folks who matter to me."

A tear escaped Sullivan's eye. "Obviously, I'm not one of those people who matter."

"I didn't say that."

"You didn't have to." She exhaled and quickly wiped the tear. She wasn't going to give him the satisfaction of seeing her cry for him. "You can't run from the truth forever, Daddy. You know these things have a way of getting out one way or another, don't you?"

Samuel's posture changed. He stood upright, and his eyes turned cold. "I hope that's not a threat, Sullivan. Don't try to go public with this. Don't forget, I know things about you too—things that you don't want to get out about that little girl. I can destroy your life as quickly as and as easily as you could destroy mine."

Sullivan's mouth gaped open. "I told you that in confidence because you're my father and I was crazy enough to believe that I could trust you! And to think that you'd stoop so low as to use your granddaughter as a ploy or a means of blackmail is deplorable."

"I wouldn't want to do it. Lord knows I wouldn't," he insisted. "But I can't let you or anybody else ruin what I've worked so hard to build."

Sullivan nodded slowly. "You know, I sat there and defended you when Vera accused you of killing Amber and trying to kill her in order to keep her quiet. I thought there was no way any father could do that to his own child. Now I can't say for sure that you didn't do it or that you aren't a murderer."

"Sullivan, that was an accident," he swore.

"It doesn't matter what you say, because I don't believe a word that comes out of your mouth." She shook her head. "There was actually a time when I felt bad that Charity would never have a chance to know who her grandfather is. Now I thank God that she'll never know what a sorry excuse for a man you truly are. It sickens me to think that a person like you has dominion over a congregation and that you have been trusted with the souls and lives of God's chosen people. You better pray that there isn't a cozy corner in hell with your name on it and that God will have mercy on you."

"Sullivan, I'm sorry it's come down to this. I really am." He kissed Sullivan on the forehead, pressing his lips hard against her skin. He knew that it was that last time he'd ever kiss or set eyes on his daughter again. "One day you'll understand, sweetheart."

"No, I won't."

Samuel nodded and turned to begin the walk to his car. Sullivan waited and watched him. A part of her was hoping he'd at least turn around for one last glimpse or to tell her that he loved her. He didn't.

Sullivan knew she had Charles's love. More importantly, she knew she had God's, but there was something about suffering another rejection at the hands of her father that Sullivan couldn't make peace with.

Burning with anger, Sullivan climbed into her car and strapped on her seat belt. "Who needs him, anyway?" she grumbled. Sullivan exhaled, and her lips began to quiver. Her vision became blurry from the tears filling her eyes. "I needed him!" she sobbed. "I needed my daddy."

Sullivan sat in the parking lot and cried. She cried for Charity because she'd never know the joy of having a strong, loving grandfather. She cried for Vera and the price Vera had to pay for being foolish enough to love Samuel and what it had done to her. Mostly, she cried for the little girl who still lived inside of her, who wanted nothing more than to know that her father loved her.

Chapter 40

*"All of 'em can go play in traffic, blindfolded,
for all I care!"*
—Sullivan Webb

Sullivan returned home to find Vera in her solarium, having coffee and leftovers from the party.

Sullivan poured a cup of coffee and sat down next to Vera at the table. "Where are Charles and the baby?"

"Upstairs somewhere."

Sullivan sighed. "You were right."

"Right about what?"

"My father. He turned out to be exactly who and what you said he was. He's gone. I think it's for good this time. He said it would hurt his family and his church and, of course, his image too much for people to know he fathered an outside child."

Vera laughed. "I ain't been wrong about a man yet!" She sipped her coffee. "But this was one time I was hoping I would be."

"I used to wonder how a man like Samuel could fall for someone like you. I'm starting to think that you were actually the moral one in that relationship."

Vera set her cup down. "Sammy ain't no different from any other man, Sullivan. Most of them are liars and cowards when it comes right down to it. It takes either a real strong or a real stupid woman to risk loving one. I stopped taking that chance a long time ago."

"Did you really love him?"

"Of course I did. Sammy is the only man I ever *did* love, and it cost me everything."

"If it matters, he claims that he really did love you, Vera." Sullivan's lip trembled. "I just wish I knew why he doesn't want me."

Vera cut her eyes over at Sullivan. "Don't do that. You know I ain't good with tears, Sully." Sullivan sniffed and wiped her eyes with the back of her hand. "You might as well stop all that. It is what it is."

"Can't I have at least one person with my blood running through their veins to love me? Why do I have to be everybody's reject?"

"Jesus Christ!" Vera uttered as she stood up. She walked into the guest bedroom to retrieve her purse. She rejoined Sullivan at the table and pulled out an address book. She dug a wrinkled-up piece of paper out of her purse, copied an address out of the book, and handed it to Sullivan. "Here."

"What's this?" She read the paper. "Who is Luella?"

"That's Luella Sullivan. She's your grandmother on your daddy's side. That's her phone number and address."

"Why are you giving this to me?" She thrust the paper back at her. "I don't want anything else to do with those people."

"Well, I'm asking that you make an exception for your grandmother."

"Why? So she can reject me too?"

Vera sucked her teeth. "Please, the woman is in her eighties. She's too close to meeting her Maker to be nasty to anyone!"

"I have no desire to test that theory. All of 'em can go play in traffic, blindfolded, for all I care!"

"If we're talking about your daddy or that witch he's married to or your no-account granddaddy, I say yes. But not Miss Luella She's different."

"Why?"

"Because out of everybody in that family, she's the only one who ever cared anything about you."

Sullivan furrowed her brow. "How do you figure that? She's never said or done one thing for me."

"Whether or not they admit it, they all knew about you," Vera acknowledged. "Of course, a whore like me wasn't good enough for Judge Sullivan and his family, but Luella came to see me right after you were born. She knew she couldn't publicly recognize you as one of her own, so she did it in private. Every time you had something at school, she was always there in the background, watching. When you went and got yourself locked up when you were thirteen, she was the one who pleaded with the folks to drop the charges. She always made sure you had Christmas presents and birthday gifts."

Sullivan couldn't believe what she was hearing. "I thought that was all your doing."

"Sullivan, you know I'm way too selfish to spend my money on you, but your grandmother did. In her own way, she loved you. She's the only one from that family I have any respect for. She was even at your wedding."

"She was?"

Vera nodded. "She sat in the back so nobody would notice her. You can hate everybody else in your family, including me, but don't hate her."

"Where is she?"

"She's still living near Savannah, over in Metter. Her address is on the paper, along with her phone number. You can call her if you want or not. It makes no differ-ence to me, but I get the feeling it'll make a lot of difference to you." Vera stood up. "Well, I guess I better be headed back. I need to get out of here before you and Charles start throwing all that religion around."

Sullivan stared down at the paper. "Vera, you know what you said about not wanting to risk loving again? I was like that too. If I didn't have Charles and God in my life, I would still be the same way."

"See? That's what I'm talking about! I'm leaving."

"Wait." Sullivan took her mother by the hand. "Knowing that God loves me made all the difference. I gave my heart to Him because I knew I could trust Him to send me a man who would take care of it. He sent me Charles."

Vera poked out her lip. "Maybe one day I'll give all this God stuff you and Charles keep talking about a try. If it saved you, there might be a little hope for me."

"I think there's a lot of hope for you, Vera."

Vera looked at Sullivan and squeezed her arm. It was the closest thing resembling a hug that she'd given Sullivan in years.

"All right, I'm gonna go tell my grandbaby good-bye and then I'm out," said Vera.

"Okay. Call me when you get there."

Sullivan sat down and looked at Luella's contact information again, debating whether or not it was worth risking her heart being broken again. According to Vera, it wasn't. Then again, Sullivan never was one to listen to her mother.

Chapter 41

"What I want is for the lies, charades, and facades to stop. If it starts with me being real about who I am, so be it!"
—Sullivan Webb

Angel met up with Lawson and Sullivan near the treadmill at the gym. "Where's Kina?"

"She left," answered Lawson, wiping sweat from her brow. "She said something about having to make an appearance at a retired educators' function."

"Are you all right?" asked Sullivan, stretching. "You look tired."

"I'm fine." The truth was that Angel was lacking energy due to excessively self-medicating. Lethargy was a side effect.

"Don't overdo it in your workout today," Lawson cautioned her. "Are you feeling any better about the baby situation?"

Angel climbed on the StairMaster. "I try not to think about it. What's done is done."

Lawson stood next to her. "I don't know if it's healthy for you to repress your feelings."

"I'm not repressing, but I'm not obsessing over it, either. I'm taking it day by day."

Lawson hopped on the StairMaster next to Angel's. "Well, you know we're here if you want to talk."

"I'll certainly be talking soon," Sullivan revealed. "I have an interview tomorrow."

"An interview?" Lawson had never heard Sullivan utter those words before. "Are you trying to get a job, Sully?"

"More importantly, has hell frozen over?" quipped Angel.

"It's not a job interview. I'm being interviewed by Keydra Parks. She tracked me down and is on her way to Savannah. She wants me to sit in for an interview about Kina."

Lawson was aghast. "Why would you agree to do that? You know that woman makes her living slamming Kina in the media."

"Has she said anything about Kina that isn't true?" Sullivan asked, firing back.

No one could say she had.

"Is this revenge for what happened with Charles, or are you acting out because of what happened with Samuel Sullivan?" Angel said. "Sully, I know you're feeling hurt and betrayed, but don't lash out at Kina for his mistakes."

"This has nothing to do with my father or bashing Kina. This is me getting the truth out about what happened to Charles and why."

"Sullivan, I'm begging you not to do this to Kina," pleaded Lawson.

Sullivan sucked her teeth. "Don't do what to Kina? Don't throw her under the bus like she did me? Don't embarrass her like she did Reggie? Don't criticize her choices like she did Joan?"

Lawson stopped moving. "Sullivan, one more scathing interview and Kina will be ruined. Her publicist has already threatened to quit on her. She can't afford to have another negative story come out."

"That's too bad," said Sullivan. "I'm not covering up anyone else's lies or upholding any more fake Christians."

Angel adjusted the speed on her machine. "You do realize that by exposing Kina, you'll also be outing yourself, don't you? Is that what you really want to do?"

Sullivan stretched across the fitness ball. "What I want is for the lies, charades, and facades to stop. If it starts with me being real about who I am, so be it!"

Kina, Angel, and Lawson huddled around the computer screen, waiting with bated breath for Sullivan's interview with Keydra Parks to begin.

"Why is she doing this?" Kina asked for the fifth time since Lawson had told her about Sullivan's plans. "Granted, we weren't back to being best buds, but after hashing everything out in the Bahamas, I thought we'd made enough progress for her not to go after me this way."

"Kina, we all know that Sullivan can be unpredictable. She's still reeling from the fallout with her father. She feels paralyzed because she can't get back at him and expose his secrets. Unfortunately, she's taking that out on you," Lawson said, assessing the situation.

Kina fumed. "Sullivan has nothing to gain by doing this. If anything, she stands to lose in a major way. I doubt that Charles is going to stand for another public scandal involving his wife, and everyone will know that Vaughn could be Charity's father, including Vaughn! Who knows how Vaughn will react when he finds out that Sullivan kept that from him?"

"I think a part of Sullivan is fed up with all the lies and secrets," said Angel. "On some level, she probably wants the truth to come out. She doesn't want to live a life of secrecy like her father."

Kina adjusted the volume on the speakers as Keydra began to speak.

"Good morning to all of our viewers out there. We're delighted to have as our guest today Mrs. Sullivan Webb, first lady of Mount Zion Ministries in Savannah, Georgia. As most of you know, we've been covering the story of the rise and fall of reality star Kina Battle as the drama unfolds. Our last guest, dancer Reginell Kerry, alluded to Sullivan Webb being the one person who could give us the truth about Kina, and she's here to give us our most revealing interview and insight into Miss Battle to date." Keydra turned to Sullivan. "Mrs. Webb, thank you so much for taking time out to come talk to us. How are you?"

"I'm great . . . blessed."

"I can see that you are. Can you tell my viewers how you know Kina Battle?"

Sullivan crossed her legs. "Kina and I have known each other since we were kids. We grew up in the same neighborhood."

"So I am right in assuming that you know Kina pretty well?"

Sullivan narrowed her eyes. "I know Kina extremely well."

"As a television audience, we've gotten to know Kina within the limited prism of the television screen. The image we have, or rather *had* before we started to learn more about her life off camera, is that of a sweet Christian who overcame the odds and inspired a nation. Is the Kina Battle we've gotten to know the real Kina Battle?"

Sullivan thought for a moment. "No, I think there are actually three versions of Kina."

"Can you elaborate?"

"The Kina we knew before the fame was sweet but insecure. As you know, she was in an abusive marriage and struggled financially for a long time. She didn't seem to really know her place in the world. Then there was the Kina on *Lose Big*. She was starting to find her voice and gain confidence in herself, and I can see how that could be inspiring to a lot of people. Lastly, we have the Kina who dwells among us today. She has the money, the fame, and a platform. She has the attention of the world, but I'm not sure that she knows what to do with it."

"So you're saying that fame has changed her?"

"I think it would change anybody who was suddenly thrust into that kind of limelight. Then again, maybe *change* isn't the right word. I think it reveals who you really are, and we're finally seeing who Kina really is."

"Interesting," noted Keydra. "What is the status of your friendship with Kina today?"

"We still talk. Admittedly, we're not as close as we once were, but I think that's just a part of life."

"Is her newfound celebrity status the reason for the change in your relationship?"

"No. Kina and I started to grow apart long before she appeared on the show."

"Now, I'll be honest with you, Mrs. Webb. Some people have suggested that Kina may have had an inappropriate relationship with your husband and that was the cause of the rift between the two of you. Do you care to address that?"

"No, I don't." Sullivan sighed. "People are going to say and believe what they want to say and believe regardless of how I answer that question."

"How is Pastor Webb, by the way? I know that your husband, who is also the pastor and former boss of Kina Battle, suffered a stroke about a year ago."

"He's getting stronger every day. He's talking now, and he's a wonderful father to our little girl. We're so thankful that God has graced him to pull through this. To look at Charles today, you'd never know that we almost lost him."

"But you did almost lose him. Our sources tell us that Kina was the one who found him passed out in his office."

Sullivan nodded. "Yes, that's true. If she hadn't been there to call nine-one-one, who knows what would've happened?"

"So she was in his office that day?"

"Yes."

"Why?"

"She was his assistant."

Keydra nodded slowly. "So she was in constant close contact with your husband?"

"Not exclusively with Charles. She worked with everyone on the church's staff."

"But her specific job was as your husband's administrative assistant, correct?"

"Yes."

"You know, there's been a lot of speculation about Kina Battle, specifically that she isn't the good girl she wants America to believe she is. First, there's her questionable relationship with rapper Cut 'Em Cali, then the drug allegations made by her cousin. We've had her lesbian lover come forth. Now there's talk that there may have been something going on between your husband and Miss Battle."

"I can assure that my husband is an upstanding man of God. He'd never stoop to sleeping with any of the church's staff members. Anyone who knows Charles will tell you that."

"Uh-huh . . . Our sources also tell us that Kina may know more about what happened to your husband than she let on to the doctors and paramedics. Some have even theorized that she's the reason he had the stroke in the first place. Do you care to elaborate on that?"

Sullivan leaned in. "What exactly are you asking me?"

"Do you think that Kina Battle had something to do with your husband's near death? Do you think she did or said anything to cause his stroke?"

Sullivan shifted nervously in her seat. She knew she had the power to expose Kina and put an end to frauds like her and Samuel. She could do it for the Veras, Reginells, and Joans of the world, who were delegated to lonely, empty corners, while people like Kina rode high on their pedestal, propped up on the backs of other people. She could make Kina pay for what she'd done to Charles and her child. She could give Kina the swift kick in the behind she so richly deserved and certainly had coming, but would she?

Sullivan cleared her throat. "A stroke can be brought on by many things, Ms. Parks. Diet, stress, and overall health all play a part. I wasn't in my husband's office that night, so I can't tell you definitively what happened between him and Kina, but I know what I *can* tell you."

"What's that?"

"I can tell you that Kina summoned help when she found Charles unconscious. I can tell you that she stayed by his side and prayed for him the whole time. I can tell you that she was there for me as a friend during his recovery. Kina has always been like a sister to me. As you may know, I'm no stranger to scandal myself, but Kina has never judged me for it or abandoned me as a friend, and I'm not going to do that to her now. I'll be the first to tell you that she's not perfect and maybe fame has gone to her head. But one thing that's real is that she loves her son, she loves her friends, and she loves her God."

Keydra waited for more. "Is that it? Is that the scoop Reginell was talking about?"

"I don't know what information Reginell thought I had to share, but that's it. That's all I have to say about Kina."

"So you don't want to address the allegations that Kina, who you've said was your best friend at one point, tried to seduce your husband, the pastor?"

"I don't know anything about that," replied Sullivan. "All I can say is that I've never witnessed anything inappropriate between them, and Charles has never said that Kina was anything but professional."

"But do you, as a woman, think that she was after your husband and your place as first lady?"

What was one more lie? Sullivan shook her head. "No, I don't."

Keydra sighed heavily. "Well, folks, you heard it here, although I'm not completely sure that we heard anything new from our guest today. I'd like to thank First Lady Sullivan Webb for joining us today. Keep your comments and your posts coming, and you can catch me somewhere in cyberspace. This has been Keydra Parks with Celebonies, and we're out!"

Kina let out a deep breath. "Wow . . . I wasn't expecting that. Sullivan could've really screwed me over if she wanted to."

"Obviously, she didn't want to, Kina. Sully is a good person at heart. We just never know when she's going to be good or do anything from the heart," joked Lawson.

"I'm proud of her," said Angel. "The one time she could've stuck it to someone else, she didn't."

"Hopefully, her act of goodwill will sway some favor my way," Kina said in anticipation. "Because at this point, barring a miracle happening, Ki-Ki's Tees will be nothing short of a colossal, epic fail!"

Chapter 42

*"I made this mess. It's time I took responsibility and
cleaned it up."*
—*Sullivan Webb*

Charles rushed into the house and found Sullivan
sitting alone in the living room. "I got your message
and came as soon as I could. What happened? Is the
baby all right?"

"Yes, she fine. She's taking a nap. Charles, I called
you because we need to talk."

He sat down beside her. "This sounds serious."

"It is. I'm sure you're not gonna want to hear it, but
it needs to be said."

"What's the matter, sweetheart?"

"We need to talk about Charity and the night you had
the stroke."

"What does one have to do with the other?"

Sullivan sighed. "Charles, I know what Kina told you
right before you went down. I think you remember too.
We haven't talked about it since I told you I was pregnant, but I think we should."

Charles tried to stop her. "We don't need to get into
all this, Sullivan."

"Yes, we do, especially in light of all this drama with
my own father." She took a deep breath. "I love you,
and you know that. But you also know that I've made
some major mistakes in our marriage, none of which

I'm proud of. Most of which, I'm downright shameful of. My affair with Vaughn is at the top of that list."

"Why are you rehashing all this? The Lord forgave you a long time ago, and so did I. I haven't thought on it again. Neither should you."

"If it was only about the sexual act, I wouldn't, but there's a child involved. As much as we'd like to pretend the whole Vaughn thing never happened, we have to face the possibility that Charity is Vaughn's child."

Charles shook his head.

"Baby, I know that she's yours in every way that matters, but there may come a time that she wants to know, or even may need to know, who her biological father is. As much as I don't want to face it, both she and Vaughn have a right to know if she's his little girl."

"Charity Faith Webb is my daughter, Sullivan. She belongs to you, and she belongs to me," insisted Charles.

"Listen, honey, I want to believe that too. I've prayed till my knees were just about bloody for that to be true, but we've got to face facts. You were practically sterile during that time. There's an overwhelming possibility that Vaughn is her biological father. I can't ignore that any longer."

Charles pulled her into a hug. "Oh, my beautiful, sweet Sullivan . . ."

"Well, I think it's safe to say your beautiful Sullivan hasn't been all that sweet," she admitted. "Which is why I think it's time we had a DNA test done for Charity."

"We don't need to do that."

"Yes, we do, Charles. The truth is, I'm not just doing this for Charity or for you. I'm doing it for me too. I'm tired of having this question mark hanging over our daughter. I'm tired of looking in her face to see whose nose she's going to develop—yours or his. I hate watching you hold her and wondering if you're wondering whether or not you're holding your own little girl or someone else's. I need peace. This is one of those times where the only way out of a situation is to go through it. I made this mess. It's time I took responsibility and cleaned it up."

"So if the test were to come back showing that Vaughn is her father, what does that mean? Are you going to leave me and take her with you to start a life with him?"

"Of course not! Charles, I love you, and I'd never take her away from you like that. My biggest concern is whether or not you'd even still want us here if the test came back that way."

"When I took those vows, Sullivan, it was forever. The only way I'm leaving you is by way of six men in black suits. You hear me?"

She smiled weakly. "What about the DNA test?"

Charles sighed. "Stay right here." He disappeared into his study and returned with a long white envelope. "You know, Charity's DNA never really mattered to me. I was going to love her, anyway. How could I not when I'm so in love with her mother? But I can see that it matters to you. Even though I thought you'd never admit it to me, I knew that one day you'd want to know who Charity's real daddy is, so . . ." He handed her the envelope. "I had a DNA test done right after Charity was born."

Sullivan was taken aback. "You did?"

"I hope you can forgive me for doing it behind your back."

Sullivan cupped her free hand around his face. "You're an awesome man. You know that, Charles Webb? After what I've put you through, there isn't a thing in this world I couldn't forgive you for! But I didn't take the test. Will the results be accurate without me?"

"Testing the mother improves the conclusiveness of the results, but it's not required," he explained. "The test results are in there. I'll let you read them alone if you'd be more comfortable that way."

She swallowed hard. "Have you seen them?"

"Yes, but like I said, nothing in that test was going to change my mind about raising Charity. She's my daughter."

Sullivan's hands were almost shaking too much for her to open the envelope. She pulled out the spreadsheet that contained the results. "What's this chart? What does all this mean?"

"Those are the genetic markers. Keep reading," urged Charles.

Sullivan scrolled down to the field labeled PROBABILITY OF PATERNITY.

"What do you see?" Charles asked.

Sullivan smiled. "The probability of paternity is greater than 99.999 percent." She lowered the paper. Tears welled up in her eyes. "She's your daughter, Charles. Charity is our little girl!"

"That's right, Sullivan. She's *our* little girl."

Sullivan threw her arms around Charles. Things were finally starting to fall into place for her, but there was still one piece missing from the puzzle. Sullivan knew where she had to go in order to find it.

Chapter 43

*"There's no point in forcing something that's
doomed to fail, anyway."*
—Lawson Kerry Banks

"Lord, I know that man looks at the outward appearance, but you look at the heart," prayed Lawson. "And in my heart, I've sinned against you, my husband, and his son. I've said I forgive Garrett, but I haven't in my heart. I can't keep living like this or forcing my husband to live this way.

God I love my husband enough to stay, but I also love him enough to let him go. Lord, you said if anyone lacks wisdom, he should ask for it. I pray that you give us both the peace and wisdom that only comes from you, and keep your hand on this family as we get through this situation. In Jesus's name. Amen."

Lawson heard Garrett's car pull up into the garage as she finished her prayer. It was Friday, so in all likelihood, he'd have Simon with him.

Garrett unlocked the door and entered the kitchen, toting Simon in his arms. "What's up, sexy?"

"A lot, actually," she replied. "Do you have a minute? There's something I need to talk to you about."

"Give me a minute to put Simon down. He was sneezing and kind of fussy in the car. I don't think he's feeling too good."

Garrett trekked to Reginell's room, which had been turned into Simon's nursery, and then returned to the kitchen, sitting down at the table across from his wife.

"I didn't see Namon back there. Where's he at?"

"He took Kenny to a basketball game at his school. They're hanging out at Kina's hotel afterward."

"That was nice of him."

"I have some good news," announced Lawson. "A school accepted my application. I was offered an administrative internship."

"Congratulations, baby! Are you doing it at your school or one of the other ones around here?"

"No, it's not in Chatham County. The school is in Jones County."

He was confounded. "In Gray?"

"Yes."

"That's quite a commute."

"Yeah, I know. Three hours, to be exact."

"So what are you going to do?"

"I'm going to accept it," stated Lawson. "It's a requirement to complete my degree."

"But it's not a requirement that you do it three hours away. What about us? How is this going to work?"

"The shadowing lasts from January until April. I'll be moving up there until I finish."

"Moving? So I don't have a say in this?"

"You can protest, but I believe we both know we could use the time apart. Anyway, the internship doesn't start for another month. Namon can stay here while I'm gone, or he can live with Mark for three months if you'd prefer that."

"This is his home, Lawson. It's yours too. I don't understand why you're doing this."

"Garrett, we need the time and the space to figure out what we want to do."

"I already know what I want. I want you, and I want to be your husband," pleaded Garrett.

"But not more than you want to be Simon's father. It's okay. I understand. Quite frankly, you wouldn't be the man I fell in love with if you didn't want to give your son your all." She paused. "Garrett, honey, I haven't been fair to you. I've tried to make you choose between your two families, and that wasn't right."

"There's nothing saying I can't have my wife and my son. Men do it all the time. Heck, you and Mark do it every day."

"We do, but the difference is that you've accepted Namon. You love him. I can't say the same for Simon."

"Lawson, in time—"

"Nothing will change in time, Garrett. I will always wonder if you're sleeping with Simone, and I'll always wonder if you would've been better off with her, raising your son together. I know that's what you want."

"I want you, Lawson."

"Babe, I know you, okay? You don't want to be a weekend dad, and I know you hate walking on egg-shells around me. You should be able to be with your son without worrying about me. I think it's better for everybody this way."

"So your mind's made up?"

"Yes. When I get back in April, we can decide where to go from there."

He nodded. "How are we going to do this? Are you going to come home on the weekends? Am I coming up there?"

"I don't think we should see each other during that time."

Garrett was both hurt and angry. "What? Why not?"

"Garrett, it'll be fine. If we're meant to be, we'll come out of this stronger. If we're not, there's no point in forcing something that's doomed to fail, anyway."

"It sounds like you've given up," Garrett replied.

"I haven't given up on us, Garrett. I'll be praying every day that we find our way back to one another, but we've got to be realistic about our situation."

"That may be the problem."

"What?"

"Being *realistic* and not trusting God to handle it." He took Lawson by the hands. "I want to pray for us."

"Honey, I've already prayed. In fact, that's what I was doing right before you came in."

"No, I said *I* want to pray for us. You can spare me that much, can't you?"

Lawson let out a deep breath and closed her eyes.

"Lord, my wife and I come to you in the name of Jesus. We call on you today to touch this marriage. We know that separation starts in the heart long before it's manifested in the physical realm, so I ask first that you'd give my wife and me a loving heart toward one another. Reveal to us areas where we have failed or hurt one another, and give us the strength to confront them head-on, not run away from our problems or let them fester. Bring about resolution in those areas and make our marriage stronger as a result.

"Lord, I confess and repent for the part I've played in damaging our relationship. I confess that I have wounded my wife very deeply. I was unfaithful to her. I broke our vows and made it difficult for her to trust me. In spite of that, Lord, I believe it's your will for us to remain with one another. If you be for us, who can be against us? Help us to remember that this marriage is a trinity—my wife, myself, and you. As long as we keep our eyes stayed on you, I know that we can trust you to bring us out.

"Your Word says that a woman is not to leave her husband, nor is a man to leave his wife. However, if we do find ourselves separated for a while, let us re-member that a separation is not a divorce, and help us to conduct ourselves in a way that is pleasing to you and honors each other. Direct our paths, Lord. Draw us closer to you and to each other. Restore this mar-riage and make it be all that you have ordained it to be. Thank you for this incredible wife that you blessed me with. I'll never stop loving her or working to make this marriage the best it can be. Amen." Garrett opened his eyes. "It's in the Lord's hands now."

"Thank you for doing that. It reminded me of how we used to pray all the time."

"Perhaps if we hadn't stopped praying together, the problems wouldn't have started."

Garrett's phone rang, and Lawson's heart sank, as she assumed it was Simone calling. As always, when-ever she and her husband started to take steps toward each other, Simone was there to make them retrace those steps.

Garrett answered the phone. "Hello? Slow down. What did you say?" Garrett listened to the person on the other end of the line for a few more seconds before hanging up.

"There's been a fire at the construction site. A couple of my guys are injured. I've got to get down there."

"Go on. Get out of here. Call and let me know what's going on once you find anything out." Garrett grabbed his keys and stopped at the door.

"What?"

"Simon . . . Simone's out of town, and I hate to drop him off on my folks at the last minute."

"Garrett, you go. I'll take care of Simon."

"Are you sure?"

"Yes, go take care of your business."

Garrett bolted toward the door, leaving his wife at home alone with Simon for the first time. She didn't know what to expect, but Lawson prayed that she could put her resentment aside long enough to care for him until Garrett returned.

Lawson went to the nursery to check on him. She looked down into the crib at Simon, who stared back at her through his round brown eyes. "You *are* kind of cute," she said with a chuckle. Simon sneezed. "Do you have a little cold?"

Simon started whimpering.

"Shh . . . ," said Lawson. She tried to give him his pacifier. He spit it out and started wailing.

"I bet you want your daddy, don't you?" Lawson patted his chest. "Go to sleep, baby Simon. He'll be here before you know it."

He continued to cry. Lawson breathed heavily and reached down into the crib and picked him up for the first time. "You're a heavy baby, aren't you?" She cradled him. Simon's cries simmered down to a whimper.

Lawson flung a cloth diaper over her shoulder and sat down in the rocking chair. "I guess keeping this old thing wasn't a bad idea, after all. I used to rock your stepbrother in this chair. Did you know that?" She rubbed his head. "You know, I'm not so bad, either. I've just been confused and a little insecure. You see, I love your daddy very much, and I was afraid of losing him to your mother and to you. You're some stiff competition, mister! I can't say I'd blame your daddy if he left me for you." Simon sneezed again.

"Bless you! You're not coming down with anything, are you?" She wiped his nose and felt his forehead. It was warm. "Oh, no, we better check your temperature."

Lawson rummaged through his baby bag until she found a thermometer. His temperature was 101.7.

Alarmed, Lawson called Angel. "Hey, chick, what are you doing?"

"The usual. Contemplating the meaning of life and thinking of a master plan. What's up?"

"What's a dangerous temperature for a baby?"

"Um, around a hundred and one or a hundred and two. Why?"

"Simon is sneezing, and he feels a little warm. It could be nothing, but I wanted a professional opinion."

"Do you want me to come over and check it out?"

"Would you?"

"Yeah, give me twenty minutes."

As promised, Angel arrived within a few minutes. She examined Simon while Lawson fretted off to the side.

Angel gave him a dose of acetaminophen and laid Simon down in his crib. "He's definitely sick," concluded Angel.

"Do I need to take him to the hospital?"

"Not at this point, but you do need to watch him. Look for any changes in his appetite or behavior. If you notice any rashes or weird spots, you definitely need to call the doctor. Keep him hydrated and comfortable."

"Let me write that down," said Lawson, scrambling to find something to write with. Simon began fussing. Lawson instinctively picked him up and began cradling him. "It's okay," she sang to him. "You'll be fine."

Angel stood back in awe.

Lawson panicked. "What's wrong? Do you see any spots on him?"

"No, I see someone who looks like a mother." She and Lawson both smiled. "I would offer to stay, but it looks like you have everything under control."

"You can go, but keep your phone on!" commanded Lawson.

"I will. Call if you need me. I'll let myself out."

Lawson kept vigil by Simon's crib all night, checking his temperature every hour, changing his diapers, and monitoring his milk intake.

After giving him a lukewarm bath around eleven o'clock that night, Lawson climbed into her bed with Simon in her arms. She was exhausted, but she knew she wouldn't be able to relax with him sick in the other room.

Lawson placed Simon on her chest and reclined in the bed. "I'll make a deal with you," she said, bartering. "If you let me sleep for a few minutes, I'll let you sleep."

Garrett came home to find Lawson propped up with pillows on their bed, holding Simon. They were both asleep.

Garrett gently roused her. "Hey, babe."

Lawson woke up. "You're back. How did it go?"

"The building is a total loss, but my guys are doing okay." He smiled, looking at the two of them. "I see you and li'l man have been getting acquainted."

"Yeah, we had quite an adventure tonight. He started running a fever." She transferred Simon to his father's arms. "He's fine now."

"Why didn't you call me? I would've come home."

"I didn't want to bother you. You had enough to worry about."

"It looks like you took excellent care of him. Thank you."

"No problem."

"Well, let me put this big guy to bed."

"I'll do it," offered Lawson.

"Really?"

"Yeah, I know you're probably tired."

Garrett handed Simon to Lawson. "That's a beautiful sight."

Lawson carried Simon to his room and checked his temperature one more time before tucking him into the crib. Somewhere between Simon sneezing and Lawson feeding him, Lawson's heart began to soften toward her stepson and, by extension, her husband. Reconciliation wouldn't happen overnight, if it even happened at all. At least now Lawson was open to the idea that she, Garrett, Simon, and Namon could be a family. She looked down at Simon, thinking that maybe Jones County could wait.

Chapter 44

"I want to smile again."

—*Angel King*

As Duke raced along the highway, weaving in and out of traffic en route to Angel's house, he had the feeling in the pit of his stomach that something was terribly wrong. It wasn't like her to not answer her phone, and it was definitely out of character for her to break a promise to one of his girls.

Duke spotted Angel's red Prius as he swerved into her driveway. He jumped out of the car and began pounding on her front door. "Angel! Angel, you in here? Are you okay?"

After getting no answer, Duke decided that the situation warranted breaking and entering. He whipped out the spare key she'd given him during their courtship and let himself in the house.

"Angel, baby, are you here?" Duke asked, wandering into her living room. The house was silent. He inspected the kitchen and bathroom. Finding that both were empty, he made his way to Angel's bedroom.

Duke stumbled upon her unresponsive body on the floor. She appeared to be unconscious. "Angel! Angel!" Duke cried, trying to rouse her. "Angel, can you hear me?"

She made a noise but didn't move or open her eyes. Duke immediately called 9-1-1.

***

Angel woke up in a fog. She didn't know where she was or how she'd gotten there. Once her vision crystallized, she noticed a nurse with a chart standing over her bed, and she realized that she was in the hospital.

"How are you feeling, Ms. King?" asked the nurse

Angel tried to sit up. "Confused. Why am I here? What happened?"

"You overdosed on hydrocodone and acetaminophen."

"I didn't even take that many." Then she remembered that she'd been taking three times the recommended dosage. "I know what you all are thinking, but I promise that I wasn't trying to kill myself."

"That's not for me to decide, ma'am."

Angel lay back down. "I guess there's no chance I'm getting out of here tonight, is it?"

"Ms. King, we're going to have to hold you here for a couple of days for observation and a psychiatric review."

"Yeah, I'm a nurse. I know the routine." The routine would include being treated and evaluated like a patient who'd overdosed as a result of trying to take her life. Most likely, it would also include her being suspended from the hospital, pending counseling.

There was a knock at her door. Duke poked his head in. "Can she have visitors?" he asked the nurse.

"Yes, but don't wear her out." The nurse looked at Angel. "Miss King, I'll be back to check on you shortly."

"Thank you."

Duke sat down in the chair next to Angel's bed. "Hey."

"Hey. What are you doing here? How did you even know I was here?"

"I was the one who found you."

"Oh," she said, a little embarrassed. "Why were you looking for me?"

"You said you were going to pick Morgan up today."

Angel cringed. "I forgot all about that! She must be so disappointed with me."

"She's all right. She wanted me to make sure you were okay. Anyway, when the school called and said she was still there, I got worried. You weren't answering your cell or your home phone, so I went by the house."

"How'd you get in?"

"I still had my key. I let myself in. You were on the floor when I got there. You were totally out of it. It scared me. It was like watching my wife die all over again."

"Duke, I'm sorry you had to see me like that, and I'm sorry I forgot about Morgan." She shook her head. "What's wrong with me?"

Duke stroked her head. "Angel, what's going on with you? Talk to me."

Sullivan and Lawson barged into the hospital room. "Oh, my God, Angel, are you okay?" Sullivan asked, sitting down on the edge of the bed. "Then again, how could you be? Look what they've got you wearing!"

"I called Sullivan. She said she'd let the others know you were here. I hope that's okay," said Duke.

"It's fine. Thank you."

Duke rose. "Here, Lawson, you can have my seat. Angel, I'll be out there in the lobby."

"You don't have to do that," Angel told him. "Go home and be with your kids."

"I'm where I want to be and where my children want me to be," insisted Duke. "The girls are fine. Worry about you for a change."

"Reggie and Kina are on the way," Lawson said when Duke left. "Sweetie, what happened? Duke told Sullivan that they think you overdosed. What's that about?"

"Suffice it to say that I've discovered a new coping mechanism."

"It was those pills from the abortion, wasn't it?" concluded Sullivan.

Angel nodded. "Not only has my in-house pharmacy nearly cost me my life, it looks like it may cost me my job as well. I'll be lucky if I get suspended instead of fired."

Lawson squeezed her hand. "We're not even going to speak that kind of talk into existence. Angel, you were born to be a nurse. God doesn't give that kind of gift just to take it away from you."

"At the very least, they're going to make me go to counseling."

"That's probably not such a bad idea," said Sullivan. "Angel, you've been through a lot. It might help to talk to somebody about it. Sometimes, talking to us isn't enough."

"I know." Angel nodded. "I never imagined that it would get this bad."

After the ladies wrapped up their visit, Duke returned to Angel's bedside. He kissed her on the forehead. "It breaks my heart to see you like this."

She couldn't hold back the tears any longer. "Duke, how did I let this happen? I feel so stupid."

"Don't do that!" he ordered her. "Don't start getting down on yourself again. That's what got you to this point."

Angel wiped her eyes. "What am I supposed to do now?"

Duke held her hand. "You let me take care of you."

She was thrown. "What?"

"Angel, you've been caring for other people your whole life. You took care of my wife when she was sick. You looked after me and the girls when she died. It's time for someone to take care of you for a while."

"Duke, you don't have to do that."

"I know. I want to."

"I'm a hot mess right now, Duke. There's a long road ahead for me to regain control of my life. I can't promise you anything."

"You don't have to. This ain't about me. It's about you getting better so we can see that pretty smile on your face again."

She nodded. "I want to smile again."

"You will." He smiled at her. "I'm going to personally see to that."

Chapter 45

"I felt like an unloved, unwanted mistake."
—Sullivan Webb

She looked at the address to make sure it matched what Vera had given her. "Thank God for GPS," said Sullivan.

Sullivan stared up at the large white farmhouse located on the outskirts of Metter, Georgia, far from the beaten path. Its scalloped trim and wraparound porch were reminiscent of houses she'd seen in old pictures and movies.

"Yep, this is it." She held on to Charity's hand as the two of them walked up the wooden stairs leading to the front door. The front door was open, but the entry was blocked by a screen door. Sullivan raised her fist and knocked on the screen door.

"Pearlie Mae, is that you?" called a voice from inside.

"No, it's Sullivan," she answered back. "My name is Sullivan Webb."

"Who?" asked the woman.

Sullivan began to wonder if she'd set herself up for yet another rejection. She scolded herself for trusting Vera's word. Since when had it done her any good?

Sullivan could hear footsteps shuffling along the wooden floor. The closer the steps got, the faster her heart raced.

A small, frail woman appeared at the door. Her wrinkled face was hidden behind large glasses, and soft gray curls covered her head. She walked with the aid of a cane. "What did you say your name was, baby?"

"My name is Sullivan Webb. Do you know who I am?"

The woman opened the screen door and studied Sullivan's face. "I know who you are. Do you know who I am?"

"Are you Luella Sullivan?"

The woman raised her trembling hand toward Sullivan's face. Sullivan jerked back, fearing the woman was going to slap her.

"I ain't gonna hurt you, child." She cupped her hand around Sullivan's face. "Why would I want to hurt my own grandbaby?" Sullivan closed her eyes, relieved. "I've been wanting to touch you again since you were two weeks old."

"You really are Luella Sullivan." Sullivan dissolved into tears. "You're my grandmother."

"Aw, hush now." She hugged Sullivan. "This is a happy, happy day."

"I didn't know if I should come. I was afraid you'd throw me away like my daddy."

She shook her head. "You have to forgive him, child. He's got too much of his daddy's pride and stubbornness in him." Charity reached for Luella's cane. "Who's this pretty little thing over here?"

Sullivan smiled. "This is my daughter, Charity. She's your great-granddaughter."

"I've got two pretty babies." Luella held Charity's face for a moment. "Come on in. I'll put on some tea."

Luella led Sullivan and Charity into the parlor. "I love this house," said Sullivan. "It has so much charm and personality."

"There's a story behind this old house. It used to belong to my daddy. They called it the Big House."

"What was your father's name?"

"Percy Johnson. My granddaddy, John Johnson, was born right at the end of slavery. He and his family lived in a little shanty down the road. He used to work all this land around here for a white man named Mr. Henry. Mr. Henry liked my granddaddy, and he allowed him to buy up all this land, including the house. It's been in our family ever since."

Sullivan sat down and plopped Charity onto her lap. "Wow! I would love to hear all about Percy and John and anything else you can tell me about the family."

"Well, you and that baby sit down there while I make this tea, and I'll tell you all about it."

Sullivan was in awe. Her grandmother, great-grandfather, and great-great-grandfather had all lived there. Twenty minutes ago she hadn't known these people existed. Now she was sitting in their parlor.

"I bet you're wondering why I never said anything to you before now," said Luella as she and Sullivan sipped hot tea.

"I've gotten bits and pieces of the story from both my mom and dad."

"Well, Sammy was courting the mayor's daughter, Martina. She was a sweet girl, and we all loved her dearly. She was a good fit with the family, and we wanted Sammy to marry her. Then he met Vera, and for whatever reason, he was smitten with her. Your mama was kind of a wild girl. She wasn't the kind of woman parents want for their son, especially if he's the only child, but she had a powerful hold over him. He just couldn't stay away from her no matter how much we pressured him.

"When Vera came up pregnant, Sammy denied it at first. I think your mama named you Sullivan out of spite. She was going to prove you were Sammy's child one way or another. We all had our doubts at first, but once I saw you, I knew you were his baby." She shook her head. "Sammy's daddy never accepted it, though. He said that whore's baby would never be welcomed in our home or our family. It wasn't much I could do after that. Times were different then from how they are now. Even though Sammy went on to marry Martina, and they gave me two beautiful grandsons, I never forgot about you, Sullivan. I've always loved you from a distance. You never left my thoughts and my prayers."

"You have no idea what that means to me," confessed Sullivan. "My whole life I've felt like nobody in my family wanted me. I didn't have a daddy. I didn't really have a mother, either. I had no relatives to step up and claim me as their own on either side of the family. I didn't know where I came from or where I belonged. I felt like an unloved, unwanted mistake. Knowing that you were covering me with your prayers and your love all that time is like having a miracle."

Luella squeezed Sullivan's hand. "I've got something I want to show you." She went into another room and returned with three large photo albums. "I want you to know who your people are. I want you to know your family." She handed the books to Sullivan. "There's about one hundred years of family history in these pages."

"Wow . . ." Sullivan opened to the first page. "This is amazing."

Luella pointed to a man in a black-and-white photograph, wearing a navy uniform. "That's your granddaddy and my late husband, Jessie Sullivan."

"He was handsome."

Luella flipped the page. "Here we are on our wedding day. That was sixty-five years ago."

"You were so beautiful," Sullivan said, gushing.

"Oh, I was a catch in my day, honey! My friends were all jealous because I was the pretty one."

Sullivan brought her hand to her mouth, touched. "I have the same problem!"

Luella pulled a tattered envelope from the back of the album. "Your mama used to send me these." She passed the envelope to Sullivan.

Sullivan opened it and found dozens of pictures of her as a child. She began shuffling through them. "My mother took these?" There were pictures of her as an infant and on her very first day of school, and pictures taken during various holidays.

Luella gave Sullivan another envelope. "I took these myself." Sullivan found a dog-eared picture of her dressed as a peach for the third grade play and pictures of her marching in the Christmas parade as a majorette with her high school's band and later at graduation. Finally, there were pictures of her smiling with Charles on their wedding day.

"I stopped taking pictures after that," said Luella. "I knew he'd take good care of you, and you didn't need me watching over you anymore."

"Vera said you were always there in the shadows."

"Now I can love you out in the open." Luella smiled down at Charity. "And this baby too."

"This has been one of the most memorable days of my life," said Sullivan, tearing up. "I can't even put into words what I'm feeling right now."

"It's a good day for both of us."

Sullivan reached over and hugged her. She caught a whiff of Luella's perfume. "That smells wonderful. What fragrance is that?"

"Oh, baby, I don't wear nothing but Chanel."

Sullivan broke into laughter. "You really *are* my grandmother!"

As Sullivan spent that afternoon getting to know her grandmother, she realized that family didn't always look the way one expected it to, and that life seldom turned out according to plan. She also thanked God for adding one more person to an already wonderful and blessed life.

Chapter 46

"No matter what I do, I'm still a loser. I'm still the one people like to kick around."
—*Kina Battle*

It was not the grand opening she'd been preparing for.

Kina stood in the middle of a virtually empty store, stacked with crisp T-shirts that would never be worn or would end up in somebody's donation pile. Ki-Ki's Tees was officially a dream deferred.

"The important thing is that you tried," Lawson said, consoling her.

"Is it?" snapped Kina.

"Yes, you had a dream and had the guts to go after it. Not everyone is brave enough to do that."

Kina looked around at the relics of a broken dream. "It doesn't matter how much money I have or how many times people see my face on TV. No matter what I do, I'm still a loser. I'm still the one people like to kick around."

Sullivan rolled her eyes. "Is this a private pity party, or can anybody come?"

"Kina, there ain't a single one of us who doesn't get kicked around by life at least once, but those whippings make for some powerful testimonies."

"That was deep, Lawson," replied Kina. "Maybe you should be the one with a reality show, seeing as how all the interest in mine has dried up. Apparently, the TV execs think I'm polarizing and insincere."

Lawson nudged her. "Aw, what do they know?"

Sullivan pressed one of the shirts against her body. "Kina, did you find out what happened to your missing money?"

Kina nodded. "I know where the money is."

"Well, where is it?" asked Lawson.

"Calin has it."

Sullivan frowned. "Who?"

"Cut' Em Cali."

Lawson was flabbergasted. "How in the world did he get his hands on your money?"

"He stole a check out of my checkbook and forged a check for fifteen thousand dollars."

"Why would he do that?" questioned Sullivan. "Doesn't he have money?"

"Apparently, not enough to cover his drug habit and lavish lifestyle," answered Kina.

Lawson shook her head. "I don't understand. How did he even have access to your checkbook?"

"He must've gone through my purse when I was in the shower," concluded Kina.

Lawson blinked. "Excuse me?"

Kina sighed. "It was one night after an event. Calin invited me up to his hotel room and—"

"You slept with him?" Lawson interrupted. "Oh, Kina . . ."

"Of course, if I press charges, the police are gonna want a statement. I'll have to tell them everything that happened. Once that gets out, what's left of my reputation will be ruined."

"For fifteen thousand dollars, I'd have to take that chance," said Sullivan. "You can buy another reputation after you get your money back."

"Kina, you have to file charges! You can't let him get away with that," protested Lawson.

"I know, but how am I going to explain myself, Lawson? First, there was Reggie's exposé, then Joan's lesbian confessions, and now this. My God, where is the bottom?"

"You're a public figure now, honey. It comes with the territory."

"I've got Uncle Sam coming after me for taxes on the show money. People thinking I'm a drug-addict lesbian nympho. Ki-Ki's Tees is a flop, and I've alienated almost everyone I care about. That show has turned out to be the worst thing that's ever happened to me," lamented Kina.

"Kina, *Lose Big* wasn't the cause of this. That television show was a blessing to you in so many ways. You had the chance to live like very few people ever get a chance to . . . at least you did for a while, anyway. The problem wasn't fame or the money. The problem was that you forgot who made it all happen."

"I forgot about God," admitted Kina.

Lawson put her arm around Kina. "We've all been guilty of that, Ki. Whether it's Sullivan having an affair or Angel getting an abortion or me screwing up my marriage or Reggie backin' it up in the strip club. No one gets it right all the time. That's why we have an everlasting supply of God's grace. It's always available for the taking."

Sullivan continued taking inventory of the store. "Maybe all hope isn't lost, Kina. With a little retooling, the right investors, and my artistic touch on these T-shirts, you might be able to turn this ship around."

"You really think so?"

Sullivan cracked a smile. "Stranger things have happened."

Chapter 47

Flawed and Fabulous

"Something smells good over here!" said Lawson, joining Garrett at the grill for Namon's graduation cookout six months later.

"And something looks good right here." Garrett leaned over and kissed his wife. "I guess we have to do this all over again for your graduation next week."

"Of course, except at mine, I don't want you wearing this apron!"

They both laughed. "Okay, but tonight I don't want you wearing nothing but this apron! Maybe a pair of heels too." Garrett kissed her again. They were both happy to have found love and fulfillment in their marriage again.

Sullivan eyed Charles suspiciously. "Don't be looking over there, getting any ideas, mister." She rubbed her protruding belly, round from six months of pregnancy. "That's how we got this one on the way!"

Charles kissed his wife's stomach. "Your grandmother needed another great-grandbaby to spoil."

"As long as you know this is it!" Sullivan stressed. "I'm closing shop after this one."

Charles looked concerned. "What if it's another girl?"

"Charles, you have an inside connection with the man upstairs. I suggest you use it!"

"There goes the graduate!" sang Lawson, stretching out her arms to Namon, still draped in his cap and gown. Her eyes welled up with tears.

"Dang, Mama, how many times are you going to cry?"

"As many times as I want! Now, get over here and hug your mama."

Namon complied and reached over and hugged Garrett too.

"Will you look at those two?" asked Sullivan, watching Reginell grinding on Mark as they danced. She shook her head. "You can take the stripper out of the club . . ."

"Oh, hush, Sully. They're in love," said Angel. "I say, God bless them for it."

"*Love?* Please!" Sullivan squinted her eyes. "I know lust when I see it. At least she's finagled her way into somebody's college. Hopefully, having an education will class her up some."

Angel laughed. "I come off suspension next week. I've been officially declared sane."

"Good for you!" cheered Kina.

"I thought the definition of *insanity* was doing the same thing and expecting a different result," Sullivan reminded her.

"Yes, Duke and I have decided that we're giving it another shot, but we're both approaching it as very different people than we were before. He's not grieving over Reese, and I'm not trying to live up to any unrealistic expectations. We're good. Besides, fourth time is the charm, right?"

"How does *Lose Big, Dream Bigger* sound?" asked Kina, hammering out a working title for her new book. Her notoriety didn't land her a reality show, but it did garner her a book deal.

"It sounds very apropos," said Angel.

As they enjoyed the late spring afternoon in Lawson's backyard, the ladies knew there would be problems ahead, just as there would be praise reports. They'd fight some more and test each other's patience, then forget what they were mad about after one or two drinks. It was all a part of the ebb and flow of life. Through it all, they thanked God for sending them friends who allowed them to be free to be who and what they really were: flawed and fabulous.

Book Discussion Questions

1. Do the characters in this book realistically portray Christian women in today's society? Explain.

2. Considering the circumstances, should Lawson have fought for her marriage? Why or why not?

3. Would Sullivan have been better off not finding her father? Why or why not?

4. Should Angel have consulted Jordan before having an abortion? Should she have asked his permission or simply informed him of what she was going to do?

5. Do you think Mark and Reginell are equally yoked, or is he better suited for Lawson?

6. Was Simone a real threat to Lawson's marriage, or was the perceived threat all in Lawson's mind?

7. Does Sullivan exemplify what a first lady should be? Why or why not?

8. Was Kina judged too harshly by the media and her friends, or was the criticism warranted?

9. Should Angel have gotten an abortion? Why or why not?

10. As a professed Christian, should Reginell have stopped working in the strip club? Does one have anything to do with the other? Explain.

Shana Burton Bio

As a child, Shana Burton, a native of Macon, Georgia, wanted to be two things: an author and a flower. Eventually, she sided with being an author. She is a two-time Georgia Author of the Year nominee and has received many awards and accolades for her work as both an author and educator. She is the mother of two children and enjoys reading, dancing, traveling, and taking long naps.

In addition to *Flawfully Wedded Wives*, Shana Burton is the author of *Suddenly Single, First Comes Love, Catt Chasin', Flaws and All*, and *Flaw Less*.

She can be contacted at:
shana.j.burton@gmail.com